'It's a sweet, funny, moving and joyous delight of a novel, full of love and full of hope, with a great big (giant hamster-sized!) heart at its centre. It may be set on the caravan park from hell, but this beautiful LGBTQ+ read is positively heavenly.' – Simon James Green, author of *Noah Can't Even*

'A warm, open and generous book with enormous heart, *Boy Meets Hamster* is genuinely laugh-out-loud funny while also effortlessly dealing with big, complex issues to do with love, family, friendship, and self-confidence & acceptance.' – Maggie Harcourt, author of *Unconventional*

'The writing is brilliant, the characters so vivid and likeable - even Margaret, who makes an excellent villain – and it made me laugh out loud several times. A really enjoyable book, and I can't wait to read what Birdie Milano writes next.' Sophie Cameron, author of *Out of the Blue*

BOY meets HAMSTER

BIRDIE MILANO

MACMILLAN CHILDREN'S BOOKS

First published 2018 by Macmillan Children's Books
an imprint of Pan Macmillan
20 New Wharf Road, London N1 9RR
Associated companies throughout the world
www.panmacmillan.com

ISBN 978-1-5098-4865-2

1 3 5 7 9 8 6 4 2

A CIP catalogue record for this book is available from
the British Library.

Printed and bound by CPI Group (UK) Ltd, Croydon CR0 4YY

For Mum and Dad
For being the truest example of true love.
And,
For Sid and Nancy,
For being particularly great cats.

ONE

The car got stuck in a traffic jam at the entrance to the caravan park, under a massive sign that read: 'WELCOME TO STARCROSS SANDS – LET THE DREAM BEGIN.'

'See, Dylan,' Mum said, pointing through the open sunroof as Dad started leaning on the horn, 'it's going to be a dream holiday after all!'

Every year I was promised a dream holiday, and every year I almost believed it. At least, just long enough to start thinking wistfully about where we might go. For example: New York would be a *seriously* prime location. I could easily dream up visions of myself checking out the view from the top of the Empire State Building, or taking pictures with the Statue of Liberty distant in the background, small enough to make it look like we were mates.

Then, every year, Mum clipped out a load of 'special offer' tokens from the newspaper, and dragged us to another caravan park in 'one of twenty-six stunning locations throughout the British Isles' for the bargain price of £9.50.

As if £9.50 could buy anyone a dream holiday. You wouldn't be able to get a stale hot dog in New York for that.

Dream holidays are the kind of thing you win on daytime TV shows by answering tricky questions like:

Who sees you when you're sleeping, and knows when you're awake?

A. The Easter Bunny
B. Santa Claus
C. My mum (no idea how; it's like she's got me hooked up to a breathing monitor).

Then they show you footage of what you can expect on the prizewinning trip: a montage of happy people with great hair mooning round picturesque Paris. Climbing the Eiffel Tower, or laughing in art galleries, clutching baguettes.

I'd *love* to go to Paris. *City of Amour.* I'm pretty sure you'd only have to step off the Eurostar and look lost for five minutes before someone elegant and bohemian would stroll by, happy to take a random boy from Woking under his wing and show him the mysteries of the Louvre.

(Not sure what that is, exactly, but it sounds romantic.)

After all, dream holidays are all about the chance for romance, right?

Wrong.

Last year, our 'dream holiday' in Wales involved finding out how long we could last without thinking about eating each other, while torrential rain kept us trapped inside a ten-foot-wide metal box that smelt of old farts. The TV was stuck on the local news channel – looping footage of grannies being airlifted off their roofs during the floods, and 'youths' paddling down the high street in recycling-bin canoes.

Mum said it was 'cosy'.

This year our dream holiday was starting in a totally inexplicable, unmoving line of cars. It was like a scene from one of those disaster movies where everyone's fleeing a zombie invasion, or an escaped dinosaur, or the meteor just about to crash to earth. Except, instead of running away screaming like any sensible person would, at Starcross Sands people were actually queuing to get *in*.

Mum looked delighted, but she had spent all week telling me that this place had won the *Caravan Monthly* Park of the Year Award three times running. Like that made it any less tragic.

Dad, less thrilled, was blasting the car horn over and over, as if he thought a headache might help the situation.

Someone from the Skoda in front of us had got out and started gesturing angrily with a pair of barbeque tongs.

In the back seat, my little brother, Jude, clambered across my friend Kayla's lap and on to mine, seconds before announcing that if he couldn't have a wee soon he would *actually explode.*

I was just looking around to see if one of the criminally embarrassing rain ponchos Mum always packed for us was anywhere within reach, when the car started inching, slowly, forward.

'I can see the sea!' Jude yelled, as we got a glimpse of caravans, cliffs, and a strip of blue beyond.

I could see the last week of my summer holiday disappearing down the chemical toilet. As usual.

The thing about dream holidays (which you'll know if you've ever been driven through a set of buzzing neon-lit gates, and found out that the traffic jam you've just been stuck in was caused by a dozen elderly Elvises in plastic quiffs and *way*-too-tight jumpsuits starting a dance-off with a giant orange hamster) is that dreams can be nightmares too.

TWO

'So, Dylan, tell our viewers: is this fabulous trip to Cornwall's Crummiest Caravan Park really the summer holiday of a lifetime?' Kayla thrust her straighteners under my chin like a microphone and gave me her best TV-host smile.

This year, after I'd launched a campaign titled: *Caravan Holidays Are Social Suicide*, and predicted a future in which I'd become a traumatized recluse, spending every day on the computer training pixelated dragons to be my only companions, Mum had let me bring my best friend along for the 'dream holiday' experience.

I flashed a cheesy grin right back at her.

'Well, Miss Flores, not quite. In fact, I might even say it was a *glummer* holiday.'

'A *slummer* holiday?' Kayla countered.

'A *scummer* holiday.' I looked over to the window, where a gang of drunken Aussies in lifeguard jackets and shades were stumbling past, slurring their way through a seriously dubious version of 'Waltzing Matilda'.

So far the trip was about as dreamy as expected.

Apparently the Elvis lookalikes blocking the park entrance when we arrived had got lost on the way to Fifties Night. Mum and Dad hadn't wasted any time in dumping me, Kayla and Jude at our 'new home-from-home', before throwing on some cringingly tight outfits of their own and dashing out to make public embarrassments of themselves at the Starcross Starlight Showhall.

My parents are both paramedics with the ambulance service. They do everything at speed. They met when they started working the same shift, but had to be separated not long after because they fought over who got to do the fast driving and turn on the sirens.

Sometimes I think they're where Jude gets his childish behaviour from.

We were left with nothing for entertainment but a delivery pizza (from this place on the park disturbingly called the Pie-O-Ria) and a tiny TV with a fuzzy, flickering screen. Definitely preferable to watching Dad twirl Mum round the dance floor in a miniskirt, but not exactly the thrill of a lifetime.

On *my* dream holiday, we'd be fanning ourselves in a luxury tent, listening to the distant roar of lions on the Serengeti. Not spending it the exact same way I spend an average Saturday night at home.

Our caravan wasn't much of an improvement on my bedroom at home, either. It was called *131 Alpine Views*, although as far as I could make out the only view we had was of a row of identical tatty beige rectangles across from us, one or two of them distinct from the rest because they had a barbeque outside, or some bunting in the window. The one opposite had a load of tacky garden ornaments too.

Flipping through the TV channels, Kayla found a talent show where a dog was juggling sausages, and sat down in front of it with her phone. We'd only been here five minutes and she already had about a million messages from her always-anxious dad.

I got started helping Jude with his stretching exercises. Sitting him on the fold-down kitchen counter, I held his feet and pushed his knees up against his chest: left then right, over and over.

He didn't mind the nightly routine, but whenever he was out of the wheelchair it was always 50/50 whether he'd do it properly or wait for a good chance to 'accidentally' kick me in the face. Today he was giggling madly and seriously determined to give me a black eye.

Every time he managed to land a blow, he widened his eyes and gasped, before – a little too late – telling me to, 'Duck!'

'Forget ducks. Do that again and I'm taking you to

the clifftop to get eaten by seagulls,' I told him, catching his flailing foot after it slammed into the side of my head for the third time. Jude had been afraid of beaches and everything on them ever since one of the £5-a-ride donkeys in Brighton chewed on his towel while he was still sitting on it, then started on his trunks.

Luckily there wasn't much of a beach at Starcross Sands, despite the name – just some grassy cliffs and a sharp drop down to the ocean.

After an initial yelp of protest, Jude took a moment to consider the gravity of the threat I'd made. Then he spotted the flaw in my plan.

'Seagulls don't eat people!' he declared, though I watched his lip waver, unsure.

Kayla broke off from sending reassuring texts and turned to look at us. 'They do in Cornwall.'

That kind of unconditional backup was why she'd been my best friend for the last four years, ever since we were cast as Aladdin and Jasmine in the Year Six panto. That had been a weird Christmas at school. I was more popular than I knew what to do with – everyone loves a main character – until we actually did the show and they found out that I can sing about as well as our hallway carpet can fly. I'd vowed never to get up onstage in public again.

I'd sort of hung on to the Aladdin look ever since though. At least, Kayla said that my mop of untameable black hair meant I looked like the Disney version (without the ab definition). Meanwhile, she'd cut her long hair to skim her shoulders not long after the show, and it had been a different colour every few weeks since. Right now it was candy pink.

Her phone beeped with another barrage of parental concern, and she paused to tap out a quick reply before shoving it back into a pocket. Kayla's dad was the unofficial third wheel whenever we hung out – not usually in person, but a constant presence on her phone. My mum complains that I must have lost her number on my thirteenth birthday, because I haven't used it since, but Kayla texts her dad almost as much as he does her. Then again, he's way more accident-prone than she is. If my dad had managed to explode a microwave, twice, when left alone in the house, then I'd want to check up on him too.

Kayla kept saying that coming away with us would be a chance for both of them to assert their independence, except now that she was several whole counties away the messaging was reaching critical levels.

Wincing and flicking off the talent show, where someone had started butchering a boy-band ballad, she came over and grabbed a third slice of Pepperoni

Passion. 'We're going to get to go out too, aren't we?' she asked. 'Check out the Starcross Sands nightlife?'

I huffed out a laugh. 'We're in the middle of nowhere! If there's any nightlife, it's either grandads in fancy dress or the kind you see on nature documentaries: black and white and lives in a sett.'

I'd been checking out the brochure Mum had left us, listing all the park's 'amusements and attractions'. It wasn't a very long list. Jude was massively excited about hanging out at the kids' club with a giant hamster called Nibbles, but the highlight of the week was meant to be something called the 'Stardance', at which the Park of the Year Award would be announced. Park of the Year? From the little we'd seen of it so far, I wouldn't have given Starcross Sands an award for being Park of This Tuesday.

I wanted nightclubs and exclusive boutiques, but it looked like I was going to be stuck with crazy-golf clubs and a tuck shop. Ever since the last Elvis-a-like had stumbled off towards the retro disco, the rest of the park had descended into the kind of deathly quiet I imagined was the sound of a thousand £9.50 holidaymakers going to bed early and wishing they'd booked Disneyland instead.

So, 'Touch my flamingo again and I'll wedge it so far up your bum you'll be spitting feathers for a week,' wasn't exactly what I expected to hear howled into the silence a few feet from where we were.

I looked at Kayla, grabbed Jude, and made it over to the window in record time.

THREE

'I won't say it again, Sandra. Put the flamingo down.'

Two women were circling each other on the lawn of the caravan across the way. When I'd daydreamed about safari holidays and listening to the roar of wild beasts, this wasn't exactly what I'd had in mind.

'You can have it back when you admit it was your Troy made our Alfie eat the urinal cake.'

'Well if your Alfie's thick enough to do it . . .'

There were lights going on in every caravan in the lane, but one in particular was glowing brighter than the rest, with its doors wide open and a small crowd gathered around outside. It was the one with the gaudy selection of garden ornaments: flamingos, gnomes, a fake palm tree.

A boy about Jude's age, who I assumed must be Alfie, was puking into an ornamental birdbath.

'Are those our new neighbours?' Kayla asked, raising her voice to be heard over the screech of one lady in a floral nightie bull-rushing the other. A teenager in a leather-effect jacket pulled at one woman's frilly sleeve.

'Leave it, Mum – the flamingo's not worth it!'

'Crank up the Gorgeous Sirens, we need to put out a red alert,' Kayla muttered to me, while Jude wriggled in my arms to get a better look over the sill.

He was seriously hot. Blond hair, broad shoulders: he looked a bit like Freddie Alton, who's Sports Prefect at our school and who would totally be my boyfriend if I wasn't totally terrified of talking to him. And if he knew I was gay and didn't majorly freak out about it.

And if *he* was gay too, I suppose. That would help.

Anyway, if we're talking ultimate perfection in human form, it's between Freddie and the blond one from the superhero movies with the shoulder-to-waist ratio of a Dorito. But the mysterious stranger trying to cool down his nightie-clad mum outside caravan 232 really wasn't bad, either.

His mum, though? She was terrifying.

'Nobody touches my ornaments, Jayden-Lee. You know the work I put into the décor.' Shaking her son off, she gave the other woman a haughty look, and sniffed. 'Some people just want to live like pigs!'

'Who're you calling a pig, Eileen Slater? You're the pig here, you . . . *piggy pig.*'

Alfie's mum might not have been that creative with nicknames, but she made up for it by plunging her hands into Mrs Slater's hair and dragging her down on to the grass. It was like watching a WrestleMania bout, but with more genuine violence.

Kayla had grabbed a chair to stand on for a better view – she's four foot eight, and puts her height down to the Filipina side of her family tree. I'd been taller than her dad since I grew three inches last summer.

'Mrs Slater's definitely winning,' she announced. 'Alfie's mum can't hold on to her – her plastic fingernails keep popping off.'

While that sounded like something I definitely wanted to watch, Jude was starting to squirm, and I didn't think it was just the usual twitches.

'I don't like it,' he complained, tipping his head back to look up at me. 'I don't want them to shout.'

'I know,' I told him, 'but this fight's not over you.'

Usually our mum is the one getting into grudge matches, or her own version of them, whenever someone says something thick about Jude. He's got cerebral palsy, which is a medical condition where his brain gets a bit muddled about telling his body what to do. He's as smart as any other five-year-old who's into ant farms and believes trains have secret lives – too smart for his own good, sometimes – but because he can't walk well on his own and he talks a bit slurry, people assume he's incapable of anything.

Mum just gets furious when they do it out loud. She's never violent about it. She just smiles. She's got one particular smile that means she's going to destroy everything that a person loves, slowly and systematically, while calling them 'sweetie'. That's how it starts.

She's verbally slaughtered people in the middle of the local shopping centre before, and once had to spend an hour in the Shopmobility reception cooling down before they let her back into Primark.

So I guess it makes sense that when people start yelling, it freaks Jude out a bit.

I was just debating whether abandoning my prime-location view of the Dramavan was *really* the kind of martyrdom that should be expected as part of my big-brotherly duties, when park security rolled up in a golf buggy to break up the fight.

Kayla *almost* forgot to keep her reaction Jude-appropriate.

'What the f-udgecake is that?' she yelped.

All three of us pressed our faces to the smeary glass of the caravan window to see. There were three security guards in beige safari uniforms that read 'Safeguarding Your Dreams' on the back, a blonde woman in a power suit, who was standing by the buggy trying to stop any of the gathering crowd of kids from taking it for a joyride, and . . .

I blinked at Kayla. 'I think that's a macho hamster.'

It was the same hamster we'd seen dancing with the

Elvises when we'd shown up at the park. Huge, bright orange, with a perma-grin and two massive buck teeth.

'Nibbles! Dylan, it's Nibbles! Can we go and meet him? Can we?' Jude's elbows needled me in the ribs. The hamster had just tackled Jayden-Lee into a decorative flowerbed, but now that the whole scene had taken on the surreal quality of something from CBeebies, Jude was totally into it.

'Nibbles?' Kayla asked. 'So I'm *not* hallucinating right now?'

'He's the park mascot. He runs the kids' club,' I told her, 'and I guess he's on some hefty hamster pellets.'

Nibbles, who my little brother was supposed to be spending the next morning with at a 'Happy Hamster Holiday Party', had just dodged a headbutt, and was now kneeling with one paw in the centre of Jayden-Lee's back, pressing him face-first into the ground.

From where we were, I could see that he'd rolled him right through one of Alfie's vomit puddles. It was seeping into his perfect golden hair.

'Looks like Nibbles is busy playing right now,' I told Jude, lifting him away from the window before he got the idea that hamsters advocated violence. 'You can make friends with him tomorrow.'

Tomorrow. Fifty pre-schoolers, too much sugar, and a ridiculous orange hamster. There was *no way* I was getting involved in that train wreck. But things were looking up: once the boy from the Dramavan washed the sick out of his hair, I was going to have the fittest neighbour in the caravan park. I whispered the name *Jayden-Lee Slater* to myself, and wondered if it was really possible to fall in love at first fight.

FOUR

Fifty screaming four-year-olds, a mountain of cupcakes a Sherpa would think twice about trying to climb, and a massive hamster clapping along to the hokey-cokey. It was literally amazing what Mum could bribe me into when she tried.

I was only getting through this nightmare scenario by picturing exactly which parentally unapproved video game I was going to buy with the proceeds. Probably something where I could imagine it was Nibbles I was repeatedly mowing down with my souped-up, stolen car. Don't get me wrong – I don't have a problem with hamsters in general. I just have a problem with ones that keep *picking on me*.

'Now everybody Hamster Hug!' yelled one of the ultra-perky party assistants, a blonde girl in a baseball cap, whose nametag said Stacie. She'd stopped the music to give the same order three times so far, and for the third time I'd turned around to escape only to run smack into a fluffy orange chokehold.

Why did he always pick *me*? Three times. Even my grandma only demanded one hug per visit. Nibbles'

Hamster Hugs were so intense that I was going to be picking fur out of my teeth for the rest of the day.

At least there was one silver lining to the dark cloud looming over the skyline of my life. Jude was currently doing the hokey-cokey with Jayden-Lee's six-year-old brother, Troy.

It looked like making your mates eat toilet freshener meant that they hung around with you less (or Alfie hadn't stopped puking yet), because Troy had spent most of the party so far playing with Jude.

Well, playing with his chair, anyway. I couldn't really blame him: having your own set of wheels is pretty cool when you're four, and Jude likes to show them off. Troy did get a bit stroppy when I stopped him trying to kick Jude out and use it for races, and then he nearly snapped the controller off while putting it in maximum gear, but he seemed all right, really.

In fact, when I went over there, he turned around and gave me a Hamster Hug too. He'd been stuffing sweets into his face not long before, so it was a bit of a sticky event, but way better than death-by-Nibbles.

'Thanks, Troy, I like you too . . . is that my gum?'

The little monster had stolen a whole pack of Wild Cherry Chew-Chew out of my pocket, and was unwrapping it right in front of me. He shoved a square into his mouth, bit down, and answered, 'Mrrph?'

Mum always says kids Jude's age shouldn't have gum because it's a choking hazard or something. And Dad says swallowing the stuff will make you blow bubbles out of your bum. But Troy was a couple of years older, and I didn't want him telling his fit brother about the funsucker who gave him a health lecture in the middle of a party, so I let him have it. Just this once. What was the worst that could happen?

Anyway, they were starting the dance up again, and Jude kept nearly running me over doing the 'in-out, in-out' bits, so I decided to get out of the circle before Nibbles got me to help him shake it all about.

I found a safe haven in the corner of the room, where Kayla was already saving me a space. She'd picked out a cupcake that perfectly matched the sugary pink tips of her hair, and was trying to eat it without the frosting giving her a clown smile.

'Hiding from another creature cuddle?' she asked, failing at even trying to look sympathetic.

'They're horrific,' I shuddered, glancing back to check I wasn't being stalked by the pet shop's finest. 'Like getting mauled by a shagpile rug. He did smell nice though. I wonder if that was Jayden-Lee's aftershave on his fur.'

'Why – jealous it didn't rub off on you?'

Sometimes she just knew me too well. OK, so I did lie awake half the night thinking about the Dramavan's hottest inhabitant. I'd even spent a while at the window this morning trying to see if I could spot him having breakfast.

I just wanted to check that he'd made it out of the fight with only minor injuries and nothing serious like, say, a broken jaw. Which might put a major dampener on any kissing prospects for the week ahead.

Not that my kissing prospects were ever more than zero. The problem came from never knowing whether the people I was interested in might be interested back. Which, I suppose, is an issue for everyone except psychics, but it's definitely a thousand times worse when you're gay.

Because, how are you supposed to know who else is gay too?

I guess a lot of people are like me and don't really talk about it. In fact, only Kayla knows. Sometimes I think I should tell more people, but it's hard. So it just follows me round, not totally secret but not *not* secret, either: the big gay elephant in the room.

But if there's loads of people keeping it hidden, like Superman covering up his skintight spandex with a suit, how am I ever supposed to know if Jayden-Lee might be one of them?

Or, more importantly, what if he's supposed to be my Lois Lane?

'He was reaching extra-spicy levels of hot sauce, I have to admit,' Kayla went on, sticking her tongue out to rob her cupcake of a bit of buttercream without putting her flawless lipstick at risk. 'Although not so much with his hair full of vom.'

'That wasn't his fault! He could probably sue that hamster for assault.'

Glaring across, I saw Nibbles was pretending to sit on the arm of Jude's wheelchair, partnering up with him for the 'arms-in' part of the dance. Which was nice, I suppose. Maybe even mutant rodents had their moments.

'Anyway, you're not allowed to fancy him, you know that, right?' I gave Kayla a look. A *remember the friends' code* look. 'I've bagsied him already.'

She gave me a look back. A *there is no friends' code and stop being a dipstick* look. 'You can't bagsie a person: he's a boy, not the top bunk of a bed. And don't you think you should try talking to him before you get any "this boy belongs to" labels made up? He might be like spam.'

'Like spam *how*?'

Kayla smirked. 'Nice shiny can, but a disgusting lump of gristle on the inside.'

I shoved her arm, wrinkling my nose at the

description. 'He's *so* not spam. And I'm going to talk to him. I just need a strategy . . . something that looks like coincidence, but—'

'Isn't that why you were chatting to his brother?' Kayla pointed a painted fingernail in the direction of the dance floor. 'Maybe he's your in.'

She was gesturing to where a boy with spiked blond hair and a football shirt that read TROY BOY 11 was whispering in Jude's ear.

'I don't think Troy's a good angle.' I put my hand in my back pocket to check he hadn't nicked my phone along with the gum.

'Come on.' Kayla tutted. 'How hard can it be to bond with a six-year-old?'

'Harder than you'd think.' I shook my head. 'Try it yourself. You're around the same height; he'll probably think you're in his class.'

'*Low blow*,' Kayla said. And for once I didn't point out that it would have to be, since any other kind would sweep right over her head. I didn't say anything. Because all of a sudden I knew exactly what my Jayden-Lee strategy would be.

Stealth.

I had to observe him closely, while staying under the radar. Like a love ninja, I'd remain invisible until I had enough information to make my strike. He wouldn't know I existed, wouldn't even know my name until . . .

'*DYLAN KERSHAW* – IS THERE A *DYLAN KERSHAW* IN THE ROOM?' A voice boomed out from the loudspeakers, and I realized that everything else had gone deathly quiet.

Stacie was in the middle of the dance floor calling my name through a microphone.

And Troy was leaning over Jude, a giant handful of chewed-up gum pressed firmly into his hair.

'AND *JAYDEN-LEE SLATER*. I NEED A *JAYDEN-LEE SLATER* OVER HERE TOO.'

The doors to the outdoor patio slid open, and Jayden-Lee stalked in, ploughing a path through the crowd of children, who were gathering round as my little brother started to wail.

FIVE

Jude has this noise he makes when he's really upset. It's not a normal sort of cry; it's more of a honk-wail, like a fire alarm being set off by a really stressed-out goose. He was having a full-on sob by the time me and Kayla reached him.

Stacie stood behind him with her microphone, looking like she'd just figured out that doing kids parties wasn't the easy shift. Beside her was Nibbles, about as useful as you'd expect a hamster to be in a crisis, with two identical little girls hanging on to his paws. From the matching pink outfits I guessed they'd have cringey rhyming names, like Florrie and Dorrie, or Jenny and Penny.

Then there was Troy, his one front tooth bared in a creepy troll grin.

His left hand was smushed tightly into Jude's hair, splatting a golf ball-sized wodge of reddish gum into his black curls, like a primary-coloured bird splat.

I should have grabbed him straight away, but I couldn't, because right in front of me stood the world's most breathtaking older brother.

I froze, caught like a startled rabbit in the headlights of Jayden-Lee's hotness. It was even worse close up. His green eyes were dotted with flecks of brown, and there was a faint white mark from an old scar at the corner of his lip, making him look a little bit dangerous and not any less kissable.

He was also looking as if the whole drama was nothing to do with him.

'Either you get your hand out of his hair, or I take it off at the wrist.' Kayla's voice cut into my love-paralysis. She was doing what I should have – squishing her own fingers into the gum to hold it to Jude's head while she peeled Troy's fingers away. I flashed her a grateful smile, even if threatening a child with dismemberment might have been a bit extreme.

'What happened?' I crouched down next to Jude's chair and took his hand between both of mine. His sobs were turning to sniffles.

'He asked if I wanted some gum!' he exclaimed, voice pitched only slightly lower than that tone only dogs can hear.

'Yeah, and he said yes!' Troy countered. 'So it's his fault.'

Jude gasped at this suggestion. 'Is not! It is *not*. I didn't want it on my *head*!'

'Should've said.' Troy folded his arms and hunkered

down solidly, looking like one of his mum's garden gnomes.

I looked up at Nibbles, the apparent authority figure in the room, but it wasn't like he could give any answers from behind two foam buck teeth. One of the twins tugged on his left paw.

'We sawed what happened!'

The other tugged on his right.

'We sawed it!'

'Jude said Troy was not *allowed* to sit on him for a ride.'

'And that's why Troy did squish his hand on Jude's hair – *squelch!*'

'*Squelch.*'

'*Squeeeeelch!*'

'Thank you Minnie, Winnie,' Stacie said. 'I think we've got it from there.'

Nibbles gently shooed the twins back towards the party as Stacie tried to look stern. Which is hard when you're wearing an orange baseball cap and have your face painted like a frog.

'I'm really sorry we didn't catch this in time to stop it, but I think both boys need to take a time out for today.'

I could sense Jude working up the energy to honk again, so I stepped in fast. 'Yeah, OK. We can just—'

'You can't ask us to go when Jude was *clearly* the

27

injured party,' Kayla interjected, rubbing her hands together to clear the lingering strands of gum from between her fingers.

I knew where this was going. Kayla plans to be a high-powered lawyer when she leaves school (though she's got a fall-back option of becoming a backing singer for her favourite band, the Deathsplash Nightmares, if it doesn't work out), and she takes any chance to practise. I stared her down, willing her to shut up before she destroyed my chances of Jayden-Lee thinking I was a normal human being with normal mates, let alone a potential love match. It didn't work.

'Really, Troy's family should reimburse the Kershaws for the price of a decent haircut, plus damages for any emotional trauma caused. However, in this instance we will accept a swift apology.'

Troy stared up at her, blinking slowly.

Jayden-Lee stared at her. Nibbles patted Jude on the back as he hiccupped on another sob, and then they both stared at her too.

I stared at the floor and wondered if they ever had earthquakes in Cornwall, and whether a well-timed one might open the ground under my feet right about now.

After a moment's silence, Troy yelled, 'YOU CAN'T MAKE ME GO WITHOUT CAKE!' and ran towards the buffet.

Jayden-Lee shrugged his shoulders. I couldn't help noticing the way all of the muscles down his arms shrugged with them.

'He doesn't do apologies. Sign of weakness.' He kicked a foot lightly against one of Jude's wheels. 'And cheer up, yeah? Crying's for girls.'

I cut in when I heard Kayla's sharp intake of breath.

'Maybe we *should* go. Everyone's upset, and sticky, and it might just be for the best.' I squeezed my brother's hands in mine. 'What do you think, Jude?'

'My hair's gone solid!' Jude declared, and broke into wails again.

'I can't take him across the park like this,' I mouthed to Kayla. This was supposed to be his holiday treat.

Kayla pursed her lips a moment, and then reached into her bag for her make-up case. 'I've got it covered. Give me five minutes and I'll sort him out.'

She put a hand on the back of Jude's chair, but Nibbles held up a paw to stop her. Then he ducked down to give Jude one of his Hamster Hugs. It didn't look nearly as smothering as the ones I'd suffered, but when he stepped back my brother was smiling like the sun coming out from the clouds.

Maybe the mutant mascot was good for something.

Jude went off with Kayla, and Troy stomped back over, a cupcake in each hand and the chocolatey remains of another one smeared across his face.

'I didn't do nothing. He was going to run me over; I was self-defending myself.'

Even Nibbles looked doubtful about that, and he had a foam face.

Jayden-Lee nodded, though, and said, 'See?'

I didn't really believe that Jude could have suddenly developed the wheelchair equivalent of road rage, hyped up on frosting and an overdose of the hokey-cokey, but I found myself nodding and making a strangled noise that sounded a bit like *yeah*.

Crisis over, I was uncomfortably aware of how close I was to Jayden-Lee, and I don't know what the problem is exactly, but when I'm near someone I like it's hard to talk properly. My tongue gets all thick in my mouth. It's like I'm allergic to sexy.

Still, at least now we could forget all this and I could go back to working out how a love ninja operates once his cover's been blown.

Except, the hamster was still waving his paws about, like he was directing traffic.

Directing us.

He pointed to Jayden-Lee, and then to me.

'HAMSTER HUG,' yelled Troy and Stacie.

'HAMSTER HUG,' yelled half the pint-sized partygoers, who'd been watching all this like it was a soap opera Christmas Special.

Jayden-Lee frowned. 'What's that supposed to mean?'

'It's a . . . thing.' I swallowed hard against the panic trying to close down my throat. 'When they stop the music, you're supposed to . . .'

I awkwardly mimed a hug.

I hugged myself. I *hugged myself*. I must have looked like the kind of person who'd sit on one arm to numb it before holding his own hand, just to see what it felt like to have a friend.

Jayden-Lee dipped his chin in a way that might either have been agreement or repulsion.

Then he said, 'Yeah, whatever. OK.'

And he stepped forward to pat me on both shoulders. That was it. A pat. Less affection than you'd show a cat. Maybe he just didn't like being ordered into PDA by overgrown house pets. Either way, my heart skipped at least two beats. I was just debating how best to act cool during a heart attack, and whether giant hamsters would be trained in first aid, when Jayden-Lee whispered something in my ear.

'Don't worry about it, yeah? Can't be easy when your brother's a retard.'

He gave my shoulder a final pat and let go. I was silent for a minute, shocked and trying to figure out a reply.

I meant to tell him that that's not an OK thing to call anybody, least of all my little brother, especially when *his* little brother thinks chewing gum makes great hair gel. I wanted to tell him that disabilities don't make people stupid, and that using someone's disability to *mean* stupid was mean and stupid itself. I nearly told him that he'd better watch what he said, because if my mum ever heard about it he'd be wishing the giant hamster had finished him off when it had the chance. I kind of wanted to punch him in the mouth.

But I just sort of shrugged and gave a guilty laugh.

And then he walked off before I could say anything at all, and I was left standing there feeling angry and not knowing whether it was at him or myself.

Then Nibbles waved his paws at me again, pushing Troy my way.

Troy yelled, 'HAMSTER HUG!' wrapped his arms round me, and threw up all over my jeans.

SIX

By the time I'd reached the bathroom, taken off my brand-new trainers and grabbed a handful of toilet roll to try and scrub the pink chunks off my jeans, I'd figured out who I should *really* be mad at.

That evil hamster.

How dense could you get? How could anyone throw kids' parties for a job and not know the number one thing you don't do to a cake-filled child. You don't *squeeze them.*

Pushed into a hug by those little pink paws, the contents of Troy's stomach had been squished out all over me, like someone trying to get the last bit out of a tube of toothpaste. Except instead of being minty fresh, I smelt of Haribo and unhappiness. And it was all Nibbles' fault.

I wondered what sort of sentence I'd get for having a hamster assassinated. Maybe I could bribe a local vet to come in and do it on the sly. In the mirror I could see that my face had turned from its usual dark olive tan to a shade as bright as the cupcake slime on my clothes, embarrassment and fury burning together under my skin. Stupid kids. Stupid hamster. Stupid, sexy, Jayden-Lee.

That gross comment about Jude should have killed my crush on him. I knew it should. *Obviously* it was a crappy thing to say, and if Mum had heard it she'd be wearing Jayden-Lee's teeth as a necklace by now. But my brain was already trying to make excuses for him. The thing was, people said ridiculous stuff about Jude all the time. Even the really well-meaning ones were always talking over him to whoever was behind his chair, as if sitting down somehow made him incapable of speech.

So it wasn't like Jayden-Lee was the only person who'd ever acted like that around him. Just, probably the best-looking one.

I dumped my trainers in the sink, kicked off my jeans and turned on the water to blast away some of the sick spatter, while I tried to figure out why that made a difference.

It's not like I'd let someone off for insulting my brother just because they had a five-star rating on the Fitness Scale. I'm not the type of person who loses his head about boys on a regular basis. In fact, I've had a total of three serious, world-altering crushes in my life so far.

1. **Freddie Alton – Sports Prefect at school.** So good-looking I physically can't form words when he's around. Like, when I'm talking to someone else and he walks past, all my vowels disappear and I end up saying something like *hnnnnngghh aaa-rrrgh.* He probably thinks I'm foreign exchange.

2. **Sam Shepherd – my next-door neighbour until last year.** We spent so much time together that Dad cut a gate in the fence between our houses. I tried a few times to tell him I liked him in a more-than-friendly way, but he never really got it. Then Sam's mum got a job in Berlin. They moved, and now we just talk on the computer sometimes, and he sent me a postcard on my birthday featuring six different kinds of German sausage.

3. **Dr Wei Liu from Woking Community Hospital.** Smart, insanely good-looking, and not necessarily too old for me either. At least, when Grandma came to visit me after I had my appendix out, she kept telling him he couldn't be more than twelve. On the other hand, he *has* looked at X-rays of my bowels, which probably didn't trigger love at first sight.

Three crushes. And it might be obvious that none of them exactly worked out. Everyone else I know has kissed someone. Half my class have been on dates or started relationships or even – in Kayla's case – had a series of highly dramatic break-ups involving compensation claims for unpaid cinema tickets, and a custody case over a goldfish.

So maybe I did have dreams of holiday romance, but really all I wanted was the chance to have what other people did. I didn't want just another crush; I wanted someone who liked me back. And it seemed more likely to happen here, where no one knew me and I didn't have to worry about a) embarrassing myself in front of the whole school b) messing up a friendship or c) getting someone struck off the medical register.

Maybe Jayden-Lee could finally be the one.

He might have a few issues, but true love was supposed to take work, wasn't it? Fairy tales didn't start at the happily-ever-after. Sometimes you had to wait until the prince stopped being a beast.

That was it. That was what this was. It was my chance to educate Jayden-Lee. To help him become a better person. I'd be building my own perfect man, only without the need for lightning strikes, surgical skills and a hunchbacked assistant.

I'd just have to get him alone and explain why

'retard' is a rubbish word to use about anybody, and how much it didn't apply to my little brother. He'd get it, if I explained. He had to. I could picture the apology already: a faint, guilty hunch to his rugged shoulders as he understood that he'd been wrong. A pleading look in his green eyes while he asked me how he could possibly make things better.

Maybe some light crying when he told me he'd do anything, *anything*, to make up for it. Nothing embarrassingly sniffly, but you couldn't go wrong with a single, manly tear.

Then I'd invite him back to our caravan to meet Jude properly, and we'd sit on the sofa and bond over Jude's DVDs of *Twinkle the Talking Train*. Our eyes would meet and we'd be startled by the electricity that ran between us as our fingers tangled together in the tin of iced gems.

It was the perfect plan. And as soon as I'd soaked the sick out of my clothes, I'd start working out how to make it happen. My trainers would probably be all right, I'd managed to soak them before any regurgitated cupcake got crusted in. The legs of my jeans still looked a funny colour, but I guessed they'd be OK once I'd dried them off.

Folding the jeans over one arm and holding them out so they didn't drip down my bare legs, I took them over to the hand drier on the wall to figure out how to do that.

It was one of those fancy new types: the kind that have a deep slot where you can put your hands in and wait while something that sounds like a jet engine tries to vibrate all the skin off them.

If I held my jeans up high enough, I could slide both legs down into the slot and blast them dry up to the knee. Except, wet denim didn't seem to set off the sensors as easily as human skin. Somehow I needed to get my hands and the jeans into the slot at the same time.

So I did what anyone would have done, if they were smart enough. I pulled my jeans on over my head and leaned forward to dangle the legs into the slot, giving myself both arms free to get the drier working.

It was quite peaceful, really. I'd never worn jeans on my head before, but it was warm and mostly dark, except for a small triangle of light coming in through the zip. As I let the jet noise rumble up my trouser legs and rattle through my ears, I relaxed for what felt like the first time all day. Everything was sorted. I was just going to have to engineer a complex, multi-layered plan to let true love take me by surprise, exactly the way it was supposed to.

'Hey, are you all right?' a voice said, right by my ear.

It turns out that the dangerous thing about the inner peace of a pair of pants is that, when you're wearing them over your ears, you can't hear if someone's opened the door behind you.

You can't hear them, in fact, until they're close enough to tap you on the shoulder and scare you into stumbling face-first into a roaring hand drier.

SEVEN

'Bad luck back there,' the voice behind me continued, as though it wasn't talking to someone with the bum part of their jeans where the back of their head should be. To someone with a freakish headbum, who'd just slammed their nose into the side of a hand drier and was trying not to hop about and yell with the pain.

I was already going to have to go and live in a cave for the rest of my life to deal with the shame. I didn't need to look *more* ridiculous.

'These parties can get rough,' the voice was saying. 'It's like entertaining a room full of tiny drunk people – someone's always about to puke, pick a fight or take an unexpected nap under the buffet table. Will your brother be OK?'

It wasn't Jayden-Lee's voice. Jayden-Lee hadn't walked in on me standing in my boxers with my jeans on my head. There was a God and he wanted me to get a date sometime in the next decade. It was probably just one of the dads from the party.

Just a friendly, concerned . . . really young-sounding dad.

I tried to pull my head free to answer him, and let out a strangled yelp.

The zip was caught in my hair. My jeans were locked tight to a clump of fringe in the middle of my forehead, trapping me in my own buttock-space. I pulled up again, experimentally, and felt a few hairs ping painfully from my scalp.

So, these were my choices:

1. I could rethink the living-in-a-cave plan and spend the rest of my life on the outskirts of civilization, just me and a specially trained assistance dog I'd send out to fetch my shopping (Tesco probably don't deliver to the depths of the woods). I'd learn which berries to pick and which mushrooms were edible, far away from the harsh stares of normal folk.
2. I could style it out.

I didn't have the patience for dog training. It was going to have to be option two. I swung my head round, jean-legs flapping in front of me like the trunk of some mutant denim elephant, fully prepared to act cool.

And it wasn't one of the dads at all. Between the teeth of my zip I could see one concerned-looking dark-brown eye – the kind of shade that's almost black, but

41

just a fraction too warm. If I tipped my head sideways, my gaze ran along a similarly dark-skinned cheek, and down to a wide mouth with the corners bitten down, like they were trying not to curl into a smile.

It took me a minute to remember that he'd asked me a question. Would Jude be OK?

'Err. Um. Mhmm?' I replied.

Which probably wasn't the clearest answer, but when I'm nervous I sometimes forget how words work.

What I was *trying* to say was that so far Jude had made it through two hamstring surgeries, a case of German measles that all joined together to turn him a frankly impressive shade of neon pink, and being stuck in the head part of an Ewok costume for seven and a half hours one Halloween. So I thought he'd probably survive the whole gum/hair trauma. He was pretty tough, after all.

Tougher than me, anyway. I'd been stuck in my jeans for less than ten minutes and I was already falling apart.

The translation process between my brain and my mouth somehow took all the things I meant to say and replaced them with a series of grunts. I added an uncertain shrug, trying not to notice that I was dripping sick-water on to the floor between us.

He had a staff shirt on. I could see the ARC part of

STARCROSS through the viewing window made by my open flies.

I had no idea how I'd missed him at the party, but obviously he couldn't have avoided seeing me taking a relaxing dip in the puke fountain. Just great. I might only have seen a few triangle-shaped fragments of his face, but they were the face parts of someone not too much older than me. My chances of using this holiday to emerge from my dire and dateless chrysalis as a brilliant social butterfly were narrowing by the minute.

I tilted my head to the side and got a new slice of facial real-estate.

He had an eyebrow bar.

I had headpants.

I was *totally* going to have to go with the cave-dwelling, grocery-shopping dog plan.

'Do you ... need any help with that?' he asked. I watched his feet shuffle on the floor. He had the exact trainers that mine were a cheaper copy of.

I was so busy trying to figure out by exactly how many degrees he outcooled me that for a moment I had no idea what he meant. I stared blankly into the seams of my jeans.

He coughed, softly. 'I mean, do you want me to get you out of your jeans?'

Everything went silent for a minute. Even the drier

finished its cycle and paused, as though it wasn't quite sure what it had just heard either.

I watched the curve of his mouth narrow out into a thin line, then quirk upwards again. 'Or, you know, the same question put less weirdly. Only, it seems like you might be getting dressed the wrong way round.'

Sucking in a deep breath, I shook my head, flapping jeans and all. 'No, it's OK. Actually, at this point I think I'm fine with no one ever seeing my face again.'

'Well, I get the appeal of being invisible, sometimes. But it seems like a shame to me.'

He hadn't stepped back much since tapping me on the shoulder, and I was suddenly really aware of the fact that we were less than a foot apart, which was much closer than *I'd* want to stand next to a bum-headed lunatic whose face I couldn't even see.

If he had been further back, I might have been able to see *his* whole face all in one go, instead of just a scrap of a really-quite-nice-actually smile.

'Also, dressing like that's probably going to lead to a few more close encounters of the nose-smashing kind,' he added.

He hadn't somehow blinked and missed me nutting the hand drier, then. I felt my nose twang as a sore reminder.

'Oh that?' I held up my hands innocently, though I

was pretty sure I looked more like the pictures of this Hindu elephant god we learned about in school once. '*Completely* intentional. I've got . . . anger-management problems. Bad ones. Sometimes I just, you know: *Grrr.*'

I actually growled at him. Like a tiger, or a lion or, you know, a complete weirdo with jeans on his head.

And the weird part was, he didn't do the sensible thing and back away muttering soothing phrases, like he probably should have. He just laughed again. I saw the STAR on his chest skip under the breath he took. 'Well, let me know if you need me to do anything. Even if it's just talking you out of assaulting inanimate objects. One of my sisters is into this mindfulness and meditation thing right now, so I've got *really* good at talking nonsense in a calming way. Just ask for Leo.'

'Leo,' I repeated, and I was about to tell him my name when the howl of feedback from Stacie's microphone screeched through the door. Both of us winced.

'*WOULD THE OWNERS OF THE TODDLER IN PINK PLEASE GET HER DOWN FROM THE LIGHT FIXTURES? THANK YOU.*'

Stacie's voice echoed through from the hall outside. It looked like the Troy incident had just been the party warming up.

'*I REPEAT: PLEASE COLLECT YOUR CHILD FROM THE CEILING.*'

Leo bit his lip apologetically. It was the only bit of his face that I could see, but it was weirdly hard to look away from.

My brain took a moment to register that he smelt nice too. I couldn't put my finger on what it reminded me of.

'Duty calls,' he told me, spinning on his heels and making for the door. Finally I had an almost full view of someone tall and long-limbed, with a head full of dreadlocks that were almost to his shoulders, messy and dark. Just the back view, though. He called over his shoulder, 'Remember, ask for Leo if you need anything!'

Ask for Leo.

Yeah, I could just tell him the boy with jeans for a face said hi. Like that was ever going to happen. As soon as I got these things off my head I was going to start looking for a cave.

EIGHT

By the time I emerged from the loos, the jeans were back on the part of my body they were designed for. I'd managed to remove a significant amount of my hair along with them, but I couldn't complain too much about that.

Not once I'd seen Jude.

Kayla had bought him a ride on the miniature version of Twinkle the Talking Train that stood outside the main doors to the showhall. It cost a pound for three minutes of Twinkle rocking gently while making *choo choo* noises. Every backward rock tipped Jude just far enough for me to be able to see the perfectly round, palm-sized bald patch right in the middle of his scalp.

'*What did you do?*' I mouthed, hoping that Jude would be too distracted by the ride to see me flapping my arms behind him. There's something about a crisis that makes me lose all control of my limbs.

'*It was welded in!*' Kayla hissed back, ducking around Twinkle and coming over to catch hold of my hands and bring them down to a safe level. 'I looked up "gum-removal techniques" on my phone, and the options were freezing it out, boiling it, or cutting it off. I thought this was the method he'd be most likely to survive.'

'Did you think about how likely *I* am to survive once Mum sees it?' My arms flapped up again. Kayla caught them. It looked like we were doing a two-person version of a Mexican wave.

Jude's prematurely balding head swung back towards me, glinting in the sunlight. I groaned. '*Sweet baby cheeses.*'

(Ever since Jude's been old enough to repeat things, all the bad words in our house have been cleaned up. Even when something much MUCH stronger – or cooler – is called for, I just can't seem to get the four-year-old-friendly versions out of my system. It's total bullspit.)

Twinkle gradually chugged to a halt, and Jude twisted round to look at me. 'Dylan! I got a haircut!'

Understatement of the century. It looked more like someone had gone after him with a lawn mower. I forced a smile. 'You definitely did! You look a bit like Friar Tuck.'

Jude screwed up his face. I couldn't tell whether he thought this was a bad thing, or just couldn't remember who Friar Tuck was. I knew we'd watched the Disney film together – it was probably where he got his love of dumb, oversized animals from.

'You know, the monk one who's best friends with Robin Hood? Giant talking mole, hits people with a stick?'

'Oh.' Jude nodded. *'Cool.'*

Kayla put more money in to set Twinkle off again and I spun around and nearly flung an accidental elbow into her nose. *'We have got to get him a hat.'*

Which was why, twenty minutes later, I was walking back to our caravan behind a mini-version of Nibbles, my own personal nemesis. Kayla had found hamster hats on the party's merchandise table, in between the sign-up list for getting your photo taken with the furry monstrosity and a giant wall poster of him. I'd considered buying the poster and using it as a dartboard.

After Kayla threatened to sue, we got given the hat for free, plus a cupcake, and Jude was put on the list for a Hamster Snuggle Selfie to be taken in a special tent at the funfair at the end of the week. Meanwhile I was somehow going to have to convince Mum that Jude would freak out if he couldn't keep his new fuzzy orange abomination of a hamster hat on at all times. Including for meals. And in bed. And the shower.

Kayla nudged my shoulder as we walked. 'I know how we can keep that hat stuck on *forever*. All it should take is a bit more gum.'

She'd been quieter than usual since bullying Stacie into the free gifts. She kept taking out her phone and glancing at it, then putting it away again with a sigh, and staring at her feet. I thought maybe it was guilt. I was just going to reassure her a bit (boiling or freezing Jude probably *would* have been worse ideas), when I was distracted by a rhythmic thudding noise, like someone boxing a brick wall.

It was getting louder the nearer we got to 131 Alpine Views.

'You don't think Alfie's mum's going mental on the Slaters' garden gnomes now, do you?' The flamingo had caused enough trouble. Gnome abuse could kick off World War Three.

Kayla shook her head. 'They all look intact to me.'

I turned to look just as Jayden-Lee's Dramavan came into view. The first thing I noticed was that she was right. The second thing I noticed was a ball flying directly at my head.

Now, there are a few things about me that not everybody knows, and one of them is this: I'm pretty good at football.

I'm *really* pretty good at it.

I don't play as much as I used to, because the problem with me being pretty good at football was that Dad got completely obsessed. He even stopped going to the Woking United games he'd always attended religiously so he could start coming to mine instead. But any time he turned up to watch me on the school team, it turned into total chaos. He coached a choir of mums to sing rude chants about the opposition and everything.

When one of his 'quiet words' with the ref at an interschool match turned into more of a quiet fistfight, I got kicked off the team for being a disruptive influence. Which was seriously unfair. *I* wasn't the disruptive influence; I was just *related* to one.

It was probably for the best, even though Dad had to give up his dreams of me being Woking's next top striker. Freddie Alton was made captain not long after that, and I don't think I could have played on his team without tripping over the ball.

I could still take a header when I wanted to, though. In fact, I could do better than that. I headed the ball directly into the side of the nearest caravan, then caught it against my chest on the return bounce. Letting it drop, I brought my leg up under it and passed it between my knee and the side of my foot without letting it touch the ground.

My keepy-uppy record is *legendary*, by the way.

While I kept the ball in the air, I looked up to see Jayden-Lee and a gang of other boys staring at me. One of them had obviously lost control and kicked it my way by accident. Lucky it didn't hit Jude – he could do a lot of things in his chair, but dodging easily wasn't really one of them.

My stomach gave a strange kind of lurch, like that moment when you tip over the highest slope on a rollercoaster.

I couldn't say anything about earlier *now*. His friends were with him, and I hadn't even told Kayla what he'd said, because I just knew she wouldn't understand. So I nodded a hello, and flicked the ball towards him off the tip of my toe.

It swooped right over his head, and over the hand he threw up to catch it. Landing smack in the awning over the Dramavan door, it rolled down one of the support struts, bounced off the birdbath and came to a slow halt right in front of Jayden-Lee's feet.

He raised one eyebrow, then the other, and said, 'Impressed.'

Then he winked at me. My stomach lurched upwards again. And I felt a part of my heart – hopefully not the part responsible for beating and pumping and all the regular coronary busywork – explode.

NINE

'Want to play?'

If they ever opened a museum dedicated to the life and loves of Dylan H. Kershaw, this moment would get its own exhibit. Probably in a little room with a gold rope at the door and signs on the wall telling people not to touch anything. This moment was precious.

Jayden-Lee nodded towards the ball, then looked back at me. 'Join in. Kev can go in goal and—'

'Actually,' Kayla cut in, 'we were just going to make sure Jude—'

'It's OK.' I couldn't let this perfect opportunity be stolen by the fact my brother had a bald patch. It wasn't like Jude was crying any more. 'You can settle him down on your own, can't you? Just stick on the TV.'

I shot Kayla a pleading look. It was hard to say exactly what the pointed glare she gave me in return was supposed to mean, but she was my best friend. I *knew* she'd want me to be happy. She'd want me to have the chance to be winked at again.

She didn't specifically *say* that, obviously. In fact she didn't say anything before pushing Jude up the ramp into the caravan and slamming the door, but it had to be true. That's what friends were for.

Jayden-Lee's mates crowded in around me. 'That's Kev,' he said, pointing to a tall boy with buzzed brown hair, 'And Dean, and the loser with the curls is Fauntleroy.'

For a moment everything went quiet as we all turned towards the boy Jayden-Lee was gesturing at. Fauntleroy's blond curls were pulled into a neat ponytail and he was shrugging so hard it looked like his head might retract into his neck. 'Mum says I'm two hundred and twenty-third in line to the throne, so she named me something noble,' he said, in a Welsh accent. 'Leroy's fine.'

Leroy got the ball and within a minute we were mid-game, a couple of ornamental flamingos having been set up as goalposts. To begin with, every time I got near the ball I'd do something fancy with it, like the Elastico – faking a kick in one direction then snapping the ball back with the inside of my foot – or the Scorpion Kick.

I knew loads of tricks. But before I'd got through half of them, I noticed that the others were looking a bit . . . less impressed. I pulled off a perfect Maradona Spin and Kev actually yawned.

So I played a bit worse after that. Quite a bit worse. Weirdly, once I started pretending to be rubbish, it seemed as though they started to like me a bit more.

We hadn't been at it long when a woman in a pink sundress rolled up in one of the hire buggies they had on the park and yelled out of the window, 'Boys! Nice Slice hour at the Pie-O-Ria! Come with me if you want to eat.'

'Mum!' Dean yelled, hi-fiving Kev before they both dived into the back of the buggy. Leroy climbed up and stood on the side of the seat, hanging precariously on to the frame.

Jayden-Lee sauntered after them, sliding into the seat beside Dean's mum.

And then there was no more room in the buggy, which was almost definitely why no one invited me to join them. I was sure Jayden-Lee would have said something about it, or at least said bye, if someone hadn't started to shout from his pocket.

'*HEY, LOSER. LOOOOSER!*'

It was one of those comedy ring-tones; I recognized it from a sketch on one of the shows Mum wouldn't let me watch. Slowly, Jayden-Lee pulled out a battered green phone, and clicked to answer it just as the buggy pulled away.

I watched until they were out of sight, then checked the time. We'd only played for twenty minutes, but I was pretty sure they'd been the best twenty minutes of my life.

'He *likes* me.' Letting myself back into our caravan, I swooned in the direction of my bedroom and draped myself over the bed. Kayla had given Jude a tin of biscuits to bribe him into keeping his hat on forever and set him up on the sofa with some cartoons. I could hear the *Twinkle* theme tune playing, but it was just background music to the song in my heart.

'*Jayden-Lee* likes me. He likes *me*.'

Kayla gave me a weird look as she came over to perch on the edge of the bed, and I sat up.

'Don't you think he likes me?'

She shrugged. It wasn't the boundless enthusiasm I'd been hoping for, but Kayla's always been more practical than romantic. She was the only girl in our class who didn't develop a crush on the French teacher's son when he helped on a trip last year, because apparently it's impractical to like someone whose mum could have a major say in whether or not you fail your GCSEs.

She really didn't understand romance at all.

'Well, he definitely thinks you're good at football. He likes your right foot,' she said, kicking her own foot out across the six inches of space between the bed and the wall.

'Apart from the fact that I'm going to pretend that trick was fully intentional *forever*, and not that I was millimetres away from booting one of the windows in –'

which I might have been – *'He likes my right foot? Seriously? Wow, well I feel really special now, thanks a lot.'*

Kayla sighed. 'I don't mean that he can't like the rest of you, just that the foot's all we have evidence for. He said he was impressed, didn't he? So, was he looking you up and down when he said it, in a "this trick shot has made me suddenly appreciate your many charms" kind of way, or was he just talking about the kick?'

Even Kayla didn't usually resort to this kind of cold shower. Maybe I should have told her about Leo from the loos, and how I had to make things work with Jayden-Lee, because the only other prospect around here thought I didn't know how to dress myself.

'So what if it was the kick? I have to start somewhere. It got him to ask me to play. Now I just need to find a unique talent for the rest of my body parts and maybe I'll have a date for something more than football.' It was totally doable. I could already wiggle my ears and raise each eyebrow independently. 'I can work on my face next; that's probably an important one.'

'Yeah, OK then.' Kayla pulled her feet up on to the bed and looked out to where Jude was singing along to 'Twinkle's Tune Time'. Something was seriously wrong.

'You don't have to feel guilty about it, you know,' I told her, snipping my fingers at the air like scissors to show what I meant. 'Jude doesn't seem to mind, and I think the hat plan's foolproof.'

'What?' Kayla frowned at me. 'Oh – no, it's not that . . .'

'And if you're worried that me and Jayden-Lee becoming Cornwall's coolest couple means I'll forget you, you're *so* wrong. Everyone needs a token straight best friend to tell them that their feet are their only attractive part.'

'That is *not* what I said.' But at least some of the fire was back in Kayla's voice. 'Though you've already ditched me for him once. But it's not that, either. I'm just . . . I'm homesick, all right?'

Obviously it was all right, I just couldn't really understand it.

'But we've been here one day.'

'I know.'

'And we're still in England.'

'I *know*.'

'In fact, we're only three hours down the M4.'

'*I know that, Dylan*,' Kayla growled, throwing a pillow at me. 'I can't help it. I've never been this far away from Dad before. What if he misses me? What if he doesn't? What if he's making toast using the ironing board again?'

The reason Kayla's so practical, really, is probably

because her dad isn't. It's been just the two of them ever since her mum went on a trip to 'find herself' when Kayla was eight, and ended up deciding that meant losing everyone else. Kayla and her dad are really close now, but sometimes it's a struggle to figure out who's taking care of who.

I stretched a leg out, and nudged her knee with my toe. 'Hey.'

She squirmed away, quickly. 'Gross. Get your disgustingly attractive feet away from me.'

Laughing, I moved to sit next to her. 'I thought you came with us so your dad would learn to cope without you.'

'I did.' She tangled a hand into her hair as though she might be tempted to start tugging it out. 'But I didn't know it would be so hard to cope without *him*.'

Slinging an arm round her shoulder, I nodded. 'OK, OK. Listen. I know Cornwall's a big culture clash, what with all the . . . fresh air and the . . . pasties . . .'

'And the seagulls. And the Elvises.'

'And the *hamsters*. And I know it's weird without your dad, but you're going to get through it. It's not even for a whole week. And you already know he misses you – how many times has he texted today?'

She held up her phone. There was a green message:

How are you?

Followed by at least six replies in blue.

Ah, fine.

Just as fine as can be expected, considering.
You have fun, Kayla! Don't worry about me.

P.S. Please email the instructions for
the TV again. I think it has broken.

Also the washing machine.

The toaster is certainly broken.
But at least not on fire any more.

P.P.S. I am doing some DIY while
you're gone. You will be impressed.

And, finally, one that had been sent just a few minutes
ago.

Please remind me, what are the symptoms
of concussion? I am asking for a friend.

I could sort of see why she was worrying. 'Did you . . . ?'

She nodded. 'I called. He really was asking for a friend . . . I had to tell him I don't think the goldfish is going to make it.'

I winced. 'Poor Flipper. But look, you've just got to keep yourself too busy to get homesick. I know last night was a washout, but there's a comedian in the showhall tonight, and it'll probably have stopped smelling of sick by now.'

'I don't know.' Kayla kicked her feet against the wall again. 'I was thinking chocolate and wallowing sounded good. Anyway, you look—'

'No way.' I was already talking over her, getting to my feet to pull her up off the bed. 'This is a holiday, not a wallowday. We're going out, and nothing can stop us.'

Then Mum burst in through the caravan door, trailing Dad and about a million shopping bags in her wake.

'Hello darling, other darling, other darling's darling friend,' she called, breezing past my bedroom and giving Dad a billion instructions on where to put the bags. It looked like they'd wiped out the local supermarket. When she found a good discount, my mum turned into the human equivalent of a plague of locusts.

I stole a quick glance out of the window to see if the lights were on in the Dramavan. The last thing I needed was for Jayden-Lee to forget his sudden appreciation of my fabulous feet in light of the fact that I'm the only fourteen-year-old *darling* in the world.

Mum hadn't stopped since she hit the tiny caravan kitchen. She was opening and closing cupboards in a kind of blur. 'You can put the corned beef away, can't you, Dylan? Six packs for the price of three!'

I didn't point out that meant two packs for the price of one, and that we were never going to want to look at a cow again after eating all those. I couldn't get a word in.

'Anyway, can't stop, your dad and I are going to watch a brilliant new comedian. *Highly* recommended by a gentleman dressed as Elvis in his porky period. You two won't mind staying in with Jude again tonight, will you? You've been partying all day.'

Yeah, with a gang of four-year-olds. But that was it. Mum turned her whirlwind back towards the door as if I'd been standing there nodding and saying, 'Yes Mum, I'd love to be trapped in a tin box for the second night in a row. I've always wanted to know what it feels like to live in a bunker. Don't mind the crying, by the way, it's only boredom.'

There was just one good thing about the visit from

62

Hurricane Mum. She was in and out so quick that she didn't even notice her youngest son had half a hamster on his head.

Dad leaned on the kitchen counter, peeled back the plastic on a pack of corned beef and ate a slice straight from the tray.

'Don't worry,' he said. 'I'll bring the good jokes back for you.'

He nodded towards Jude and his orange hamster hat. 'Later, Ginger.'

Then to me. 'Later, Rudolph.'

Then he was gone too. The caravan looked somehow emptier than before, even though it was now full of carrier bags and cheap beef. On the sofa, Jude lifted one hand and waved.

'Hi Mummy. Bye Mummy.'

Kayla sighed and patted me on the shoulder as she walked past me towards the kitchen carnage. 'I'll get the chocolate.'

TEN

'What did he mean, "Later, Rudolph"?'

Dad's jokes could be bad, but it was seriously out of season for reindeer. Although, I wasn't sure he'd have made any more sense in December. I followed Kayla to the kitchen. 'Did I grow antlers or something?'

She pulled a face. 'Well . . .'

'I *did* grow antlers?' I reached up and started rummaging through my hair. Maybe something fell on me. Maybe I'd been walking round looking like an escapee from the New Forest all day.

'No, Dylan, don't be ridiculous. It's just – well, doesn't your nose *hurt* at all?'

It didn't, really. But when she mentioned it, I realized that it hadn't been feeling quite *right* for a while. Not since it had violently introduced itself to the hand drier in the loos. I covered it with the palm of my hand, then yelped, unprepared for the burst of pain that spiked up into my skull.

'It was getting redder and redder the whole time we were walking back. I didn't want to say anything, you know, after you saw Jayden-Lee . . .'

After Jayden-Lee saw *me.* I sat down heavily on the floor, head (carefully) cradled in my hands. Kayla crouched beside me. 'It's not that bad, really. Want to see?'

I puffed out an anxious breath between my knees. 'Maybe. But if you're lying, then you've got to help me dig the hole in the ground I'm going to bury myself in.'

'Deal.'

She returned a couple of minutes later with a mirror. I took it, cautiously, then nearly flattened her with a panicked wave of my arms. 'IT'S HUGE.'

'It's a magnifying mirror,' Kayla said, patiently. 'Look in the other side.'

It was still horrible. There was a purple ridge across the bridge of my nose, which must have been the impact point. Everything below that was a swollen, throbbing red. It looked like the middle of my face had been swallowed up by the world's biggest boil.

'He wasn't impressed by my kick,' I said slowly, as the truth finally hit me. 'He was impressed by the actual volcanic eruption on my face.'

'It's not—'

'*Look at me,*' I snapped, not wanting to be reassured when I knew it was a lie. 'Better take a few steps back before molten lava starts pouring out of my nose.'

Kayla clicked her tongue and stole the mirror back so

I couldn't keep staring at my hideous disfigurement. I was just wondering how realistic it would be to pretend I was my own ugly twin when she held a hand out. 'Come on, we'll cover it up.'

Along with every Deathsplash Nightmares lyric, and about a dozen reasons why homework should be classified as child labour, make-up was one of the things Kayla knew best. She tidied the small herd of sliced cattle Mum had left us into the fridge, restocked Jude's biscuit supply, then shepherded me into the bedroom carrying a make-up bag the size of Mars.

Kayla's bag went everywhere with her. Sometimes I thought she had a closer relationship with the things she smeared on her face than she did with me. She rummaged inside it for a minute, then pulled out a tube so big it looked like you could hammer nails in with it.

'Coverclear Concealer,' she announced, holding the thing out like it was the top prize in a game show. 'This is what's going to make you beautiful again. Now, hold still.'

I held still. The next few minutes were dark and unsettling, as she spread what felt like thick cake batter across my face. I had a feeling that if I peeked, I'd find her using a trowel.

She got it from the internet, the concealer stuff. I knew because I still remembered the day she'd turned up in class looking totally different. No lipstick, no mascara. She just looked really . . . skin-coloured.

Because, before that, she didn't. Kayla's got this birthmark, kind of an unusual one called a port wine stain. It looks a bit like someone's splashed a big glass of it all over her. The whole of one side of her face is covered in splotches of red.

Obviously, when she started school, none of the other kids knew what a port wine stain was. So they called her Ketchup Face.

Kayla was shorter, and a few dress sizes bigger than most of the other girls, but she seemed to brush off any dumb comments made about that. It was Ketchup Face that stuck. So, as soon as she found a way to cover her birthmark up, she did. I just had no idea it took this much work.

'Are you nearly done yet?' I growled through gritted teeth, trying not to let the muscles in my face twitch and mess everything up. 'I think I feel it starting to set. You know, like concrete?'

'Nearly done,' Kayla replied. 'Just putting on the blusher and eye shadow.'

'WHAT?' *Every* muscle in my face twitched as I opened my eyes and tried to push her away, but she was already doubling over with laughter.

'Your face! As *if* I'd do that to you. Well −' she

quirked one eyebrow – 'not unless you think Jayden-Lee would like it?'

I scowled, lightly shoving her away. 'Have I ever told you how unfunny you are?'

'All the time. That's how I know when I've achieved genius. And speaking of genius, take a look.'

She held up the mirror. I peered into it, prepared for the worst. But I looked . . . normal. A bit suspicious and squinty-eyed, and my nose was still a few centimetres bigger than usual, but mostly I looked normal. Skin-coloured. I looked up at Kayla, gratefully. 'I could *so* give you a Hamster Hug right now.'

'No thanks – I saw what happened during the last one.' She started putting her magic kit away again. 'Anyway, unless you get it wet, that stuff's set like . . . well, yeah. Like concrete. You never did tell me how you messed your nose up, by the way.'

'I had an accident with my jeans.'

Her eyes widened.

'Not *that* kind of accident.'

There was no way I was telling her all the details of how I'd embarrassed myself. She was going to stop letting me out on my own. I tugged on her arm, instead. 'Come on; let's see if anything's happening in the Dramavan. It might be the only entertainment we get all night.'

When we went to the window, though, the caravan opposite was deserted.

'Oh well,' Kayla shrugged. 'It's too early for a fight, anyway. Fancy a beef sarnie?'

Four hours later we'd eaten three corned-beef sandwiches each, watched two DVDs of *Twinkle* (I was mentally picking out the most romantic episode to play when Jayden-Lee made his big apology), and I was just coming back from putting Jude to bed when I found Kayla standing at the window again.

'What are you looking at?' I asked. 'The whole park's dark tonight.'

Literally *everybody* must have been in the showhall. We were missing a comedy legend.

Kayla pressed her palm to the windowpane. 'That's why I'm looking. Tonight you can see the stars.'

I watched her for a minute, thinking. 'You know what I said about going out tonight?'

'Nothing's going to stop us? Yes, that went well.'

I shook my head and caught her hand in mine. 'It was just delayed, that's all. Come on, we can at least get a decent view.'

We only went a few steps. Just far enough to be able to lie down in the grass. You really could see the stars. The sky looked broader and there seemed to be more of them than there were in Woking. I turned my face towards Kayla. She looked more delicate in the moonlight than she ever let herself appear by day. 'The view's better, right?'

'Yes, and the glow-in-the-dark flamingos really add to the ambience,' she deadpanned. But her mouth turned up at the edges.

'It's just nice that, wherever you go, you can look up at exactly the same stars.'

'Unless you go to Australia, or anywhere in the southern hemisphere, really, where they have an entirely different set.'

'Really?' I leaned on my elbow to look down at her. 'I mean – stop spoiling it! I'm trying to say your dad could be looking up at the same stars, right now. He's not that far away.'

Kayla smiled at me. 'I know what you were trying to say, even if it was horrifically corny, and I think you might have got the idea from a cartoon mouse. But thanks. I just need to remember I have a bit of home here with me, too.'

'Is it in your make-up bag? Because that thing's massive. Did you bring the kitchen sink? OW, no need to kick me!' We were both trying not to admit we were laughing. Kayla had her arms crossed over her chest to keep from shaking.

'*No*, I meant—'

'I know what you meant. Me too.'

'I hate you.'

'I hate you too.'

I flopped on to my back again, looking up at the millions of stars. Australia was totally missing out: just then, I wouldn't have wanted to be anywhere else.

ELEVEN

Kayla was right about her magic make-up. The next morning my nose hurt more, but it was still mostly the same colour as my face. I carefully washed around it to preserve the effect. It was like having one of those peel-off facemasks that supervillains use as disguises, except this one just made me look like myself.

I emerged from my room and did my now-habitual check of the Dramavan, trying to catch the Slater family sitting down to their cornflakes. Jayden-Lee probably looked *amazing* with morning hair. I smoothed my hands back through my own bedhead, trying to calm down some of the weird angles it liked to stick up at while I slept.

Jude's coat was missing from the hook on the door, so he and Dad must have gone out early. Meanwhile Mum was in the kitchen, picking at a slice of corned beef on toast in between ironing some sort of evening dress that looked like it was made from tinfoil, and beating the contestants to all the answers on a TV quiz show.

From the smile she gave me when I joined her, she

hadn't discovered Jude's new hairdo yet. I wondered if I could convince her that monk-chic was in.

'Laika!' she exclaimed, before I could say good morning. 'First dog in space!'

We both turned to the TV to watch a nervous girl in owl glasses repeat the same answer seconds later. Mum looked triumphant. 'Ha!'

She reached out to ruffle my newly smoothed hair. 'Morning, my crumpled sweetheart. Congratulations on managing to join us in the waking world before noon. Then again, you did have a busy day yesterday, didn't you – Jude hasn't *stopped* talking about the party.'

She offered me a corner of beefy bread, and I screwed up my nose. Even if I'd wanted to eat it, not knowing exactly what Jude had said was making my stomach turn over in uncomfortable ways.

'He even wore his new hat to bed. I never – The artist was Caravaggio! Yes! – knew he was so *enthusiastic* about hamsters.' She shook her head, popping the bit of toast into her own mouth.

I tried not to sigh with relief. 'Yeah, I *totally* don't understand the appeal . . . Mum, about yesterday . . .'

I stopped. Part of me really wanted to tell Mum exactly what had happened with Jude, with the party, my nose – everything. If I just explained now that Jude had gotten into a *quite literally* sticky situation, and the brutal scalping that Kayla gave him with her nail scissors had been the only way out of it, then she might not take the news too badly.

If things went well, I probably wouldn't get stuck babysitting my little brother for the rest of the holiday.

Though, if they went badly, I might not be allowed to see the outside of the caravan for the rest of the holiday either.

And I was starting to like Starcross Sands. I still couldn't understand how its dated decorations and pitiful excuses for entertainment had ever qualified it for Park of the Year, but there were a few positive points. I liked the fact that it hadn't rained yet. I liked the Pie-O-Ria's double pepperoni. And the brochure had been right about one thing: it *did* have spectacular views.

As if on cue, there was a loud screech from the direction of my favourite view in the whole park. Mrs Slater had the kind of high-pitched siren scream that made it sound like we should all start running for a bomb shelter. '*JAYDEN-LEE, WHAT HAVE I TOLD YOU ABOUT KICKING YOUR BALL AROUND THE CARAVAN? YOU'VE TAKEN THE FACE RIGHT OFF MY LOVELY GNOME!*'

I wondered which of her gnomes the lovely one was. It couldn't have been the angry fisherman, or the scary gardener, or the coal miner who looked like he needed the loo.

Mum looked up from her ironing. 'Mozambique, to win the round. Are they starting *again* over there?'

On screen, the girl in the glasses failed to take the trophy home. Mum had won the quiz. But, as she turned off the TV and switched the radio to *Ultimate 80s Classics* to drown out the sound of another argument starting up across the way, I got the feeling she didn't really approve of our neighbours.

Which reminded me what the real downside would be if I chose to tell Mum the truth about what had happened yesterday. Hearing what Troy Slater did would send her straight over to the Dramavan to have a word. And Mrs Slater might have been good in a fight, but I doubted a single gnome would survive if anyone made another comment about Jude.

Did I want Jayden-Lee seeing Mum in full on Boss Battle mode?

No. No. If I dealt with it myself, I could fix every-thing . . . eventually. So when she turned back to me and asked, 'What was that about yesterday?' I'd made my decision.

'It was *so* unfair.'

I'd deflect.

Because obviously the best way to get rid of any guilt

I felt about hiding things from Mum was to make *her* feel guilty instead.

'Do you know how *boring* it is in this caravan?' I waved an arm around, managing to gesture to the whole tiny room in one movement. 'There's nothing to *do*. Even the TV's only got three channels. It's exactly like living in the Middle Ages. If you'd wanted me to spend the whole holiday trapped in one room, you could just have left me locked in the cellar at home. At least I'd have had my computer.'

I was really getting into my stride, pressing home my point by standing and pacing the six whole steps it took to get across the floor and back, when I noticed Mum wasn't arguing. She wasn't even looking annoyed, or guilty, or however she was supposed to look when she realized she'd been neglecting her eldest child. She was just standing there, hanging her dress on one of the cupboards, calm. Then she dug out a brightly coloured leaflet from under her breakfast plate, and flapped it at me as I paced back to the kitchen counter.

'While I doubt that depriving you of social media and satellite television counts as the human-rights violation you seem to think it is, your dad and I did think you and Kayla deserved a night to yourselves. So we picked this up at the show last night. It looks fun, don't you think?'

Slowly, I reached across to tug the leaflet from between her fingers. *ARE YOU A STARCROSS SINGING SENSATION?* It asked, in bright gold lettering.

I held it at arm's length, as though it might bite me. 'Singing?'

'Karaoke!' Mum beamed like it was Christmas morning and I was unwrapping a brand-new bike. 'Dad wanted to go at first, but lost interest when they told him football anthems aren't allowed. It seems they've been responsible for one or two little disagreements in the past.'

'Yes, but . . . Karaoke?'

I couldn't sing. I really couldn't. If my one-time-only starring role in the school panto had taught me anything, it was that my singing voice was bad enough to break glass and make dogs run away whimpering. I lip-synched the hymns in assemblies. Why would I *ever* want to do karaoke?

'We'll be taking Jude to the water park for the day, then out for dinner. You two can enjoy yourselves.'

'At karaoke.' Somehow, Mum was missing the blank horror in my voice. I tried a different, desperate tactic. 'You know, the water park sounds fun. And this is a *family* holiday, so maybe we could all go . . . ?'

Mum gave me a sugary smile, which was always a

bad sign. 'Of course, darling. Are you going to tell Kayla, or shall I?'

At that moment, the door to the caravan's third bedroom flew open behind me. The intro music to a death metal power ballad filled the room.

Kayla was standing framed in the doorway, her hair backcombed and a hairbrush clutched in one hand to form a makeshift microphone. She looked like she'd styled herself by sticking her finger in a plug socket. And she was staring right at me.

'Tonight, Dylan Kershaw, you and I are going to be *stars!*'

TWELVE

The showhall looked different at night. Like the 'after' segment on a makeover show, it was the same place, but with a few new sparkly curtains hung up to disguise the dowdy bits, and a glitterball/smoke machine combo working hard to distract anyone from looking too closely at the rest.

There was a queue at the door when we got there, so we stood and listened to the playlist of slightly out-of-date pop music banging through the walls.

'Told you they wouldn't have anything by Deathsplash. It's going to be a total cheddar-fest,' I told Kayla.

I'd managed to talk her out of planning a full-scale assault on the stage to 'preach the gospel of rock', and I was pretty sure I'd done the right thing. Most of the other people waiting weren't quite Mum and Dad's age, but they were definitely over the hill when it came to appreciating decent music. Kayla's hair had calmed down a bit, too, and she was looking kind of incredible in a mermaid-coloured glitter dress. She was a magpie for sparkly things; apparently it was tough to find plus-sized dresses that were shiny enough for her taste, so when she found something, she bought it on the spot.

I'd gone for black jeans, instead of blue, and a grey T-shirt I was almost sure had been washed before I packed it. I thought it really gave off the image I was going for: *please no one look at me.*

Kayla was singing scales under her breath. She was approaching karaoke with the dedication of a trained athlete. 'I can adapt my talents to cater for all tastes,' she told me. 'I'm going to do power ballads. I'll power ballad their ears off.'

'That's what I'm afraid of.'

She pushed me, and I laughed. Then I hiccupped. Then I choked.

Jayden-Lee was joining the back of the queue. Jayden-Lee, in a white T-shirt and his black faux-leather jacket. He looked just like the antihero from a black-and-white movie. A rebel without a cause.

Suddenly I wished I'd made a bit more of an effort. I wanted him to find something other than my right foot impressive. Though I stuck it out a bit, anyway, just in case.

Somehow, Kayla hadn't noticed him. She obviously didn't hear the same angelic choirs I did whenever he was nearby – and she was glued to her phone, *again.* I elbowed her, urgently, and she followed my tractor-beam stare to its source.

'Has he seen you?' she asked. 'He's coming this way.'

And he was. My right foot must have had magical properties, because Jayden-Lee skimmed the back of the line altogether and started walking our way. He was wearing sunglasses even though it was dark, which should have been stupid, but just made him look even more gorgeous somehow. Like he needed them just to handle his own radiance.

Then he tripped straight over my foot. He stumbled, grunted, and pushed the glasses up into his hair as he turned and gave me a dismissive look. 'Watch out, yeah? You might want to straighten up a bit.'

Walking past me, he hooked an arm around the waist of the girl at the front of the queue, and disappeared into the smoke. It was like witnessing a grand entrance happening in reverse.

Watching him, I felt my chest tighten up and realized I'd stopped breathing the second we'd made toe-contact. Now I wasn't sure I wanted to start again. I'd read that people who were oxygen deprived sometimes had amazing hallucinations just as their brain started to give up. Maybe, right before I went into a coma, I could hallucinate that someone I fancied would ever actually give me a second look.

Then Kayla smacked me on the back and hissed at

me to *inhale*, and I sucked in an involuntary gasp of air. Fantastic, now I wouldn't even get a hallucinatory date. I had the worst luck.

'He's got a girlfriend,' I said, staring down the line of people at the empty space where Jayden-Lee used to be. A group of women dressed in fairy wings and sashes with *CHANTAL'S HEN PARTAAAAY* spelled out in rhinestones had taken his place. I wanted to crumble into dust.

Kayla wrapped her arm around my shoulders, which I knew meant she was standing right on the tips of her toes. 'Or he's got a me.'

She did have her arm round me, and we definitely didn't fancy each other. I couldn't argue with that. It just didn't really make me feel any better.

'Don't be so fatalistic,' Kayla said. 'You don't know who that was. It could have been his friend, or his sister, or anyone. How likely is it that he'd have found a girlfriend in a couple of days, anyway?'

She kissed my cheek, then scrubbed away the glitter lip gloss she'd transferred, before turning her attention back to another beeping text message.

Maybe she was right. Though it definitely wasn't his sister: I'd been observing the Dramavan like a birdwatcher on the trail of a rare tit. There were definitely only three people in it.

I didn't want to think about how unlikely it might be for Jayden-Lee to have found a girlfriend in a short stay at the park. Because however slim the odds on that were, they had to be worse for him finding a *boy*friend. The days Mum's £9.50 payment had entitled us to already felt like they were ticking down fast.

Maybe she *was* just a friend. People thought me and Kayla were together, sometimes, even though I'm even less her type than she is mine.

As we moved further down the line, Kayla glanced up, examining my expression. 'Feeling better? You're still coming in, aren't you?'

I sighed and nodded. 'I suppose. Although you just want to make sure I'm there to film you ballading people's bits off.'

'History should not go unrecorded,' she confirmed with a grin.

Once we got to the front, it was obvious why it was taking so long to get in. As well as Stacie, who was selling tickets on the door, there was a huge security guy checking the contents of everyone's bag.

I was kind of disappointed that it wasn't Leo. It would have been interesting to see what the rest of his face looked like.

Kayla put her bag on the table to be checked, and Stacie clipped off two tickets for us, then stamped both our hands with black crosses. 'No fighting, no aiming projectiles at the performers, and no alcohol to be consumed if underage.' She reeled the list off like a station announcement system going through stops on the train.

Kayla nodded her head and, after a moment's delay, I did the same.

I hadn't been to many places where people were drinking before. Someone once tried to smuggle it in for a school dance, but the teachers were on to that. One of them went round at the end of the afternoon walloping everyone's gym bag with a kendo stick, and the owner of the one that made smashing noises was sent home immediately to wash the smell of Malibu off their football kit.

Then there was Rohan Ward's birthday last term, where he tried drinking 0.5 per cent alcoholic mouthwash, and ended up puking minty green.

Just as we headed in, the music changed and somebody started wailing an off-key version of 'I Will Always Love You'.

I'd rather have puked minty mouthwash than had to get up and sing in front of strangers.

Fortunately, there was no way that was going to happen.

THIRTEEN

'FLEAS ROVER HAIR,' Kayla yelled over the music as we tried to shove our way through the crowd. It turned out that people *loved* karaoke. The whole place was rammed. She put her hand on my shoulder, just in case we got separated. It would have been like losing a blade of grass in a forest.

'FLEAS WHAT?' I screamed back. 'IS THERE A DOG IN HERE?'

Trying to talk and walk clearly wasn't working. I bent my head down to Kayla-level, bringing my arms in on either side to make a little soundproof bubble in the middle of the melee.

Well, sort of soundproof. I could still hear the woman onstage yodelling the letter 'I' as if it had twenty separate syllables (*III-EE-AAIII-YEE-III WILL ALWAYS LOVE YOUUUU*), but it wasn't quite as deafening.

'I said, *she's over there*,' Kayla repeated, tutting at me. 'The girl Jayden-Lee came in with is over by the bar. Alone.'

My head snapped up like a meerkat's. I'd been not-so-subtly keeping an eye out for my new love rival. I wasn't exactly scoring highly in the avoiding-embarrassing-situations stakes lately, and the last thing I wanted to do was walk straight into Jayden-Lee with his tongue down someone else's throat.

I mean, obviously I didn't want to walk straight into Jayden-Lee at all, but if I did I'd rather it was one of those romantic movie moments where he'd spill his coffee and I'd drop my study notes all over the floor. And then when we both bent down to get them, our noses would bump in an adorable, definitely not nosebleed-causing kind of way.

But I hadn't brought study notes with me, or any kind of prop. I was completely unprepared for romantic collisions.

The girl at the bar was ordering something that came with a cherry and a little umbrella on the side of the glass. I narrowed my eyes, trying to find something to hate about her, but it's really hard to dislike a person based on the fact that they've touched the arm of the person whose arm you want to touch.

'Go and talk to her for me?' I turned back to Kayla, desperately, only to find her attention had wandered already. I grabbed the phone from her. 'Seriously, can you get off this thing for five minutes?'

Her dad couldn't need *that* much babysitting.

Kayla looked stung for a moment, then snatched her

phone back. 'You talk to her. What am I supposed to say?'

'Ask her if the person she came in with was her boyfriend! *I* can't do it – what if Jayden-Lee comes back?' The girl had taken a seat now, running a hand through her neatly curled red hair. She had to be waiting for somebody. 'Come *on*, Kayla.'

Kayla rolled her eyes at me. In fact, she rolled her whole head. Little sprinkles of glitter shook out and mixed in with the shimmer of her dress.

'I'm going to start billing you for my time,' she told me. 'Every act as your intermediary will be charged at a flat rate, and you should be grateful I'm not backdating fees or you'd be liable for quite a sum.'

I looked blankly at her. She knew I was no good at translating her legal jargon.

'What I'm saying, Dylan, is that you're going to owe me *big time* for this. Fine, I'll talk to her. But you have to go and put my request on the sign-up sheet. I'm not missing my big moment because of your love life. Or lack of one.' She tossed her hair, and vanished into the crowd.

I wanted to stay where I was and watch Kayla's progress with the mystery girl, but the hall was so packed I knew if I didn't fight my way to the front now, I'd never get there. And I had to get her name on the sign-up sheet: I owed her one.

The sheet was kept on the edge of the stage, right under the microphone, and 'Whitney' finally finished her number just as I was picking up the pen. There was a moment of glorious silence. My ears had never felt so good.

Then a man in a red velvet jacket, with a black moustache that looked like it was made from curled liquorice, walked over and started talking into the microphone, practically ordering everyone to give the last singer a round of applause. 'Wasn't she wonderful, ladies and gentlemen? I'm sure we'd all like to have been the inspiration for that passionate little number, heh heh heh.'

Puke. I tried not to grimace at his sleazy laugh, and looked over my shoulder to see how Kayla was doing. Immediately, the gang of hen-fairies I'd seen in the queue surrounded me, giggling and daring each other to sign up. One made a grab for my pen, so I held it up out of reach. I hadn't finished adding Kayla's name.

The host was pacing the front of the stage above me, leaning out to peer across the crowd. 'So if Alex Turville would like to take the mic, we're ready for you now. Alex? Come on Alex, baby, don't be shy, step on up.'

It sounded like someone had chickened out of their song. I didn't blame them. The list was mostly Elvis numbers with a couple of 80s classics thrown in – some of those weren't so bad, but that didn't mean I'd want to screech them at a crowd.

I tried to get back to putting Kayla's details down, but yet another fairy went for the pen. I waved it in the air again. 'No, I'm using it now.'

She yelled something I couldn't quite hear, so I shouted back, trying to make her understand. 'IT'S MY TURN NOW.'

'There you are, Alex. I thought we had a runner!' the host cheered.

I glanced up, hand still raised over my head, curious to see exactly how terrified Alex looked. But the host was staring straight at me. 'There he is, folks, let's get him up onstage. Give a big hand for Alex Turville and his brave choice of song.'

I didn't know what a brave choice of song was supposed to be. All I knew was that my name wasn't Alex, and I wasn't brave enough to sing *anything*. My voice got anxious-squeaky when I was forced to read bits of Shakespeare aloud in class. I even mimed my way through 'Happy Birthday'. No way was I about to sing in front of all these people. No. Way.

But I felt a set of hands on my shoulders pushing me, and the crowd were starting to chant: 'Come. On. Alex. Come. On. Alex.'

'But I'm not—'

No one could hear me. No one cared that they couldn't.

'COME ON ALEX! COME ON ALEX!'

There was no escape route between the crush of bodies. A fairy made another dive for the sign-up pen, and I was almost grateful when she managed to prise it from my hand – until she started using it as a weapon, prodding me towards the steps to the stage.

I tried to dodge the needling pricks of the biro jabbing at my ribcage, pleading my case. 'I can't! I don't even sing in the shower because it wouldn't be fair on the rubber ducks. *Please.*'

'*COME ON ALEX!*'

The crowd's roaring turned into a deafening cheer as two more fairies grabbed my arms and dragged me up the steps into the sparkly-curtained setting of my worst nightmares.

FOURTEEN

I must have looked like someone approaching the electric chair, because as soon as the fairies abandoned me on the stage, the host dived in to grab my arm. He kept patting my hand and saying what I thought were meant to be reassuring things, but he had a grip like steel around my trembling wrist, and it's really hard to feel reassured when you know you're about to cause grievous eardrum injuries to a whole hall full of people.

I stared out from the centre of the stage, trying to spot Kayla anywhere among the sea of faces staring back at me. That was a mistake. It felt about as terrifying as looking over the edge of a ravine into a pit full of snakes, knowing you're about to jump in.

Everybody seemed to blur together into a single mass of make-up and big hair. If I looked really closely, I could just pick out an Elvis jumpsuit, or a fairy wing.

'You know, I was sure Alex was going to be a girl. You're full of surprises.' The host massaged my shoulders like I was a boxer going into a fight, and not just someone who looked too scared to stand close to the microphone in case it bit him.

91

What had he meant about it being a *brave choice?*

The music started with a quick electro beat and the crack of thunder, and suddenly I got it. I knew why it was brave. I knew why he expected me – Alex – to be a girl.

'Go get 'em, Tiger,' the host chuckled, and vanished behind the curtain as the big screen in front of me flashed up the first verse of 'It's Raining Men'.

I knew the song, obviously. Everybody knew the song. It got played at least once an hour on the 80s radio station Mum liked to torture us with on long car rides. People were screaming now, just from hearing the intro.

I cleared my throat and leaned into the mic. 'Um, the thing is, I'm not really familiar with . . .'

But that only made them scream more. I was having Aladdin flashbacks: back to the first time I went on in my costume to cheers and applause, right before everyone found out how terrible I was.

It was a bit like being a rock star, if rock stars only performed because they were scared the crowd might pull a couple of their limbs off otherwise. Those fairies looked feral.

There was no way out. I was only getting off stage once I'd sung the stupid song. Screwing my hands into tight fists at my sides, I took a shaky breath and half spoke, half whispered the first line.

Luckily it was quite a talky song, at least in the verse bits. I was just trying to remember exactly how high the notes were in the chorus when I finally managed to pick Kayla's pink hair out of the crowd. She was staring at me, her mouth open so wide you could fit fifty Pringles in it (which I'd tried to do once on a school trip, when she'd fallen asleep and started snoring on the coach).

Next to her, the red-haired girl didn't seem to be paying any attention at all. She was tugging on someone's arm – another boy her age. He was blond, but he wasn't Jayden-Lee. I knew immediately, because looking at him didn't make me feel a bit vomity with love.

They looked like they were fighting. I couldn't tell exactly what was going on, but trying to figure it out made me nearly forget what I was singing. By now I'd hit the chorus and was howling at the top of my voice about wanting to be surrounded by soggy men, or something.

Which, considering I wasn't exactly public about the fact that I liked boys at all, felt like a weirdly dramatic way of announcing it. Not that announcing I was gay was something I ever really planned to do. I had dreams sometimes where I went to school and everyone already knew, without me having said anything at all. Sometimes that felt terrifying, and sometimes it was almost a relief. Talking to Kayla about it had been surprisingly easy, and I knew I'd say something to Mum and Dad eventually, when I'd picked the right time. But the idea of telling other people I was gay always left me feeling kind of panicked, like I couldn't catch my breath.

But it couldn't stay a secret forever. Otherwise I'd never get to walk through town holding someone's hand, or share one of the giant chairs with them at the local Caffe Coffee, or kiss them. Which were my top three things I really wanted to do with someone someday, so I'd have to tell everyone I liked boys eventually.

The original singers of 'It's Raining Men' were *definitely* clear about liking boys, but I didn't want to make my announcement in song. Stomach loop-the-looping, I dropped my voice to a growl and tried to sound like one of those croaky blues singers with lyrics about how nothing matters because you're going to die anyway.

Which fitted, kind of, because I'd definitely rather have died than do what I did next. Which was spot Jayden-Lee watching me from the crowd.

I caught his eye. For a few seconds the world narrowed to just me and him.

Then he started to laugh. It was like getting a shock

of cold water thrown right in my face. My skin prickled with the beginnings of a painful blush. There couldn't be anything worse than this – nothing. I screwed my eyes tightly closed, not wanting to look.

But I had to. I opened just one eye, in case the pain of watching him fall apart with laughter could be halved if I only saw it with my right-hand side. Blinking in the glitterball lights, I slowly refocused on the crowd and managed to pick Jayden-Lee out of it again.

Just as he was knocked sideways by a massive orange bum.

Nibbles had hit the dance floor, and he was wobbling about every bit as enthusiastically as he had been at the children's party. The strangest thing was that everyone seemed to be loving it. Loads of people were joining in to throw his hamster shapes.

Jayden-Lee didn't look like he was loving it much though. He glared after Nibbles, then turned the dark look in my direction. I was still rasping my way through the song, growling out a warning about feeling stormy weather moving in.

I met Jayden-Lee's eyes again without even meaning to, and found myself watching as he was grabbed by the collar and shoved across the floor.

It was the blond boy I'd seen with the redheaded girl earlier. Now they were fighting over her? Life was so *unbelievably* unfair. Jayden-Lee stumbled back from the shove, but stayed on his feet, and the next minute he'd launched himself at the other guy and they were rolling together on the ground.

And that seemed to set off some kind of chain reaction.

It was like watching a game of angry dominos. Someone knocked into someone else, who knocked into a whole new chain of people. Within seconds, half the room seemed to be fighting instead of dancing. I heard a glass break and tried to see if Kayla was still over by the bar, but she'd vanished.

Unsure what else to do, I stumbled through a couple more words.

Then a fairy leaped up onstage, grabbed the mic stand and swung it over her head, yelling at someone out in the crowd, 'DON'T YOU TOUCH HER – SHE JUST GOT HER NAILS DONE!'

A girl with a broken wing climbed up and tackled her solidly to the ground, then growled at me, 'What're you looking at?'

I ran.

FIFTEEN

Throwing myself off the side of the stage, I tried to get into the crowd to find Kayla, the exit, anything, but it was like trying to complete an assault course. Every couple of steps I had to dodge a thrown fist, or climb over two people dragging each other across the floor. Someone threw a karate kick sideways and almost got me in the stomach with a sequinned stiletto.

I'd seen a couple of fights at school before, but they had nothing on this. I just didn't know how it had all happened so fast. Maybe everyone at Starcross Sands was seething with inner rage about not getting to go on a *real* holiday, and this was what had made it bubble over.

I couldn't see Kayla anywhere. I looked desperately for her pink hair, but all I could see were flying fists and furious faces. It was karaoke carnage. I ducked under a misfired swing thrown by a woman in a leopard-print miniskirt at someone wearing a 'Birthday Boy' badge, who looked about fifty.

'WHAT DID YOU GET ME FOR *MY* BIRTHDAY?' she was yelling. 'FLOWERS FROM THE FLIPPING GARAGE!'

Turning, I checked whether anyone would be able to get out by climbing back over the stage, but the anxious-looking host was lowering a thick grey safety curtain. I noticed there were stains splashed across it from what looked like a decade of thrown glasses of wine and beer, and a few rusty-looking marks that might have been something else.

So maybe this evening's outbreak of violence wasn't a total one-off.

A growl from behind me pulled my head around towards a purple-faced stranger. He charged at me, like he was a bull and I was something flappy and red. I held up my hands, skittering backwards. What had I done to upset him? Murdered his favourite song, perhaps.

There was no time to ask questions. Penned in on all sides, my escape route had to be either up or down.

Or both.

I went with down first: ducking and sliding between two sets of legs, narrowly avoiding ending up with a trainer logo permanently stamped across my forehead. The next part of my strategy meant going *up*. Reaching the bar, I clambered to my knees on top of it, giving myself a bird's-eye view of the fight. It looked like I'd lost him.

There were bursts of sound and flashes of colour all

around me, shifting like a kaleidoscope, but no angry shade of purple. And no pink. No Kayla. Where was she?

I had to duck to the side as something was tossed on to the bar not far from me.

No. Not something.

Some*one*.

Jayden-Lee. He seemed to have shaken off the guy he'd been fighting with and picked up two furious hen-fairies instead. One of them had taken off her wings and was whacking him with them.

'Is he causing problems?' The growl was low enough that I could hear the words rumble like thunder under the rest of noise in the room. It was the huge man who'd charged at me. Now he was talking to the fairies, moving them aside with his meaty hands and stepping between them to pick Jayden-Lee up by the deep V of his collar.

Without even thinking about it, I grabbed the fire extinguisher off the side of the bar and stood up brandishing it. 'Get your hands off him!'

Jayden-Lee stared up at me, lips parted like a fish desperately gulping in air. The man who had hold of him barely gave me a second look, but that didn't matter. This was my moment. It was the first chance in my life to be the one to save the day, and I was taking it.

This romance was playing out *exactly* like a fairy tale: one where I'd finally overcome enough obstacles to earn my place as the hero.

I'd never hit anyone in a way that might hurt before – or wanted to. The idea of it made me hesitate for one precious second before a plan clicked into place.

Jumping down from the bar, I swung the extinguisher up and back, ready to bowl it along the floor and sweep big-n-beefy's legs from under him. The next moment I was moving forward, an unstoppable force.

And the moment after that I was being dragged back again, with a pair of arms wrapped tightly round my waist. As I panicked and struggled to set myself free, I managed to set off the extinguisher, spraying a burst of white foam out in front of me.

Funnily enough, the arms that had me in a steely grip seemed to be made of foam too.

In fact, they weren't arms at all.

They were paws.

'Not *now!*' I shouted, trying to kick my way clear of the unwanted embrace. 'Do you really think this is the right time for a cuddle?'

The hamster didn't answer. He just tipped me sideways and scooped one arm under my legs, sweeping me off my feet the way princes rescue their damsels in distress. As my world tilted, I caught sight of

Jayden-Lee watching me being saved against my will by something from the mutant petting zoo.

At least, I think it was Jayden-Lee.

He was covered from head to toe in white, flame-retardant foam. It looked like he'd been hit by a million custard pies. At least it seemed to have distracted the man who'd been choking him. He'd vanished somewhere back into the room, along with any chance I'd ever had of impressing Jayden-Lee.

My one shining moment of heroism had just been buried in a fluffy white mess.

Jayden-Lee wiping foam from his flawless face was the last thing I saw before the hamster started rushing me towards the door. The crowds parted in front of him like the Red Sea in front of a massive, rodent Moses. Anyone who didn't get out of the way just bounced off his orange padding as he ran.

'Get off me! Let me go – my friend's in there!' I yelled. But either my voice was too quiet compared to the rest of the shouting going on, or nothing got through the hamster headpiece, because Nibbles just kept carrying me onwards.

A frazzled-sounding Stacie started giving instructions through the tannoy. '*Thank you for living the dream with us this evening. Due to unforeseen circumstances, the showhall will now be closing for the night. Please could all*

patrons make their way to the exits and vacate the area in a
calm and quiet manner.'

She added, *'Come again!'* just as Nibbles swept me
through the exit and into the dark outside.

SIXTEEN

The cool air felt like a slap after having been trapped in the hot, crowded showhall. Nibbles slid me back on to my feet next to the wall, and I immediately slumped against it. For some reason it felt like all the bones in my legs had turned to jelly. My pride was still smarting from having been princess-carried away from my own rescue attempt, but I'd have to regain my balance before I could do anything about it.

As my eyes slowly adjusted to the dark, I noticed that I wasn't the only one standing there.

'Dylan?'

I took a huge, relieved breath and sighed out, '*Kayla.*'

Then I turned to Nibbles to ask how he'd known exactly where to take me. But he was gone.

'That's one heroic hamster,' Kayla said with a dreamy smile. 'As soon as the fight broke out, he just picked me up and carried me out here. He's been bringing people out ever since, like a knight in furry armour.'

So that was it. Nibbles was just rescuing whoever he happened to bump into, whether they liked it or not. I couldn't believe Kayla was fluttering her eyelashes over him. 'I don't think knights just snuck into battles and kidnapped people, did they? It would be a pretty inefficient way to fight.'

As I spoke there was the sound of glass smashing, and two men staggered out of the showhall with their arms locked round each other. I couldn't tell whether they were hugging or fighting, but I edged Kayla a bit further away from the door, just in case.

'He saved *you*, didn't he?' Kayla asked, eyebrows lifting.

'He *ruined my life*. You have no idea what that hamster just did.' As I ran her through the bullet points of my own tragic transformation from heroic to helpless, a collage of images formed in my mind. Jayden-Lee's face as he spotted me on the stage, his lip curling before he broke into a laugh. The look he gave me as I lifted the fire extinguisher, like he was seeing me in a whole new light. And the disdain in his eyes as they emerged from the foam, that light extinguished. Literally.

'Well, I still think he's knightly. He didn't know he was interrupting a "moment", did he?' The look on Kayla's face worried me.

'Don't you dare. You *cannot* be falling in love with Sir Prance-a-lot.'

'I'm not!' she huffed. But her smile didn't go away.

'Kayla, you can't. You can't fall for somebody who spends all day in a hamster suit. He's probably got fleas.' Honestly, *one* close encounter and she was getting all stupid over him. I still wanted to shove him on to his big orange behind.

'You don't even know him,' I went on. 'You don't know what he really looks like – it could be a girl in there for all we know.'

'Wouldn't matter to me,' Kayla said, like that made any sense. 'Anyway, you think you're in love with Jayden-Lee, and you've never even had a proper conversation.'

I took a quick, urgent look around to check no one was standing too close. 'Shut *up*. Oh my god, people will *hear* you.'

I couldn't believe she was willing to risk exposing my crush just to prove a point about a hamster. 'It's different with Jayden-Lee. At least I've seen his face. And haven't you ever heard of love at first sight? Being totally into someone you know nothing about means it's *real*, unlike your freaky thing with the hamster.'

'That hamster saved me tonight. Where were you?' Kayla was raising her voice in a way that I knew was dangerous. Usually this was where I'd know not to wind her up more, but she was *so* wrong. About the hamster, about me, and especially about Jayden-Lee.

'You know where I was,' I protested.

'Yes. You were looking for *him*. Because he was more important than me, *again*. Do you know what that girl told me, the one you made me speak to?'

Of course I didn't. I'd forgotten all about her. But the same painful twinge was back in my chest as soon as Kayla brought her up. 'Is she dating him?'

'*No*, she's dating someone else. Someone who wasn't very happy about Jayden-Lee using her to get in ahead of the queue. I don't know whether you could see anything from up on your high horse – sorry, I mean, from up on the stage – but you might have noticed the punch that started the whole fight. The boy is spam, Dylan. He's complete spam. And if he hadn't been here tonight, none of this would have happened.'

All she was doing was proving my point about her wrongness. 'You just said someone else started the fight. I'm amazed you managed to look up from your phone long enough to notice *anything*, but you've got it wrong. It's not fair to say Jayden-Lee—'

'I'll tell you what's not fair!' Kayla was really shouting now. People were starting to sidle away in case another riot kicked off out here. 'What's not fair is I didn't get to sing tonight because you're obsessed with that jerk. What's not fair is that girl probably getting dumped by her real boyfriend because Jayden-Lee told Stacie they were together. She didn't even know him! None of that's fair – you just can't see it. Or maybe you just don't care about anything else when he's around. You certainly don't care about me!'

She stared at me hard for a moment, daring me to claim otherwise. Then she turned away, walking a few steps before starting to run in the direction of Alpine Views.

I stood there, feeling like I hadn't avoided being punched tonight after all.

The showhall doors opened again and more people ran out, shepherded by a figure in a giant fuzzy suit. Among them were the red-haired girl and the boy Kayla had said was *really* her date. As I watched, they stopped running, took each other's hands, then he wrapped her in a tight hug.

Which just showed that Kayla had got it all wrong. There must have been a misunderstanding somewhere, and it wasn't Jayden-Lee who was to blame.

A shadow blocked out the light coming from the showhall, and I looked up to see Nibbles looking over at me. It was *him*. He'd destroyed everything. At least for me.

He gestured between me and the space where Kayla had been. I could tell he was trying to ask a question.

'She's gone,' I said, the words feeling like a hard lump in my throat.

I had to bite my lip to keep from adding: *and it's all your fault.*

SEVENTEEN

The next morning, Kayla was gone before I got up. Mum said she'd found out about some open-air yoga sessions on the cliffs, and had left early to go and practise her downward dog.

According to the brochure, that's the name of one of the poses they do, and not as disgusting as it sounds.

'And since you've got nothing else to do,' Mum said, just *assuming* that without Kayla I'd be incapable of organizing my own social life, 'you and your dad can take Jude to the playground.'

She and Jude had spent the morning building Lego creations on the caravan floor. Mum's was a massive castle, complete with balconies and a tiny, waving queen. Jude's was a very enthusiastic blob, inside of which a model train had set up home with a family of Sylvanians.

I had grievous Lego injuries to the soles of both my feet just from getting to the sofa, and was already feeling indignant (and a little bit sulky about not being asked to join in). 'Me and *Dad*? Can't I just take him on my own?'

Handling Jude was nothing compared to handling my dad. He loved a playground. One of my earliest memories involved being stranded on the bottom bit of the see-saw, while he showed off how high he could get on the swings. It had only been a see for me.

Jude looked up from his building site. 'I want Dylan *and* Daddy!'

He tugged the hamster hat down on his head and gave me a *look*, which if I didn't know better, I'd have taken as blackmail.

'You'll both go. You can take this time to memorize your father's face before we lose him to the football screenings at the Dog and Duck. And since you barely seem able to look after yourself –' Mum flicked her fingers at me like she was brushing off dust – 'perhaps between the two of you, you'll make one responsible adult. Go on, go.'

She'd noticed the state of my nose first thing. Without Kayla to give me a fresh coat, it was looking all mottled and splotchy again. Although that was an improvement on the purple of two nights ago, when my nose hadn't just been the same colour as an aubergine, but almost the same size.

And Mum had a point. Two points, really.

I was incapable of planning a social life on my own.

And we did see less of Dad once football season

properly kicked off. He even organized shifts at the ambulance station around important fixtures. If there was a good game on, he couldn't be trusted not to try and tune the emergency radio in to *Sports Extra*.

We both loved football, but I never went to the pub with him any more. It got lairy in there on match days, and some of the jokes that went flying round were really hard to smile at.

Here's something you'd think was a fact if you only watched the Premier League: gay players don't exist. There aren't any gay footballers in the major teams. Although that's not what gets said whenever a striker misses an easy chance to score.

Being able to kick a ball really well and fancying other blokes are two qualities that never ever occur in the same person, apparently, so I must be a scientific miracle. I think it's just that no footballer wants to come out because of the things they know will be yelled at them. It's so *stupid*.

But I guess it makes some people uncomfortable, the idea of having gay people around while they're watching football. They just want to be left alone while they spend ninety minutes staring at other men running about in little shorts. Anyway, the whole atmosphere at the pub just meant that the only football me and Dad really watched together was on the highlight shows at home. At least there I didn't have to deal with anyone else seeing what he was wearing.

Dad's football-watching outfit and his going-to-the-playground outfit were exactly the same. Full kit. Stripy socks and boots with studs, even though they're difficult to walk in. And because Mum doesn't let him buy a new season strip every year – or any year – he wears the same one. The shirt has the name of some mulleted player out of ancient history on the back, and the fabric's worn so thin on the shorts that you can practically see the hairs on Dad's legs.

That's what he was wearing when we set off from the caravan. I'd put on a hoody and was trying to vanish inside it, like a turtle with a fleecy shell. Dad had accessorized his humiliation mufti with an ancient khaki coat we liked to call his Jurassic Parka. It didn't really improve the look.

I watched the curtains closely as we passed the Dramavan, letting out a tightly held breath when not one of them twitched. I might have blown all my chances away along with a blast of extinguisher foam last night, but at least I could try and make it through one day at Starcross Sands without actively increasing my total-loser rating.

Ducking my head low, I kept up with Jude's chair. He looked up at me from under the hamster hat.

'Is Kayla *very* cross with you?'

I frowned at him. 'Kayla isn't cross with me at all.'

Which might have been true. Maybe she'd find her inner zen at yoga and come back too chilled out to be angry any more.

But by then Dad was looking over his shoulder at me. 'Seemed like it, running off to be a dog this morning.'

God, I hoped he never said that to her face.

'Really?'

'Couldn't get out fast enough. Asked if I should wake you, but she said yoga's all about expanding your horizons.'

That didn't sound *too* angry, to me.

'Said it required an open mind, and you don't have one,' Dad went on.

Oh.

So maybe she was still a little bit angry. I swallowed around a tightness in my throat. Dad watched my chin dip down to my chest and punched me in the shoulder, which he seemed to think was a good way of comforting someone. 'You want to talk about it, you know who you can ask. I've got years of experience talking to women.'

I made a face. 'Yeah, I've been talking to Mum for years too. Thanks though.'

Inside I was wilting a bit. I couldn't help wondering

if he wished I *would* talk about girls with him. I didn't want to talk about Kayla, though. I just kept going over how she'd said I didn't care about her. Of *course* I did. It wasn't my fault that her jealousy of me and Jayden-Lee was making her completely unreasonable.

Not that me and Jayden-Lee was ever going to happen now.

'Anything else you want to talk about?' Dad nudged me again.

He just wasn't going to leave it alone this morning. For a moment I actually thought about telling him everything, the same way I'd nearly spilt it all to Mum yesterday. I could tell him about Nibbles and how he was ruining my life. And about my fight with Kayla and everyone's massive fight with everyone else last night. Maybe even about Jayden-Lee, and how I'm definitely gay, even though I was Man of the Match six times in one year at school.

But then I thought about his mates in the pub, and what they'd have said about seeing me up onstage at the karaoke, and I just couldn't do it. It wasn't the right time.

We stopped at a set of child-sized traffic lights to let the miniature train that ran around the park chug slowly by. I scuffed a foot into the dirt and shook my head.

Dad patted me firmly on the shoulder. 'Well, you know I'm always here if you – ONE SWING LEFT.'

And the next minute it was just me and Jude, watching Dad sprint through the gates of the playground to bags the last swing. Jude twisted in his chair to look up at me. 'Kayla's not *really* going to be a dog, is she?'

I just about stopped myself from clapping a palm across my face. 'No, and you'd better not call her that, unless you've lost the will to live.'

Jude nodded solemnly, looking like a little wise old man with a hamster growing out of his forehead. 'OK. Let's get Dad to do it.'

I laughed. 'Sure. But first, let's go kick him off the swings.'

EIGHTEEN

As soon as Jude rolled through the playground entrance, two pink and purple blurs threw themselves off the climbing frame and raced towards us. I remembered them from the party a few days ago. Polly and Dolly? No, Minnie and Winnie.

I could see their mum getting talking to Dad while he was pulling some stunt moves on the swings.

'It is our *birthday*,' panted Winnie or Minnie, making it to us first.

'We are a *year older*,' breathed Minnie or Winnie, when she caught up.

'And,' they both said in unison, 'we gotted *pony princess* outfits.'

Which did explain why they were both in ball gowns, with pink and purple fuzzy ears clipped into their hair. I hadn't said anything for the same reason Mum hadn't been too fussed about Jude wanting to live in his hat. Four-year-olds are *strange*.

Although, I had spent last night karaoke-ing with a hamster and a pack of attack fairies, so maybe it wasn't just them.

Jude was looking at the twins curiously, tilting his head as though he was trying to puzzle something out. I thought he might be wondering what kind of ponies came in pink.

'Don't you like them?' he asked.

And then I noticed that the two little girls were frowning identical frowns.

'We *love* them, but . . .' The twin princesses turned around to show big rips in the back of each of their dresses, and wailed, 'TROY TOOKED OUR TAILS.'

Troy Slater was a menace to society. I didn't know what he had against hair exactly, but first he ruined Jude's, and now he was up to no good with a couple of rainbow-coloured pony tails.

I didn't know if the police could do much about six-year-olds with antisocial behaviour issues, but as far as I was concerned, that kid should have been clamped. I was going to have to tell Dad and the twins' mum what had happened to Jude. Maybe if the Dramavan had *two* sets of angry parents descending on it, Jayden-Lee wouldn't think my mum was totally bizarre.

And I could let Dad break the news gently to Mum that her baby boy looked like he should be colouring in Bibles in a monastery.

I was going to do it. I had to. I marched over to Dad, ready to tell him the bald truth, when a yell from outside the park stopped me in my tracks.

'*Oi, Leroy, on yer head!*'

Somewhere just beyond the edge of the play park, a ball flew up into the air and seemed to hover for a split second, then vanished downwards again. It didn't reappear – Leroy's head obviously didn't get to it in time.

There was a rattle of laughter. Kev, Leroy and Dean must have been having a kickabout. I looked at Dad, who was still trying to swing himself over the top bar, totally unprepared for the news I was about to break. I *could* use this moment to tell him what had happened to Jude's hair, *or* I could tell him I wanted to play football with some new friends. I knew which one he'd be happier about.

It wouldn't be a bad idea to get to know Kev and the others better, either. Especially since Kayla had decided yoga was more fun than me. They hadn't been as impressed by my trick shot as Jayden-Lee was, but I had loads more up my sleeve. I could offer to teach them, and then maybe we could all hang out together. Then they could put in a good word for me with Jayden-Lee, and he'd realize I'd never meant to foam him in the face. He seemed like the understanding type. I was sure that under his tough, bad-boy surface there was a gentle heart just waiting to be allowed to care.

'*Troy? Where are you, you little git? What have you done with my phone?*'

If I had a superpower, it must have been the ability to conjure someone up by wishful thinking.

I knew that voice. I knew it the same way Kayla knew all the words to the Deathsplash Nightmares' new albums the day after they came out. I knew it because I spent all day listening to it in my head. Remembering the little rasp in it, and the way he clipped off letters he didn't seem to need.

'*Get out 'ere before I kick in your PlayStation, you runt.*'

It was the most amazing voice I'd ever heard. And it belonged to someone I'd last seen looking disgusted with me through two inches of foam.

Leroy and Kev were calling over to Jayden-Lee. There was no time to befriend them now. No time to prove I was more than a bad aim with a fire extinguisher. No time for anyone to put in a good word.

I wasn't ready.

Throwing myself over the safety barrier at the only non-walled edge of the play park, I crashed straight into the bushes of the woodland area beyond, just as Jayden-Lee came stomping through the gates.

The bushes were quite comfy, which was good, as I was seriously considering making them my new home. I couldn't face the world again, not if Jayden-Lee had seen Dad in his see-through shorts.

At least, the bushes were comfy until I noticed the thorns. I'd wedged myself firmly into a narrow, V-shaped gap between two branches, and now couldn't make any sudden movements if I wanted to keep my skin attached. I thought about how long I could stay out here. If I made myself a comfy bed of leaves and lived off the half-empty crisp packets that blew out of the bins, it could be a sustainable thing.

My stomach made a soft groaning noise at the thought of food – I'd opted out of another helping of beef on toast that morning – but I could still see the very top of Jayden-Lee's head from where I was sitting. His golden hair caught the light like his own personal halo.

It wasn't safe to leave.

I'd just stay in my bushes until the coast was clear, listening to the birds singing, the branches snapping, the leaves crunching . . .

The last two didn't seem quite right. It sounded like an animal was in there with me, but not a small, cute, normal animal like a hedgerow mouse. More of a massive, stompy animal, like a bear. I froze. I'd heard that you shouldn't run if you happened to encounter a wild animal because it only gave them something to chase.

There was a zoo not far from the caravan park. They

must have had an escapee. The bear must have come down here looking for picnic baskets, which I always thought was a myth, but maybe all those cartoons were based on fact. Maybe bears only murdered people if they didn't have a bag full of pork pies and cucumber sandwiches.

I could see the headlines now: *BOY DIES IN BRITAIN'S FIRST BEAR ATTACK: IF ONLY HE'D BROUGHT SOME LUNCH.*

The bear tapped me on the shoulder and whispered, 'Have you lost something?'

And, after I'd yelped embarrassingly loudly, I figured out that it probably wasn't a bear. It was a voice I knew. It was Leo, from the loos.

NINETEEN

Leo had jumped back when I cried out, probably not expecting to be taken for a ravenous zoo creature. I couldn't turn around to look at him without being viciously stabbed by the thorns on the bushes I'd burrowed into, but I heard the leaves crackle as he stepped towards me again, and a hint of amusement in his voice.

'Sorry, I didn't mean to surprise you. I just caught a glimpse of your top and climbed in here thinking it might be one of the kids from the playground. We've had to get runaways out of the trees before.'

He was speaking in a slightly hushed tone, probably because hiding in a hedge had finally managed to cement my crazy-person status. As if the headpants hadn't been bad enough.

Next time, I'd just dig a pit and bury myself in it instead. 'No, I'm fine. I mean, I haven't lost anything. And I haven't escaped from anywhere.'

You know, except a straitjacket at the local Victorian asylum. I was almost glad he couldn't see how flushed my face was.

'So you just like to hang out in hedgerows?' he asked. I could hear him kneeling down somewhere behind me. 'Is it a communing-with-nature thing?'

'Yeah. I mean, no. Not really.' I tried to think of a good reason why I'd be communing with nature. Birdwatching? No – then he might expect me to actually know something about birds, when in fact I had difficulty breaking them into more complex categories than little and hoppy, or big and squawky. Or, worse, he'd just think I was the most boring person on the planet.

'It's just . . . peaceful, isn't it?' I started. 'So it helps. With my . . . anger-management problem.'

Mum says liars are always caught out by forgetfulness, but I remembered the lie I'd used before perfectly. Then again, most people's lies don't make them sound like they might have rage blackouts in their local branch of Homebase.

'Oh, right. Of course.'

I could hear a shuffling noise behind me, which I took to be the sound of a hasty retreat. I didn't turn round to watch him leave. It wasn't worth getting prickled by a thousand thorny branches just to catch my first glimpse of what Leo's face looked like – not with the expression I was sure would be on it.

Then something pressed up against my back. It was

his back. He'd sat down and was leaning up against me.

I was immediately hyper conscious of every little shift of our bodies. If he moved an arm I could feel his shoulder slide with it. He was really warm, like he'd just stepped out of a patch of sunshine. I sort of wished I wasn't still wearing my hoody – I didn't feel like being a turtle any more.

'What are you doing?' I asked.

'Seeing if it works.' He lowered his voice to a whisper. 'The peace and quiet. I've had a couple of crazy days too.'

I could feel his back arch like he was reaching for something, before he added, 'And I was looking for a place to have my lunch, if you don't mind the company. Chicken?'

A hand ducked backwards into my space, dangling a little white sandwich triangle. I knew I should probably have turned him down politely, since it was his lunch and everything, but my stomach had started doing backflips of hungry desire. I needed the sustenance.

And I definitely didn't mind the company either.

'Um, thanks.' I stuffed a good half of the sandwich into my mouth in one bite, still grateful that we couldn't see each other and I didn't have to worry about my chipmunk cheeks. It was a great sandwich too. A little bit spicy – not like Mum's version, which tasted mostly of beige. 'So, what's been so crazy around here?'

I could feel his shoulders lock up. It must have been bad. 'Have you heard of the Park of the Year Award?'

'You mean the one Starcross Sands has won three times? The thing that's on all the leaflets and printed on a poster by the gates?' I paused, then shrugged. 'No, don't think so.'

He laughed, and I grinned to myself as a little of the tension in his back released. 'I wish I'd never heard of it. We're shortlisted for a fourth time, so there are undercover judges on the site, and the manager's acting like winning is the kind of historic event that would put walking on the moon in the shade. We're all being run into the ground with new rules. I got a written warning for helping someone the other day.'

It was the first time I'd heard the warm, easy tone of his voice falter.

'You got written up? It wasn't for the . . . chewing gum . . .?' I'd feel really guilty if something that had started out in my pocket might have got him in trouble, even if it technically happened via Troy.

But he was already shaking his head. His dreads brushed against my shoulder. 'No, it was the karaoke last night. According to the rules, the right thing to do would have been to alert security and stay out of the way while people pulped each other on the dance floor. I just couldn't do that.'

Oh, no. He was *there*? If he'd been around for the fight, then he couldn't have missed my performance. The weird thing was, I'd been looking out for him too, a little bit, but I hadn't seen a thing.

'The karaoke.' My voice had gone up in pitch enough that I could probably have hit the high notes I'd avoided last night. I coughed to try to get it back to normal. 'Yeah, I think that was probably a bad night for everyone.'

Jayden-Lee and that girl. Me and Kayla. That stupid hamster.

'Even if it was just the part where they had to listen to me.'

'Hey, I thought you were sounding pretty good until that fairy clocked you with the mic stand.' I could feel his laughter bumping up against my spine. Somehow it didn't make me feel awful, like Jayden-Lee laughing at me had. It actually made me laugh a bit too.

'Well I'm glad someone enjoyed it. I thought it must have been as painful to listen to as it was to sing.'

'No – it was different, that's all. And you kept going, didn't you?' The aftershocks of Leo's laughter were still chasing themselves across my skin in little shivers. 'That's the main thing. Or, I think so, anyway. Mum wasn't too delighted when she heard about what happened though.'

126

'Your *mum* was there?' For a moment I was terrified I might have trampled her in the stampede. But Leo shook his head again.

'No, she runs the Pie-O-Ria. She keeps them well behaved in there – just worries about me getting into trouble. If I'm not careful she'll have me serving up slices with her, just to keep an eye on me. Can't go too far wrong selling pizza.'

'I don't know . . .' I leaned back a little, until I could just make out his silhouette against the branches. 'I think letting people order pineapple as a topping ought to count as a crime.'

Leo snorted. 'OK, that's fair. Although speaking of crimes, I'd better get going. The worst one round here is being late. *"You don't win Park of the Year through tardiness, Leo Smith."'*

From the high, snippy voice he put on for the last part, I could tell he was doing an impression of something said to him before.

I almost decided to brave being torn to shreds by the thorny bush and twist round to look at him, then – before he could go, and take away my chance to find out what he looked like with him. Part of me really wanted to know. Well, a *lot* of me did. But it had been so much easier talking back to back, instead of face to face. So I just nodded, and let the tug of my shoulders answer him. 'I'll stay here a bit longer.'

'Good idea,' he said. 'Just until you're sure you won't rage out and karate kick a bench.'

I spluttered. How was I going to take that lie back without sounding even weirder? *No, I love furniture. I cuddle my sofa every day.*

So I didn't say anything until I heard him getting to his feet again. Then I tipped my head back until I could almost see him. His shadow was falling over my face. 'Thanks for the sandwich. I think I might just have been hangry, after all. Now Starcross Sands will be spared my wrath.'

'Remember to mention that on the customer service survey. I might get a bonus.' He paused, as though he wanted to say more, but then I heard him treading his way carefully back through the branches. He was gone.

Just in time to miss the sound of some bone-chilling screaming coming from inside the playground.

TWENTY

I leapfrogged back over the barrier so fast, I almost crashed face-first into the slide. Stumbling to a stop, I stood there panting and tried to figure out what was going on.

It didn't *look* like anyone was being murdered.

Dad and the twins' mum were ignoring the screams completely. They now had a swing each and seemed to be engaged in a very serious competition to be the first over the top bar. Jayden-Lee had vanished as suddenly as he'd arrived.

Jude and the twins had formed a small circle around a bend in the miniature train tracks, where they ran across one corner of the playground. The noise I could hear seemed to be coming from somewhere in the middle of it.

My heart had stopped trying to punch its way out through my ribs as soon as I'd seen that Jude was OK, but I dashed over anyway. It sounded like they were sawing somebody in half. Jude had seen a magician do that for his last birthday party, so it was always possible he'd try to recreate the stunt.

'You're not torturing anyone, are you?' I asked, putting a hand on his arm.

'Uh-uh.' He moved back to let me see. 'We're *playing*.'

And there was Troy Slater, tied to the train tracks like an old-fashioned damsel in distress. The girls had used two pink skipping ropes to hold him down: they were tied round his wrists in big loops. Troy was twisting and kicking like he was doing a horizontal version of Riverdance.

He saw me and yelled, 'GERREMOFF! GERREMOFF!' in a way that suggested that if his hands were free he'd be bulldozing everyone in the playground. I eyed the skipping ropes nervously.

There was a whoop of delight from somewhere behind us. Dad had figured out how to twist the ropes of his swing so that it spun him in circles as it unravelled. Hopeless.

'THEY'RE GONNA KILL ME. I'M GONNA KILL 'EM!' Troy wailed, not really encouraging me to release him.

'We're not killing you,' said Minnie or Winnie.

'We're just going through your pockets,' agreed Winnie or Minnie.

They'd already reclaimed their tails – each of them had a large neon-pink bundle of artificial hair sticking out of a princess-dress pocket. I thought for a minute that Kayla might like one to match her hair, then remembered how she'd vanished off to downward dog and salute the sun without me, and that I totally wasn't bothered about her any more.

As well as finding the missing parts to their birthday outfits, the twins had uncovered a huge pile of other strange things, most of which looked like it belonged to someone other than Troy. He must have had pockets that ran right down his legs.

Hesitantly (because anything Troy had touched was likely to be sticky from an unknown source), I picked up a sparkly kitten toy that meowed when I squeezed it. 'Is this yours, then?' And then a pair of wire-framed glasses like the kind my nana wears. 'Or these?'

'NO,' Troy snarled. 'I FOUND THEM, THASSALL. LEMMEGO.'

Letting him go just then would probably have been a bit like letting a bull into a china shop and then throwing in a grenade. I tutted softly.

'Shame, the glasses might suit you. I don't think *any* of this is yours, though, is it?' I rummaged through the pile of contraband again. One square of my cherry chewing gum lay at the bottom of the heap. 'Which just makes me wonder what you're doing with it. It's an awful lot to have just *found*.'

'Everything OK, kids?' Dad's voice made me jump. I twisted round to find him and the twins' mum standing over us. Neither of them looked particularly worried that their children had Troy Slater helplessly at their mercy.

With his klepto-collection, I could probably have had Troy thrown into the caravan park equivalent of juvenile detention. Jayden-Lee might even thank me for it. He hadn't sounded too pleased when he was looking for Troy before.

Then again, he might have the same kind of rule I have about Jude. We fight sometimes, obviously, but the only person allowed to be mean to my little brother is me.

I chewed on my lip, trying to figure out my next move. 'Troy was just . . . explaining his good deed for the day.'

'He was?' Minnie asked.

'*Was* he?' asked Winnie.

Troy grunted, and looked just as surprised as they did.

'Totally,' I said. 'Look at all these things he's got that don't belong to him.'

Dad, Jude, the twins and their mum all looked suspiciously at the glittering collection. I dropped the toy kitten back on top of a dragon's hoard of squeaky dolls and dog chews, somebody's swimming trunks, a plastic Elvis quiff, and a single blue suede shoe.

'He must have spent *all holiday* collecting up people's lost things so he could return them to their rightful owners. But that's hard to do all alone.'

'He can give it to lost property!' Jude declared, beaming forgiveness down on Troy now all had been explained.

'We can take it! Mummy, can we?' The twins each pulled on one of their mother's arms until she nodded and agreed to stop at the park office on the way to pick up their cake. She and Dad arranged for Jude to stop by their caravan later for a slice.

Then Dad rested his hands on the back of Jude's chair, and they turned towards the playground gates.

'WAIT!'

Troy had finally found his voice once the twins had gathered up his treasure pile and everyone looked ready to go.

'WHARRABOUT ME? WHARRABOUT THE TRAIN?'

There was a distant ringing sound. It was the kind of ringing that might have been made by the warning bells of a miniature train coming along the tracks.

'You can get up, silly,' Jude said.

'Probably *before* you're runned over,' added one of

the twins, as the other nodded seriously.

'It will be harder to get up *after*.'

'BUT I'M STUCK! HELP! HELP! I'M TIED UP!' Troy's face was slowly going red.

I leaned over and lightly tugged on the end of one of the skipping ropes. The knots fell away in my hand. 'Yes, Troy. But they only tied you up with bows.'

With all that kicking, he hadn't really tugged on the ropes around his arms at all. When he did, the remaining ties easily unravelled.

I held out a hand. 'You really had better get up. Being squashed by a tiny train covered in bunting would just be embarrassing.'

Ignoring my offer, Troy scrambled to his feet and backed away. 'I'll get you,' he hissed, and then pointed to me and Jude. 'I'll get *you* double!'

He ran out of the playground, presumably to work on some fantastically evil vengeance, but just then I didn't care. I'd spotted something in the bundle of goods that Minnie was holding.

A battered green mobile with a shattered screen.

'I think I know who this belongs to. I'll give it back.'

I tucked it into my pocket quickly, before Dad could ask, or anyone could see my hands shaking. *Jayden-Lee's phone.* It had to be. I'd just accidentally managed to secure an all-access pass to the backstage area of his brain.

I could find out anything I wanted about him, if I could just get past the feeling that it would be really wrong of me to look.

I tried to talk myself out of having morals the whole way back to the caravan. I was concentrating so hard on it that I didn't even notice that someone I didn't recognize was standing in front of our door.

Not until she turned around and in a brisk, sharp voice said, 'Good afternoon. I'm the park manager. Would one of you be Mr Dylan Kershaw? I very much need to have a word.'

TWENTY-ONE

She was wearing a shiny, royal-blue power suit that looked like she'd pulled it out of a portal to the 80s, and holding a serious-looking clipboard. There are two types of clipboard in the world: ones that make people look like they're going on a Geography field trip, and ones that look like they're full of Very Bad News.

This clipboard definitely seemed to be the bad-news kind. Besides, she'd never have made it through a field trip with those shoulder pads.

I had no idea what the park manager could want to see me about. Except, as she clipped back down the ramp towards us, my mind ran an instant action-replay of everything that had happened in the three days since we'd arrived. By the time I could see that the badge pinned to her tailored jacket read *Call me Margaret!* I'd remembered a hundred reasons she might want to see me.

Maybe Troy had already reported me for trying to turn him into the human equivalent of leaves on the line. Or she'd had a call from lost property about a missing phone. She might have come to throw me out of the park before I could start another riot with an off-key power ballad.

Or—

'Has something happened to Kayla?' I gasped out the question before I could help myself, my heart feeling like it had crawled up into my throat to choke me. I knew I was the emergency contact in her phone because I was slightly less prone to panic than her dad.

She might have had a yoga accident. Ruptured something while doing sun salutes, or tied herself in a knot instead of a lotus. 'Kayla Flores?'

I'd never forgive myself if there'd been a yogatastrophe.

'What are you saying about me?' Kayla pulled open the caravan door and looked out with a glare hard enough to crack concrete. My heart sank right back into my chest. She was fine, but it looked like she still hated me.

Then Mum appeared behind her, clutching a gigantic, steaming dish of something that looked a bit like she'd just caught it falling out of a cow's backside. 'You're back just in time for lunch – we're having mystery beef.' She frowned as she caught sight of Margaret's crisp blonde curls. 'Can I help you?'

'I really do need to speak to Dylan Kershaw,' Margaret the manager said, somehow unfazed by

Mum's toxic meal planning. 'If somebody could possibly clarify who that might be.'

'It's me.' I stepped forward. If I was going to be charged with crimes against karaoke, or worse, we might as well get it over with.

'Mr Kershaw.' Margaret stuck out her hand. I waited for Dad to take it before it clicked that she was still talking to me. After a minute, she lowered it again, then peered into Jude's chair as if he was a specimen in a laboratory jar. 'And this must be Judy.'

'*Jude*,' said Jude, who'd heard that name from the kids at school before, and not the ones he liked.

'Ah yes,' Margaret went on, ticking something off on her board like we'd just passed a test. 'I thought that was an *unusual* name for a little boy. And this is the one to whom the incident occurred?'

'Incident?' Dad asked.

Margaret stared at her board. 'Yes, ah, the . . . most unfortunate, deeply regrettable personal injury event in which your sons were involved. I believe Dylan was the supervising familial persona.'

She was making less sense than Kayla did when she broke out her legal-eagle talk. A *personal injury event* sounds like something on the schedule of the Bad Luck Olympics. I said, 'Excuse me? I'm what? What incident?'

Margaret tapped her teeth with the end of her pen.

'The report I have here informs me that you were responsible for the care of your brother at one of our Happy Hamster Parties.'

She was here about Jude and the gum. The penny dropped with a thud, then rolled off quickly down the road just to avoid having to be there when Mum found out what I'd been hiding from her.

The words *responsible for your brother* rattled around my head.

'Oh, that.' I spluttered, folding my arms tightly across my chest to keep them from flapping as I spoke. The last thing I needed to do was accidentally smack the park manager in the face. 'That wasn't an incident. No one was hurt or anything – it was more of a . . . minor redesign?'

Kayla would have known the right word to use, if she was still talking to me. Kayla wouldn't have made it sound like Troy gave Jude a new shelving unit and some fancy wallpaper instead of the worst haircut of his life. *A minor redesign?*

But Jude's hair wasn't the worst thing. The worst thing was that it was all my fault.

Margaret sucked a breath in between clenched teeth. 'Mr Kershaw, I have *several* statements here assuring me of the course of events, as well as your involvement. This one, for instance, states that—'

'Jude,' Mum's voice rang out from the caravan doorway so sharply that Margaret lost track of her notes. 'Darling, take off the hat.'

For a moment I'd almost imagined that things couldn't get any worse. That I might be able to talk my way out of this. My only chance now was to grab the back of Jude's chair and make a run for it. We'd cross the border into Devon and live like outlaws, surviving off our wits, and building new lives for ourselves under assumed names. Mum *never* had to know what was under that hat.

But Jude had tugged it off almost before I could move. His bald patch gleamed accusingly in the sunlight, a little bit sweaty from being stuck under all that orange fur.

Mum headed down the ramp. I tried to calculate how long I had to live.

She still had the stinky beef dish in her arms. Maybe she'd try drowning me in stew. Or she could just force me to eat it: that might be worse. I held my breath as she stopped in front of me, cleared her throat, then spun round to face the manager, wearing her most threatening smile.

'Well, Margaret. I do appreciate your concern, though as you can see the *personal injury event* was limited to a rather large chunk of his hair – which is why I've decided to take no direct action about your staff's inability to manage the children in their care. I've heard it's a quite important week for you, with all this Park of the Year business, so I'm sure you wouldn't want there to be any *unnecessary fuss*.' Mum's voice was sickly sweet, but so clipped that it sounded like she was biting off the end of every word, and might bite someone else in a minute.

My mind was racing to catch up. Mum knew? She didn't blame me?

She knew?

I looked up at Kayla. Surely she wouldn't have said anything about this, even if she did hate me now. She was looking as surprised as I was, although she tried really hard to start glowering again when she saw me watching.

Mum looked back at me, her smile softening to something less deadly. 'I know you think I don't notice anything. I notice *everything*, sweetheart. And Jude and I had a long conversation this morning about the hygiene problems involved in wearing a hat in the shower.' She ruffled what remained of his hair. 'He's booked in for an appointment with the on-site salon this afternoon.'

'A session that we will of course provide entirely gratis, complimentary and free of charge,' Margaret jumped in to add, the mention of the Park of the Year Awards seeming to have transformed her completely. 'And I'd like to issue your whole family with free tickets to our fabulous Stardance.'

She fanned out a handful of shimmering golden tickets. Mum hefted the pot of mystery beef into the crook of her elbow and plucked them from between Margaret's fingers.

'There are only four of these.'

Margaret nodded anxiously. 'A little gesture of goodwill.'

'Four. There are five of us.'

Still looking like she'd just handed over the keys to a brand-new car, Margaret nodded again. 'Obviously, accessibility issues when the venue is at full and total capacity for our evening events mean wheelchairs aren't permitted due to fire-safety policies, but there will be a crèche you can—'

'Abandon him in? Are you calling my little boy a *fire hazard*?' Mum's shoulders squared up like a boxer getting ready to deliver the knockout blow.

Margaret seemed to be missing the warning signs, but Dad hadn't. He scooped Jude out of his chair and carried him into the caravan, loudly humming the *Twinkle* theme tune.

Mum wrapped her arms round the pan of beef like a

war drum. 'You're trying to apologize for spoiling my son's party by offering us tickets to one he can't go to? Because *he* might cause an accident? Have you ever heard the word *discrimination*, Margaret, because I have to tell you—'

YOU'RE A LOSER!

A voice from inside my hoody interrupted Mum mid flow. She spun round like a whirlwind and I stared blankly back at her.

LOOOOSER! HEY! LOSER!

Something was vibrating and shouting in my pocket, making it seem like I was yelling insults at the park manager from somewhere in the region of my hip. My phone had different ringtones set up for everyone, so I could avoid answering when Dad's *Match of the Day* theme played, and pick up when it was Kayla's 'Hard Rock Hallelujah'. Mum knew that.

YOU'RE A LOSER!

But this wasn't my phone.

LOOOOOSER!

It was Jayden-Lee's. And it was his ringtone. I couldn't answer a *stolen phone* right in front of the park manager. What would I say? *Oh, I just robbed a child so I could find out if this boy I like likes me too*. The situation couldn't have been any more impossible.

'OI, KERSHAW! ON YOUR HEAD!'

Until I saw Jayden-Lee standing outside his caravan. It was like I'd summoned him with the power of pure panic. Praying that he was too far away to hear the muffled sound of his own ringtone, it took me longer than it should have to even notice the football hurtling straight towards me.

Or, not straight towards *me*. Jayden-Lee really wasn't that great a shot.

Swallowing hard, I grabbed the phone inside my pocket, groped blindly to try and make the wretched thing turn off, and yelped out, 'Sorry, I need to pee!'

Shoving past Kayla, I made it halfway up the ramp just as the football impacted with Mum's pan, and the world exploded in a shower of flying beef.

TWENTY-TWO

There's only so long you can stay in a toilet without looking weird, or like you have clogged-bum issues. That's especially true when you can hear everyone outside trying to clean up after a shower of beef stew. Still, I tried to drag the time out as long as I could, picking bits of beefy shrapnel off my hoody. I'd listened to the shouting between Mum and Margaret for a while without really being able to make out any of the words, but things had gone quiet now.

Jayden-Lee's phone had one missed call on it, from someone called Daisy. There weren't any texts afterwards to ask what he was doing, or why he hadn't picked up, but I still wondered who she was.

Was Daisy a girlfriend-sounding sort of a name?

There was no passcode on the phone, so all Jayden-Lee's messages were *right there* waiting for me to look at them. All I'd have to do would be quickly check how many kisses she ended her texts with to know if it was a love thing. There might be pictures too. It would be so easy. I just had to press one button . . .

My finger hovered over it.

145

I touched it really, really lightly, so that if the messages did open up it would be more like an accident, really.

Nothing happened.

I pressed a bit less gently.

Someone hammered hard on the door. 'Are you coming out anytime soon, or does everyone else have to clear up your mess, *as usual*?'

Kayla was leaning on the doorframe when I opened it, after making loud handwashing noises and very carefully turning Jayden-Lee's phone to silent. She wasn't smiling. If she had decided to speak to me again, it looked like it was only to start another fight.

I got in before she could. 'What do you mean, *my* mess? I didn't kick the stupid ball.'

'No, you're just the reason it was kicked. And you didn't exactly try to stop it.'

In the kitchen, Dad was at the sink washing beef out of Mum's hair. Kayla had escaped the worst of the debris, but she had little brown polka dots all over her previously plain yellow dress. She'd worn weirder things, honestly.

'If I was fast enough to have stopped that ball, I'd be in goal for England,' I told her, folding my arms and trying not to notice the weight of the phone dragging at my pocket. Could guilt make things feel heavier? If it could, I was going to be walking with a limp before long.

Kayla would know if Daisy was a girlfriend sort of name. All I wanted to do was ask her about it, but I couldn't. There were too many other things I needed to say first, and I didn't know how. Everything I tried seemed to get stuck somewhere on its way out, words and sentences bunching up uncomfortably in the base of my throat. I didn't have clogged-bum problems, just verbal constipation.

Kayla must have taken my pained expression as guilt. She glanced over at Mum and Dad. 'She wanted to go home straight away, but your dad talked her out of it. Said she should stay and get her money's worth for the holiday.'

'What, £9.50?'

Kayla shrugged. 'It probably helped that the manager left looking like she'd taken a swim at the local sewage works. The mystery beef landed on her head.'

I felt better knowing that it had been Margaret, not Mum, who'd caught the worst of the beefsplosion, but I knew why we were really staying. Jude was happily on the couch watching cartoons, and he'd already pulled his Nibbles hat back over his head. Looking at him just made me sigh. 'He totally loves that hamster.'

'I'm quite a fan myself,' Kayla said.

She was *still* going on about that? Jude might have adored him, but she knew that Nibbles was the bane of my life. 'Because of the other night? He wasn't in any danger, you know. He wears more padding than the riot police.'

'He still saved us,' she retorted. 'I don't know where you were, but I for one was glad to be swept up in his tiny hamster arms.'

'I WAS ON STA—' I started, before realizing my voice was creeping up to a shout, and my parents weren't far enough away not to hear it. Quickly I stalked towards my bedroom, beckoning Kayla to follow.

Then I whispered, 'I was onstage having the most humiliating experience of my life. Maybe you didn't notice?'

'Maybe I didn't,' Kayla said, hands on hips. 'But then I've never been to the centre of the universe, and that's apparently where you think you are. We were supposed to be having a night out together. After Jayden-Lee turned up it was like you barely noticed I was there. At least Nibbles helped me get out without a black eye.'

It didn't matter that I'd been looking for her, that the first thing I'd thought about when it all kicked off at the karaoke was making sure she was safe. Nibbles had got there first, and now it seemed like Kayla thought he was

Superman with a new choice of costume. I couldn't believe it.

'Oh my god, you really are in love with him. You don't know anything about him!'

She scoffed. 'You can talk.'

'I know more about Jayden-Lee than you do about that hamster. I know more than you think.' Or I could, if I just got up the courage to go through his phone. I could feel my face heating up as I tried hard to keep my voice to an angry whisper. 'For all you know, Nibbles has a girlfriend in every caravan.'

'For all *you* know, Jayden-Lee has a girlfriend at home. Anyway, I don't think Nibbles would be like that. He's family friendly, after all.'

Kayla's words felt like a slap. I *didn't* know whether Jayden-Lee had a girlfriend at home. I didn't know if that was who Daisy was. I didn't know if he had a boyfriend, either, or if there was any way he might want one.

But I had a way of finding out.

I could barely look at Kayla any more. 'Fine – fall in love with someone who dresses as a six-foot rodent. They make late-night documentaries about people like you. But whatever; do what you want. Maybe he'll take you on a date in his great big plastic ball.'

She started to draw herself up into a four-foot-eight

column of blazing fury, but I didn't want to stay around to hear what she had to say. I'd listened to so many of her crush stories: the guy with the really amazing beard who turned out to only be twelve, or the one working at the corner shop who was gorgeous until he got a spider web tattooed right over his face. Jayden-Lee was the first person I'd *ever* told her I liked, and she'd just decided to hate him for no reason.

I wasn't going to listen to her drool over a hamster. Before she could even open her mouth I'd stormed out, slamming the bedroom door behind me.

Not really thick enough to be slammed, the door made a sort of clanging sound and burst open again, leaving Kayla staring open-mouthed as I left.

TWENTY-THREE

Mum and Dad called after me as I thundered back out of the caravan, but I didn't want to speak to them either. What would be the point? I hadn't pulled off the save of the century by putting myself between the ball and Mum's stew, and I didn't have a time machine handy to go back and do it now. I felt like I'd just missed a penalty in a critical game.

Mum might have been fuming over the tragic waste of beef, but that wasn't my only problem. Troy was probably off reloading with gum somewhere, priming himself to launch at me from the shadows like a disgustingly sticky six-year-old kamikaze. Kayla and Jude had dumped me for a hamster. I had nothing left – nothing.

Except Jayden-Lee's phone, burning a hole in my pocket.

I walked without really knowing where I was going, or what I'd do when I got there. Pacing down the long rows of caravans and past the playground, I stopped for a minute to let the miniature train pass by. It was empty apart from two old ladies with their grey hair pinned back under nylon scarves to keep from getting windblown by the half-a-mile-per-hour thrill ride.

I considered getting back in the hedgerow and staying there until the worst holiday of my life was over. But I could hear people inside the playground. Ordinary, happy people, who had friends who hadn't abandoned them. So I kept walking.

Soon I was back outside the Starlight Showhall, like a thief returning to the scene of his most embarrassing crimes.

There were posters for the Stardance pinned up everywhere. They were going to have a semi-finalist from a celebrity cooking show as a special guest, and, along with the Park of the Year Award, they were also announcing the prize for the best Elvis tribute. The music was being done by someone who was a Radio 1 DJ back in the dark ages. It didn't look like the party of the century, really. Still, something felt like it was twisting up inside me as I read.

I'd been to dances at school. I knew how they worked. The boys stood at one end of the assembly hall and stared at the girls at the other end for the first half of the night. Then gradually people sort of drifted together and paired off.

I usually skipped that part, and hung out with the

other people who were trying not to be noticed at the edges of the room. I could have found someone to pair up with, probably, but it never seemed like it would be fair to pretend I was interested when I wasn't. Not in any of the girls.

And boys danced with girls at school. That was just how it was.

So I knew what standing on your own nodding your head to the music was like. And I knew what it was like when everyone rushed the floor for the big songs with routines you couldn't help but know. But I didn't know what dancing with your arms round someone else felt like. I'd never done that at all.

Jude wasn't going to grow up thinking he didn't fit in at dances too. No way. I'd just reached up to tear down the poster when a pair of paws grabbed me tightly round the waist.

Not again. It was like getting mugged by a fuzzy armchair. *Nibbles.*

He spun me round before I even knew what was happening, and raced off down the path. Seconds later he was followed by a small gang of shrieking little girls in party dresses, who must have been on their way to see Minnie and Winnie before they decided to play hunt the hamster.

As I watched, Nibbles dived in through the showhall

doors, and the whole crowd vanished after him, giggling and screaming.

Fangirls were obviously all part of the job for the world's most huggable hamster.

Well, they could have him. I tugged down the Stardance poster, crumpling it into a yellow ball in my fist and throwing it in the direction he'd gone. Then I did the same to the next one. Then another, and another. Soon I'd gone through the whole row of them. There were scrunched-up pieces of yellow paper all down the path, like angry confetti.

I should have left then, before someone came out to find all their hard work screwed up and tossed on the floor. But I didn't want to. Part of me *wanted* to get caught. Maybe it would be the final straw, and they'd throw me out of the park. Jude could stay. I'd just get a coach back to Surrey and live on Doritos and that cheese that comes in tubes from the corner shop until everyone came home.

It sounded like a really appealing prospect.

While I waited for someone to show up and hand me a lifetime ban from terrible caravan park holidays, I wandered over to the Twinkle ride outside the main showhall doors. I didn't have a pound for a go, but there was nowhere else to sit, so I hopped up to use the passenger carriage as a makeshift bench.

The phone in my pocket made a soft clunking sound as I bumped it against the side of the train. Who wouldn't put a passcode on their phone? It was as if Jayden-Lee *wanted* me to find it. He could have done the whole thing on purpose: given the phone to Troy and told him to get caught with it, just so I'd end up having to take it back.

What if this whole thing was *Jayden-Lee's* secret plan? Mine had been totally messed up thanks to Nibbles, and Troy, and the disaster on karaoke night, but maybe Jayden-Lee had taken matters into his own hands. Maybe this was his way of telling me I hadn't blinded him with extinguisher foam, but with love.

I thought about how he'd winked at me when I kicked his football back. How he'd been *impressed*. And he'd been trying to get my attention again today, hadn't he? He hadn't meant to turn the stew into a weapon of mass destruction.

He'd probably wanted me to check his phone the whole time. I fumbled it out into my hands and brought the cracked screen back to life, smiling stupidly at its wallpaper of a BMW exploding in *Carjackers 2*.

He liked gaming. I liked gaming. So we had something in common already, *and* I knew more about him than Kayla thought.

I swiped into the message from Daisy.

> mum sez to tell aunty eileen to bring
> her back some ciggies from yr holiday.
> Do they do duty frees in cornwall?

No kisses.

It sounded like she was some kind of cousin. I felt my heart soar. The sun parted the clouds to beam a spotlight down on me. In the distance, birds were singing.

Then a new message flashed up. From Kev.

> Hv u asked him yt?

And another.

> Do it mate! Get urself a date 4 tonite haha

It was like my body had forgotten how to use its lungs. I wheezed out a breath and tried to take a fresh one, but the air didn't go anywhere, just got stuck painfully in my throat. My brain was too busy to tell my organs what they were supposed to be doing. It was just flashing up the words ASKED HIM. DATE. TONITE on the screen behind my eyes.

ASKED HIM?

DATE?

TONITE?

156

It *couldn't* mean me. But what if it did? Had Jayden-Lee talked to his mates about me? We'd played football together, after all. They'd all seen how impressed he was by my skills. What if he felt the same way about me as I did about him? I had to know. Choking down any lingering guilt over invading his privacy, I opened up the message app on his phone and scrolled down again.

I found Kev's name.

And then I ducked, seconds before a football thudded against the wall where my head had just been.

'Oi, Twinkle. You got cleaned up quick. What're you doing with my phone?'

TWENTY-FOUR

I went straight into crisis-management mode. I needed to play for time. I had to find a swift, strategic response to deflect Jayden-Lee's attention from the fact that I had his phone at all, giving me the chance to come up with a flawless excuse for getting caught looking through it.

'Twinkle's the train, actually.'

That was it. That was all I managed. My brain's version of crisis-management mode just involved stating the ridiculously obvious, then completely shutting down.

Jayden-Lee was looking at me as if I'd just admitted that *Twinkle* was my favourite show, and that I spent every afternoon on the sofa in a onesie, singing along with the 'Choo-Choo' song and crying over heart-warming messages like *'Friends help keep you on the right track.'*

Which was totally untrue, obviously. I almost never did that. But since my little brother was a massive fan, I couldn't help picking up a few *Twinkle* facts, here and there. The problem was that my mind had suddenly emptied of everything else. The only conversational option I had was to launch into all of them.

'Except in the German version, where Twinkle's called Funky. I think that's a translation thing, or maybe it's because Germans have problems with Ws. Did you know they show *Twinkle* in over twenty-one different countries? Apparently it's because there aren't any cultures who get offended by trains, although there are four of them where her voice is dubbed by a man.'

Jayden-Lee was looking at me the way I look at my shoes when I've trodden in something unpleasant. But then, I had just revealed myself as the weirdest trainspotter on the planet.

I definitely wasn't redeeming myself for having effectively gunged him at the karaoke any time soon, even if he had sort of paid me back in beef stew.

'Whatever,' he said, finally. 'My phone. Where'd you find it?'

And, somewhere buried deep in my grey matter, a single brain cell sparked back into life.

'Oh, is this yours?' I held it up, the screen having reverted to black. I'd never even had the chance to click back into the messages. 'It was lying on the ground out here. I was just checking the contacts to find out whose it was.'

I was a genius, an actual genius. It was the perfect excuse.

Jayden-Lee dragged a hand through his hair (which fell back immediately into a flawless sweep, as if he was walking around under an invisible blow-drier) and growled, 'That little . . . he's going to pay for this.' He snatched the phone with a huff and inspected the shattered screen. 'Least it's not broken.'

I curled my fingers back to brush against my palm where he'd touched it.

'Jude's the same – a total nightmare with my stuff.'

Jayden-Lee's lip curled into a question mark. 'Yeah, I'm sure he *runs off* with things all the time.'

He laughed, and I almost caught myself joining in, not because it was funny, but out of some weird feeling that it might make him like me more. But my mind flashed back to the party, and how sick I'd felt about laughing then.

This was my chance though. The opportunity I'd been waiting for to put him straight about Jude. In five minutes I'd be comforting him as he sobbed over how ignorant he'd been.

'You've never seen him on the walker he uses round the house. When he's nicked my crisps, he can get away like he's doing the hundred-metre sprint.' I'd start small, I decided, and build up little details until Jayden-Lee got it.

He wasn't looking at me, just staring in through the

showhall doors, so maybe the guilt was getting to him already.

'You know, some people get the wrong impression of him. Just because he—'

'Has that hamster gone wonky or something?' Jayden-Lee muttered.

I paused. It was a bit off topic, but might be something new we had in common. 'When hasn't that hamster been wonky? I can't be the only one having nightmares about his buck teeth coming for me in the night.'

Jayden-Lee laughed again, and it was a better sound now. A sound that made me want to punch the air. Now I could add my sense of humour to my right foot in the portfolio of things he liked about me. I was nailing it. 'He ran by here a little while ago,' I added. 'Probably on his way to cause more childhood traumas.'

'Well he's in there now.' Jayden-Lee tapped on the glass. 'Looks like he's gone off on one.'

I slid off Twinkle and went to see what he was talking about. Leaning in to peer through the dull glass, I held my breath as our shoulders touched.

It took a moment to figure out what was going on inside. But I didn't think it looked wonky at all.

'I think he's doing ballet,' I said.

Part of Nibbles was doing ballet, anyway. Whoever

was usually inside the furry monstrosity had taken off the bulky costume and was just wearing the head and paws. From the neck down he was covered by a black, clingy leotard that ran all the way to his wrists and ankles.

It was strange. I'd always thought the person inside the tubby, bumbling hamster would be tubby and bumbling too. He wasn't. He was tall and lean and muscular. He looked more like an athlete than someone's pampered pet.

And he *was* doing ballet. As we watched, he kicked a leg lightly up until his ankle touched his ear. It was incredible.

Jayden-Lee let out an explosive laugh. '*That* has to be the gayest thing I've ever seen.'

I tried really, really hard not to flinch, but I must have done somehow because suddenly our shoulders weren't touching any more.

Inside, Nibbles had launched himself from what must have been warm-up exercises into an actual routine. He leaped and spun without stumbling once, but I was barely watching. I'd found my own reflection in the glass and stared at that instead, willing my face to look the same as usual – not hurt at all.

Falling in love felt a lot like falling into a canal. A sudden shock as you're plunged into murky depths, with all kinds of unexpected dangers just below the surface. I was starting to think that I might like to climb back out.

Beside me, Jayden-Lee was fumbling with his phone again. I could see the reflection in the screen, flashing up Kev's messages. He seemed to be considering something, tapping the phone against his chest.

'You going to the pool party tonight?' he asked.

I glanced around quickly. Besides me, and the distant figure of a dancing hamster, there was no one else he could be directing the question to.

I just needed the right response. Not too eager. Casual, yet cool.

'I hadn't heard about it, but I'm pretty sharp at snooker so—'

'Not that kind of pool, you div. Swimming pool.' He rolled his eyes back in his head and spoke more slowly, as though English might not be my first language. 'They're shutting out all the kids who like to pee in the shallow end and playing some tunes. Wave machine, all that. You going?'

I hadn't been planning to, clearly, or I wouldn't have thought Jayden-Lee's idea of a good time might involve something my grandad played in the pub. It was lucky I hadn't gone really wild and suggested a round of darts.

No, this was a proper party. And he seemed really interested in me being there. But was asking if I *was going* the same thing as asking if I wanted to go *with him*? It was a small yet vital difference.

I shoved my hands in my pockets and tried to act like it wasn't the most important question I'd ever been asked in my life. 'Uh, yeah. Might do.'

'You should,' he said, looking me up and down.

I stared back. I couldn't help it. This close up, he barely even seemed real. He was like an artist's ideal of beauty, painted in tiny, perfect brushstrokes and then breathed into life. It didn't seem possible that he could be asking me, with my swollen nose, and weird obsession with talking trains, and my beefy family, if I wanted to go out with him.

He nudged my foot with his. More of a kick, really, but he probably didn't know his own strength. 'Come on. Least you won't have to worry about anyone catching fire.'

I swallowed down a nervous squeaking noise and cleared my throat. 'Yeah, um, sorry about that. I was trying to . . . anyway, sure. I'll come. I'll see you there.'

He nodded, once, turning back up the path as he started pressing a reply into his phone (probably about ME, his date with ME). 'Good. See you.'

I watched his reflection in the glass door until he was

out of sight. Inside the showhall, Nibbles was still dancing – pushing up on to one foot and spinning in a dizzying pirouette that summed up in one motion exactly how I was feeling.

I didn't think it looked gay, or strange. I thought it looked beautiful.

But the whole world looked beautiful to me, just then.

TWENTY-FIVE

I was going to a pool party.

(With Jayden-Lee.)

A party, at a pool.

(That Jayden-Lee had asked me to go to.)

(With him.)

I drifted away from the showhall and headed along the path up to the cliffs in a kind of daze. He hadn't said it was a date, exactly, but that didn't matter. He still wanted me to go. He wanted me to be in the same place as him, at the same time.

Just me, him, and however many people fit around a half-Olympic-sized pool. It was going to be *amazing*.

I hadn't been to anything resembling a pool party since my sixth birthday, when Dad set up a giant inflatable paddling pool in the garden. In hindsight, it had been a mistake to serve so much of the party food on those little pointy cocktail sticks. The garden was a swamp for days after the pool exploded, and we never did find Jack Benjamin's trunks.

This party was going to be a much more grown-up, sophisticated affair. There probably wouldn't even be any sausages on sticks. Instead they'd have a barbeque, and drinks in coconut shells, and songs about summertime for everyone to dance to in their swimsuits.

But, just when I should have been thinking about the tropical heat, I felt a prickle of cold sweat at the nape of my neck.

I pictured it again. Sun loungers for catching the artificial rays, and a wave machine lapping at the non-slip pool edge. People pushing each other into the water, splashing around in their bikinis and trunks.

A shiver ran through me.

It's not that I'm insecure about the way I look. I'm fine – I'm just wiry rather than stacked. Dad says I'm built for speed: perfect when I'm racing up the length of a pitch. But Jayden-Lee was easily twice as broad as me, and I couldn't stick a note to my bare chest to explain the difference between slow- and fast-twitch muscles.

Or, I could, but I wanted one night *without* totally humiliating myself.

It just wasn't quite what I'd imagined for my first not-a-date. Most people don't start off a relationship by seeing each other in their pants, and maybe I'm old-fashioned, but I think that's just fine. I tried to picture Kayla being reassuring about it. When the girls in our class had started a 'bikini body' diet fad, she'd shown up to one of their parties in a bikini of her own, looking amazing, to point out that any body could wear one. Even a body that had eaten peanut-butter pancakes for breakfast.

Kayla wouldn't reassure me. She'd tell me to go in Speedos. But somehow her confidence was comforting all by itself.

'*You can't pretend to be someone you're not,*' Imaginary Kayla said. '*Or you'll never know if he might have preferred who you already were.*'

I hmm-ed, unsure.

'*Also, false advertising is a crime. He'll either end up dumping you or reporting you to the Trading Standards Office,*' she added.

She might have been a figment of my imagination, but she was right. Besides, it wasn't like I could show up to the pool party in a disguise. That was the entire problem.

There was a long bench set up on the clifftop, next to a sign warning people to stay away from the crumbling edges. The seat looked like it had been carved out of the trunk of a single fallen tree. I sat on it and stared out to sea, trying to get some perspective.

Everyone would be in swimwear. No one was going to care about mine.

'*Exactly,*' Imaginary Kayla interrupted. '*And what else are you going to do, Dylan – turn up dressed for scuba diving?*'

That was an idea. I could pretend I'd thought it was fancy dress.

'Dylan!' Kayla yelled.

'I know, I know. Where would I even get a last-minute wetsuit from?'

Actual Kayla tilted her head and looked at me like I'd gone completely round the bend. 'I know you're upset, but I didn't think it was bad enough to make you run away to sea.'

She must have followed me up here. I hadn't even noticed her coming up behind the bench, too busy worrying how the rest of me was ever going to match up to my 'impressive' feet. I was so startled I didn't have time to figure out whether I was still supposed to be angry.

'I'm not. Not in just a wetsuit, anyway.'

She sat down on the opposite end of the bench. 'Rowing boat?'

'I was thinking something less likely to give me bum splinters. Do you think they do luxury yachts at Starcross Sands?'

'I don't think they do luxury loo roll. Actually, I know they don't. You could use the stuff in the showhall loos as tracing paper.' She pinched her lips together in a way that I knew meant she was trying not to smile. I couldn't understand why she was even talking to me again, and I wasn't sure I wanted to ask, just in case she stopped.

I tried, 'Did you want something?' instead, and hated how nervous my voice came out.

'I did want something, as a matter of fact,' she said. And I waited for her to tell me to leave her alone forever, or book her a taxi back to Woking, or something. But she didn't. She shifted closer to me on the bench and said, 'I want us to be friends again.'

'But you hate me,' I protested. 'Back in the caravan you were looking at me like I'd spat in your cornflakes.'

'I didn't have any cornflakes, Dylan. The only thing your mum bought for breakfast was sliced meat,' she said. 'I don't hate you.'

'You hate Jayden-Lee,' I tried.

She gave me an uncertain look, like she wanted to deny it but couldn't quite get the words out. 'I don't *like* Jayden-Lee. But I respect your decision to love horrible things. I never say a word about your T-shirts.'

'Just because you don't understand *style*.' I tried to narrow my eyes at her, but now it was my turn to bite down on a smile. 'Your love for that hamster is turning you against me.'

Kayla shoved her shoulder into mine in a way that was more friendly than violent. 'I'm *not* in love with Nibbles. Not to be mean, but that much body hair isn't for me. I just don't think he's the devil incarnate, that's all.'

I thought about how unexpected it had been to see Nibbles practising ballet moves – doing something quiet and graceful, instead of crashing around making my life miserable. For some reason I wanted to keep the memory of it to myself. Jayden-Lee hadn't understood it, so it was probably a stupid thing to like.

'Maybe not the devil,' I conceded. 'Something a bit lower on the evil scale, like a zombie or a werewolf. He could be a hampire.'

Kayla laughed, and I felt as though a tight band that had been wrapped around my chest since last night had suddenly snapped open. Me and Kayla were a team. Spending all day without her had made me feel like I was missing a limb. An arm, maybe. My smarter, more sensible arm, which always knew the right thing to do.

'I think I know what you do hate,' I said carefully.

I could feel her studying the side of my face. 'What's that?'

'Being left on your own. You haven't got your dad here, and I don't think I've been here half the time, either. I'm sorry. If it helps, it turns out I really hate it too.'

Kayla was quiet. In the fields that ran up the slopes of the cliff, they were setting up for the end-of-season funfair. I watched the big wheel start to turn and chime out a celebratory tune, as Kayla reached for my hand and slipped her fingers through mine.

'OK,' she said.

I looked at her from the very corner of my eye. 'Does OK mean we're friends again?'

She almost started to nod, then stopped herself. 'It means we're working on it. We're in the negotiation phase of re-establishing boundaries and terms.'

'You're going to draw up a contract, aren't you?'

She looked innocent. 'I might. Don't worry – you'll only have to sign it. I'll deal with all the small print.'

'That's exactly what I'm worried about. But there are visitation rights in the contract, aren't there? We have to hang out with each other to check we can still get along . . .'

'In a civil manner?' Kayla finished for me. 'Yes, that will definitely be part of the negotiation package.'

'*Great.*' I grinned. 'Because I know *exactly* where we're going tonight.'

TWENTY-SIX

There was a strong smell of coconut and chlorine in the air at the Splashdown Swim Centre, and I wasn't sure whether it was that or the knot of nerves in my stomach that was making me feel so sick. Kayla seemed fine – she'd grabbed a lemonade on our way through the door and was sipping it through a twirly straw, already having stripped down to her pink-frilled swimsuit.

After some heated debate (Kayla *totally* told me I should go in Speedos), I'd settled on some long board shorts and a Hawaiian shirt.

Well, a black shirt I'd let Kayla draw pineapples on in glitter eyeliner.

They must have turned the heating up to full power to match the tropical theme. We'd been there ten minutes and I was already sweating. Everyone was sweating. People in the pool were probably sweating. The whole place was a kaleidoscope of glistening skin.

Kayla stopped and dipped a bare toe in the water. 'A few more rubber duckies and this would be good for a bath.'

'Rubber alligators don't count then?' I pointed across

to where some impromptu races were being held: two pot-bellied lads who *had* decided to go with the Speedo option were straddling a couple of giant gators and paddling them the length of the pool. There were loads of inflatables in the water: a couple of lilos, several plastic palm trees, and a giant two-seater banana.

Not to mention enough ornamental flamingos to send Jayden-Lee's mum into a frenzy. I wondered if she was here. Trying to spot anyone specific in a crowd of half-dressed people wasn't easy though. For one thing, I didn't know what Mrs Slater looked like without one of her nylon nighties on. And for another, I really, seriously, didn't want to think about what she'd look like out of them.

Even picking out Jayden-Lee turned out to be impossible. If he'd turned up at all. I looked for the tell-tale golden glint of his hair among the dancers on the other side of the pool, but all I could see was that ridiculous hamster doing the hula in front of the DJ stage, with a group of girls who might have been the karaoke fairies trying to throw flower garlands over his oversized orange head.

Looking at Nibbles now, it was almost impossible to remember how graceful the person inside had looked, tripping lightly through ballet steps in the hall.

Kayla dug me in the side. 'There he is.'

'I know,' I said. 'I'm just going to make sure I'm on the other side of the pool from him at all times. They say evil things can't cross running water. It was in a film.'

'I'm not sure a wave machine counts as *running*,' Kayla said, 'And while it's reassuring to know that you have *some* life skills, even if they only amount to protecting yourself from fictional vampires, *I meant Jayden-Lee.*'

My head snapped round to see where she was pointing. Of course I'd ended up telling her about my maybe-a-date, and even though she still thought Jayden-Lee was one evolutionary step above pond scum, she said she was happy for me. That was how I knew our friendship was getting back on track.

I hadn't told her about the ballet, or Jayden-Lee calling it gay, though. That would only have made her think she was right about him being wrong all along.

That was the problem with Kayla. She'd write him off over one tiny flaw when – as I confirmed when I finally saw him, standing with Kev, Leroy and Dean, and laughing with his mouth open between bites of Kahlua Pork – he was otherwise perfect in every single way.

Just as soon as I'd talked him out of using insults like gay, or retarded, she'd be totally out of excuses to hate him.

'Is he picking food out of his teeth? Urgh, Dylan, you want to kiss that?'

... OK, just as soon as I talked him out of calling people gay, or retarded, and into some less caveman-like behaviour. *Then*, he'd be perfect.

I watched him drag his finger and thumbnail over his teeth, pick out a strand of pulled pork, examine and then eat it. Kayla was squirming beside me. Did I still want to kiss him?

I had to, didn't I?

That was the point of love. People who were in it could overlook each other's flaws and just see the good bits, and Jayden-Lee had tons of those. Like ... the incredible angles of his jawline. And those little dark flecks that peppered the green of his eyes.

And OK, maybe I could admit now that some of what I felt for Jayden-Lee was more to do with the shape of his mouth and the way his autumn-gold hair fell into his eyes than anything else. But love had to start somewhere. Why couldn't it start with his little lip scar and my right foot, and grow from there?

While I was watching, he looked up. As though his focus was being guided by fate, I saw him tilt his chin in my direction and start scanning the faces around me. I held my breath, waiting for the jolt of electricity when our eyes finally met across the deckchairs. I could picture it: he'd hold out a hand and walk towards me, and I'd walk towards him, like heat-seeking missiles with each other as a target.

He smiled as his gaze settled on . . . a girl right next to me, whose friend was trying to re-tie her bikini strings after a slight wardrobe malfunction in the pool. He hadn't noticed me at all.

He'd been looking, though. And now he was headed my way, so he'd have to see me, any minute. And I suddenly felt strange about that.

'Do you want to get in the water?' I asked Kayla urgently.

'What? But he's—'

'I really feel like taking a dip. Who goes to a pool party without getting wet, anyway?' I was dragging her with me to the pool edge as I spoke, getting out of the line of Jayden-Lee's sight as quickly as I could. I still wanted to see him, obviously. Just, not yet.

Not until I'd figured out what I wanted to say.

Every time I thought about speaking to him at all, my throat seemed to seal shut. At this rate I'd open my mouth and only be able to emit high-pitched squeaks, like I'd been learning how to speak fluent Hamster and wanted to show it off.

'Dylan, you're still wearing your shirt,' Kayla was protesting.

'No problem!' I croaked, with the last bit of oxygen I had left. 'We don't even need to get wet.'

Kneeling down at the side of the pool, I grabbed one end of the giant floating banana and climbed aboard.

A moment later, after passing over her lemonade for me to hold, so did Kayla.

'See!' I said, only sounding the tiniest bit panicked. 'This is nice, isn't it? They've done a good job with the decorating – it really looks like a beach.'

'Oh, yes,' Kayla agreed. 'If you ignore the big signs telling people not to run, and that the water will change colour if you pee in it, it's just like our own personal paradise. And what *is* the matter with you, exactly? I don't think you should be in charge of this banana if you're in the middle of a breakdown.'

I was doing a great job of steering the banana, as it happened. With a few initial bumps and scrapes, I'd managed to paddle us almost three feet away from the side of the pool.

'I'm not having a breakdown,' I hissed over my shoulder. 'The thing is . . .'

The thing was, I wasn't sure I *did* want to talk to Jayden-Lee tonight. I thought about him all the time, and that was brilliant, because in my head he always said and did exactly the right thing, and he liked me the same way I liked him. He was great, at a distance, like when I was watching him across the pool, or hanging around outside his caravan. Because then he really was perfect. Silent and unreachable, like the kind of star you make wishes on that you never expect to come true.

I'd imagined him asking me out so many times in the last few days.

And now I didn't want it to happen. Because it wouldn't be how I'd pictured it. Because every time he opened his mouth, a little bit of my image of him got spoilt.

If nothing ever happened between me and Jayden-Lee, then neither of us could ever mess it up, and I could keep the vision of us as the caravan park's perfect couple in my head forever. The realization that I didn't want to find out that the daydream I had of him wasn't the actual reality hit me like a bomb.

Then so did Jayden-Lee, with his knees bent up to his chest, cannonballing straight into the water beside us.

TWENTY-SEVEN

In the wake of Jayden-Lee's tidal wave, Kayla tipped back off the banana and hit the surface of the pool with a splash of her own. The back-and-forth motion of the water was almost enough to make me seasick, but I managed to stay afloat with my knees gripping the banana, and her glass of lemonade held above my head.

Kayla was treading water, head down and taking deep breaths. The fall must have knocked the wind out of her.

Twisting round, I held my other arm out to help her back on board. 'Here, come back up.'

Kayla shook her head without lifting it. 'No, I'm not getting back on that fruity death trap.'

I didn't think it was exactly the banana's fault, but Kayla and I were still in the new stages of being friends again, and if I could let a pool toy take the blame for me dragging her out on the water, I was going to do it. 'I think it was built for speed, not security. Are you OK? Do you want me to get you a lilo?'

She hadn't looked up yet. She was peering down into the water as though there might be a treasure chest at the bottom of it, instead of a few floating plasters and someone's verruca sock. 'No –' she took a deep breath – 'I'm fine. I think I might just swim for a while.'

I frowned. 'Kayla?'

'I'm *fine*,' she repeated, in a tone of voice that only proved she really wasn't. 'Just turn around.'

'But—'

'*Turn around.*'

I didn't want to start a new fight over how not-fine she was. I turned around.

'Hey, Twinkle.'

. . . Just in time to see Jayden-Lee cruising up beside me, now astride an inflatable alligator.

Was Twinkle supposed to be a permanent nickname? I really didn't think I liked it. Even the way he smiled when he said it seemed wrong, turning his mouth into an ugly sneer.

I didn't want to complain about it and sound like the Starcross branch of Trainspotters Anonymous again, though. What I had to do was give him a nickname back. Something a little bit flirty, like *Tiger*, but somehow meaningful at the same time.

'Hey, Twonkle.'

In my head it had sounded a lot cooler.

It didn't even rhyme properly. It was like my brain had just let a massive fart out right through my mouth, and Jayden-Lee looked like he'd smelt it.

'Is that supposed to be funny?'

He gave me a dangerous-looking glare, and I shook my head several times, fast. 'No, I – I don't even think it was supposed to be a word.'

I considered slipping backwards off the banana and joining Kayla underneath the water. It wouldn't be the bravest thing to do, but maybe it would make a good first not-a-date story for me and Jayden-Lee to tell our friends, if things somehow took a better turn later. *How did it go? Well, first I forgot how to speak English, and then I had a really good go at drowning myself out of shame. But otherwise, fine.*

Jayden-Lee was still looming over my banana. He leaned across, but not in a romantic, wanting-to-be-close-to-me sort of way. It didn't feel like he was going to yawn and stretch and end up with his arm around me as if it was an accident.

It felt a little bit like a threat.

'You do though, don't you?' he said. 'Think you're funny.'

A jeering laugh went up from the side of the pool, and I looked across to see Kev and the rest of Jayden-Lee's mates standing in a huddle, watching.

I swallowed nervously, almost sure by now that this not-a-date was really just Not. A. Date.

'I don't. I promise – I really don't think I'm funny at all,' I stammered. 'You should hear me at Christmas; my cracker jokes go down worse than the sprouts.' That wasn't true, I *slayed* with 'What's orange and sounds like a parrot' last year. But for some reason I felt I had to defend myself against the idea that I had a sense of humour. I didn't know what Jayden-Lee thought I'd been joking about, but it didn't seem like he was laughing. 'I'm very serious, actually. Like . . . maths. Or cancer.'

I was trying to think of other serious things to compare myself to when he interrupted.

'Do you always talk this much rubbish?'

My jaw got very tight, my teeth clamping shut so firmly that I couldn't pry them open to make any more words. My cheeks were burning too, but not in embarrassment. It reminded me a little bit of how I'd felt when I'd tried to tell my friend Sam that I liked him, right before he moved to Berlin, and he'd said he liked me too, 'but not in a gay way, obviously'. And then laughed.

And I'd had to laugh and pretend that, *obviously*, that wasn't what I'd meant at all.

So I nodded slightly to answer Jayden-Lee's question, because my stuck-fast teeth wouldn't let me do anything else. Yes, OK, all I did was talk rubbish. He could think that if he wanted, because all *I* wanted was to get out of the stupid pool and walk barefoot back home if I had to.

He was still giving me that same sneer-smile that turned him from something beautiful into something mean. And he didn't seem to be going away, despite me directing a thousand LEAVE ME ALONE thoughts right between his eyes.

I knew it. I knew if I talked to him tonight, then everything would be ruined.

'I see you watching, you know,' he said, very softly. It took a moment for the thudding of my pulse in my eardrums to quiet enough for me to hear him properly. 'Every morning I see you looking out, like a little stalker. So either your TV's on the blink, or you're trying to get a look at something else.'

'I –' I managed to get a single syllable out before I realized I didn't know how to explain. How could I tell him that I just liked knowing he was there, not that far away from me? I liked feeling like we were a tiny bit close, that was all, so I'd check when he was in, sometimes. Sometimes I might have checked for a little bit longer than I really needed to.

Jayden-Lee nodded, slowly.

'The thing is, my mates think it's about time I asked you – do you *fancy* me or something?'

Right at that exact moment, looking at him made my

insides churn in a completely non-romantic way. No one had ever asked me that before. Which made sense, because it's not like people look gay on the outside. Some people might joke about it, but it's not like anyone ever says, 'Wow, that guy looks soooo heterosexual.' So no – no one I'd actually fancied had ever asked me about it.

And the only person I'd ever told was Kayla.

There were so many other people who didn't know. A lot of the people I cared about most in the world. And now Jayden-Lee was asking if I fancied him, in public, right at the moment when I'd suddenly become unsure.

But I looked at the way his hair had turned dark bronze now that it was wet, and how it perfectly highlighted his tan. I looked at how straight and elegant his nose was, and the curve of his lips that I'd thought about kissing maybe twenty . . . hundred times.

And I said, ' . . . Yeah.'

TWENTY-EIGHT

'YES, GET IN!' The yell was loud enough to make several people turn and look at us, while I tried to look anywhere *else* because

1. I didn't want any of this to seem like it was anything to do with me, and
2. I couldn't quite believe that shout of delight had come from *Jayden-Lee.*

He twisted round on his alligator and called his mates' attention with a long whistle. As if everyone our side of the pool wasn't already staring. 'OI, KEV. YOU OWE ME A FIVER, MATE. I *TOLD* YOU HE WAS A TOTAL GAYBOY.'

And then he sat there and grinned at me, as if he'd just guessed the punchline to my joke.

'I told him.' He chuckled. 'Told him you was. All that looking at me. Your sparkly shirt.'

I looked down, slowly, at the glittery pineapples that Kayla had drawn to give my usual plain outfit a kind of 'Hawaiian Gothic' feel.

'I mean, you can just tell, can't you?' he crowed, like I was going to agree.

I couldn't do anything. I couldn't even move. Half a pool full of people suddenly knew something about me that I hadn't even been able to tell my mum, and I was pretty sure I could feel every single pair of their eyes on me. If I could just stay perfectly still and quiet, maybe I'd become invisible, and their focus would drift right past. I didn't think I could form words, anyway. My brain was operating on two levels: fight or flight. My fists balled up by my sides. I wanted to hit him, and I wanted to run – and stuck between the two options, all I could do was sit there, looking like a waxwork model of a teenager that had been sculpted at the precise moment his life had ended.

'Oh, of course.' There was a loud splash behind me as Kayla pulled herself back up on to the banana, like a vengeful mermaid dragging itself on to the rocks. 'Of course you can tell when someone's gay. It's so obvious, they may as well all be walking around wearing badges saying "I'm a homosexual – ask me how." No wonder you figured it out.'

Jayden-Lee stopped smiling. He looked the way I must do when I panic and all the words spill out of my head. Like I'm trying to pick the right ones out of a puddle on the floor, but everything I'm coming up with is useless and mismatched.

' . . . He's not wearing a badge,' he said, finally.

'Isn't he?' Kayla snapped from just over my shoulder. 'My goodness, so he isn't. Well you must feel very, very clever then, for figuring out something that's none of your business and shouting it to the whole world.'

The alligator squeaked between Jayden-Lee's legs as he shifted uncomfortably.

'Look, if he's going to decide to be a gaylord then you can't blame me fo—'

'Decide to be?' Kayla cut him off. '*Decide to be?* I don't think you understand how these things work. Or maybe you do. When did you decide to be straight, exactly?'

Jayden-Lee's eyebrows hunched into a furrow of confusion. 'I didn't. Just always have been, yeah?'

'Are you *sure* though? Really?' Kayla was on him like a dog mauling a squeaky bone.

I wanted to turn and watch, but I was scared I'd interrupt her flow.

'Because you don't *look* straight to me,' she continued. 'I mean, why don't you try being gay for a while? You probably just haven't met the right boy yet. I'm sure that, when you do, you'll realize this whole deciding-to-be-straight thing was just a silly phase.' She paused for one long, deep breath. 'And now you know how *stupid* you sound.'

Out of the corner of my eye, I could see that Jayden-Lee's gang of friends had edged closer along the side of the pool and were straining to listen. Jayden-Lee had the look of someone on the kill-screen of a game, who'd just run into an enemy area and realized he was all out of ammo.

Pretty desperate, in other words.

He worked his jaw slowly, looking from his friends on the poolside and back to Kayla again. All out of defences. Then he said, 'All right, splotchy, calm down. I'm not the one who spat the ketchup in your face.'

That was when I turned round. I should have realized why she'd been keeping her head down, and why she hadn't wanted to climb back on the inflatable with me. The chlorinated water had washed off all her Coverclear. It had been so long since I last saw the deep red stain down one side of her face that I'd almost forgotten what it looked like.

She made a strangled sound in the back of her throat that could have been the beginning of a sob.

Before I'd thought about what I was doing, I'd taken the glass of lemonade I'd been holding on to for her since she fell, and thrown it straight into Jayden-Lee's face, twirly straw and all. Then I shoved him off his alligator. Hard.

He toppled backwards, a flail of arms and legs

vanishing under the water, while the gator sped away in the tide his fall caused. And there must have been something in the lemonade that triggered the colour-changing dye they used to show up when little kids had wet themselves in the water, because by the time he'd come to the surface he was surrounded by a cloud of billowing red.

'*Gross*,' a girl near us called out. I thought she was the one who'd had the bikini malfunction before. She turned and started paddling away fast.

In seconds, the whole of our side of the pool was doing the same thing. The banana was tugged along by the crowd swimming around Jayden-Lee with repulsed expressions, all rushing to get out at the side.

The banana suddenly got a lot lighter as Kayla climbed out too. I called after her, but she broke into a run towards the deep end as a voice that sounded like Stacie from the children's party started crackling through the tannoy.

'*Could the gentleman who has urinated in the water please report to the shower room immediately. That's the gentleman with the weak bladder, reporting to the showers for a hose down.*'

Safely out of the water, people were starting to laugh. I had to push my way through a mass of them, including Jayden-Lee's friends, who were loudly pointing him out to anyone who'd listen.

'*Ladies and gentlemen, please do not be concerned. Chlorine kills most known infectious diseases. The festivities will continue once more has been added to the pool.*'

I was just in time to see Kayla vanish through the door of the girls' changing room, her shoulders heaving. Racing after her, I smacked right into a furry, orange blockage.

Not *now*. Nibbles must have been the only person in the pool who *hadn't* heard what Jayden-Lee yelled at me, and probably thought I was taking advantage of the distraction to sneak in and watch girls getting undressed. As if I would.

I yanked myself out of the vice-like grip of his pink paws. '*Fine* – I'll wait for her outside.'

And, while Stacie's disembodied voice reassured everyone that pee probably wasn't one of the *really bad* biohazards, I headed for the door.

TWENTY-NINE

Emerging from the bright lights of the pool, I slammed into total darkness outside. I had to put a hand out to the wall to get my bearings while my eyes adjusted to the change.

I needed to find Kayla, as soon as possible, and make sure she was all right. I couldn't believe she'd climbed on to that banana in front of everyone. For me.

In the distance, I could just pick out lights from the caravans in their neat, straight rows, like very orderly constellations. Slowly, though, they were blotting themselves out, as their inhabitants decided to go out for the evening, or go to bed. Mum and Dad and Jude were down there somewhere. Jude with a freshly buzzed head of prickly black hair, and Mum restocking the fridge with a few less heavily protein-based snacks.

She'd told me the beef bomb wasn't my fault, and that I wasn't who she was angry with. Though she did expect me to be more helpful in clearing up any future leaked stewage.

I still felt bad though. None of it would have happened if I'd watched Jude more carefully. If Mum hadn't had to step in to defend me. Now it was happening again – Kayla never even answered the phone without her make-up on, but she'd confronted Jayden-Lee without it for my sake.

All I'd done since we got here was obsess over my imaginary love life with the imaginarily perfect boy-next-door. I didn't even listen when she tried to tell me who he really was. I'd forgotten to ask how her dad was, or if he'd burned anything down yet. I'd even stolen her slot at the karaoke.

The only thing I'd cared about all holiday was Jayden-Lee, and he didn't even like me. It had taken me way too long to understand why she hadn't wanted me to like *him* either. He was spam, just like she'd said.

I didn't know *how* she'd been able to tell that, though. It must have been some kind of psychic superpower.

I heard the door open behind me and spun round quick, one hand waving to attract her attention in the dark. 'Kayla?'

A set of bony fingers pinched around my wrist. '*Mr Kershaw*, I did have a sneaking suspicion that you might be found at the heart of this *disturbance*.'

Margaret the manager's yellow hair loomed out of the darkness like a dimly lit halo.

'Is a disturbance worse than an incident?' I asked, and she gave a whinny of irritation, the way a horse might if it was getting ready to aim a swift kick. I scrambled for something else to say as a distraction as I tried to tug my hand free. 'Oh and, um, sorry about the beef.'

It might not have been the best thing to go for. She probably wouldn't want to fondly reminisce about her day spent smelling like gravy. Her hand closed tighter, locking like a human handcuff. I half expected her to frogmarch me out of the park right there.

'You do appear to be at the epicentre of a number of these ... incidents ... disturbances ...' She drew in a breath so deep I worried she was preparing to blow out flames. 'These *catastrophes*, Mr Kershaw. You are, quite simply, a magnet for disaster. And I'm sure you can appreciate that it would be imprudent for me to allow such antisocial behaviour to continue. The judges for Park of the Year are among us as I speak. We have *standards* to uphold.'

I couldn't believe I was being told I lowered the tone of somewhere with a restaurant called the Pie-O-Ria.

'I haven't been antisocial! Trying to be social's what's caused all the problems in the first place!'

'*That is not the point*,' Margaret hissed, somehow managing to shout and whisper at the same time. It was frightening, but a little bit impressive too.

She started listing things. And from the way her fingers were twitching around my wrist, I could tell she wished she had a clipboard to tick them off on. 'A four-year-old attacked with scissors at a children's party,' she started. 'Another child left in the path of an oncoming train . . .'

Obviously Troy had found a less sticky way to take his revenge, the little snitch.

'Come on – that train goes at the speed of a racing snail. And *I* didn't tie him down!'

'You encouraged dangerous behaviour in persons younger than yourself. Do you really imagine that is an improvement? Then of course there was the karaoke event, which you turned into an act of affray.'

I hadn't been acting. I didn't even know what a fray was. 'I was just *singing*.'

'I have run this park for three years, Mr Kershaw. Never before has one song contributed to the breakdown of civilized society. And what, exactly, do all these events have in common?'

Was she saying *I'd* started the karaoke riot? 'I don't know! I didn't get onstage and start swinging the mic stand at people, if that's what you mean.'

Trying to pull my arm free only dragged her in closer, until her face was barely an inch from mine. 'Perhaps not. But what all these events have in common, Mr Kershaw, is definitely *you*.'

And when I opened my mouth to deny it, I realized

she was right. OK, most of what had happened hadn't been directly my fault, exactly. But I'd been there, every time, right in the middle of it.

I should have watched Jude better.

And blocked Jayden-Lee's ball.

And told the twins it was wrong to threaten other children, even the really rubbish ones.

And picked a better song.

And just not come tonight at all. I should have known real life didn't happen the way I dreamed it would.

I'd been blaming the hamster for most my problems so I wouldn't notice the truth: it wasn't Nibbles who was destroying my holiday – it was me.

At least now that my crush on Jayden-Lee had sunk without a trace, I might start being more aware of what was going on around me. It was like my brain had been on autopilot for days. I could still eat, and talk, and walk about like a functioning person, but all the time my only real thoughts had been about what it would feel like to hold his hand.

Now I was out here in the cold, holding Margaret's. And I couldn't even tell her she was wrong. I gritted my teeth. 'Sorry.'

'I'm afraid that's just not good enough. You see, I simply cannot permit your endeavours to spoil this park's prizewinning chances. We consider all our guests to be shining stars, but you appear determined to fall to earth in a destructive ball of flame.'

That seemed dramatic. 'Are you kicking me out of the park?'

She let a breath hiss between her teeth: in the darkness it sounded like a snake rearing back to strike. 'Not as yet. But I am hereby banning, barring and prohibiting you from attending any event within it, until the announcement of the Park of the Year Award. Should you fail to comply, I have some very interesting security footage of you vandalizing our advertising displays this morning. Perhaps your parents would be interested in watching that?'

She gave me a smile so sharp it looked like she chewed razorblades for fun.

The Stardance posters. I tried for a moment, but I couldn't really regret ripping them down. Still, I wasn't sure that Mum and Dad would understand that I'd been doing it for justice. 'Fine. I'll just stay in the caravan until we go home, all right?'

Margaret abruptly released my wrist. 'Very good. This ban of course includes our prestigious, exclusive and glittering Stardance. You can discard your complimentary ticket.'

'You mean the dance you already banned my little fire hazard – sorry, my *little brother* from?' I hoped the darkness hid how close I was to starting another incident right there and then. 'That's fine by me.'

'Wonderful. So long as we're absolutely, positively clear. I shall look forward to never having to see you again, Mr Kershaw. *Do* enjoy your stay.'

Without another word, she squeaked round on her heels to clip back inside and clear up my latest 'disturbance'. I thought I might hate her more than the hamster.

Actually, I was almost sure I did.

I tipped my head back with a long sigh, and tried to pick out patterns in the impossibly black night sky.

'The trouble with being under the same stars as the people you love is that you also have to be under the same ones as people like her.' Kayla stepped up beside me, nudging her shoulder against mine.

She'd redone her make-up, but seemed somehow paler than before, and she hadn't managed to hide the rims of red around her eyes.

Carefully, I reached for her hand and tucked it into mine. 'I heard they're different in Australia, though. I'm up for moving if you'll come with me.'

Without looking across to check, I could sort of *feel* her smile.

'Maybe one day,' she said. 'Now come on, you great big menace to society. I'll walk you home.'

THIRTY

We didn't talk much on the walk back to 131 Alpine Views, but Kayla's shoulder bumped against mine the whole way.

Breakfast the next morning was weird though. Mum and Dad usually had noisy arguments over who got to read which bit of the paper, but today they were being overly polite and giving each other fair turns with the crossword. I thought they might have been trying not to mention anything about my and Kayla's fight, or the beefsplosion from yesterday. At least there was none of it left, except for a few gravy stains on Mum's clothes, and a strand of carrot clinging to the outside of one window, too high up for anyone to reach.

Kayla had her head dipped low over a bowl of cereal. Her make-up was back to being as flawless as always, all signs of what had happened yesterday smoothed away.

I wasn't sure the same was true for me. I felt different. I even worried I might *look* different. If my sexuality was usually a big gay elephant standing in the corner of the room, then last night Jayden-Lee had sent it on a stampede. Any minute it might burst in and start trumpeting again.

Which meant I was stuck. We had another whole day and a half at Starcross Sands, and I'd have to do what Margaret wanted and stay inside for all of it, otherwise I'd never know if I was talking to someone who'd heard Jayden-Lee call me a *gayboy*.

I'd always thought the most difficult thing about being gay was not being able to tell who else might be. I was so wrong. It was way worse feeling like the whole world had been given a free gaydar, and that the beeping noise it made was coming directly from me.

Luckily, Jude was happy to fill in the blank space of no one else talking. He loved his new tough-guy buzzcut and was looking forward to showing Nibbles that afternoon, when he'd been promised he could get a Hamster Selfie at the fair.

He only settled down when Mum and Dad went out for a morning of intensive crazy golf, after setting him up on the sofa with a pot of crimson paint and some glittery heart stickers. He was busily making what looked suspiciously like a Valentine's card for Nibbles.

'Dylan?' he waved his paintbrush to get my attention. 'Can hamsters get married?'

'. . . Only to other hamsters,' I told him, scooping the last of the cereal bowls into the sink.

His lower lip jutted out in disappointment.

'OK, I'm off to salute the sun.' Kayla swept back in from the shower, wearing sporty leggings and a cropped top. 'I could really get into this yoga thing, you know, and I've met some great people. You should try it – it might help you chill out a bit.'

She threw the towel she'd wrapped round her head at me, and I caught it seconds after it collided damply with my face. 'Thanks, but I think I'll give it a miss for today.' I watched her go to comb her hair in the mirror. 'You look . . . different.'

'Do I?' she asked.

'Sort of.' It's not like it was something she could have missed. 'You haven't put your stuff back on.'

Usually redoing her concealer was the first thing she did in the morning, and after a shower, and she slept with it on at night in case there was a fire in the early hours and she needed to look her best while screaming for help. She'd had it on earlier. But her face was bare, now.

Turning towards me with a startled look, she started patting herself down as though she thought I was talking about her clothes. I sighed dramatically.

'You know what I mean.' After last night I expected her to be wearing a double layer from now on.

'Kayla's a different colour,' Jude interrupted, looking up from his paints.

I winced.

'Less orange,' he concluded.

Kayla laughed, ruffling her fingers through her hair to fluff it up before going to sit next to Jude, pressing her finger to one of his stickers and attaching it to his nose. 'You're right. Does it look OK?'

He nodded.

'Good. Because I think I'm going to be this colour more often. I was starting to feel like a hypocrite, covering it up all the time.'

All I could think of was the way her face had crumpled last night when Jayden-Lee said what he did. I couldn't care less about her birthmark, I just didn't want anything to make her cry again. 'If it makes you comfortable, what's wrong with that?'

'Nothing at all – it's just not how I want to be. Don't you think people comment on other parts of me?'

'Well, you have got pink hair.'

She clicked her tongue. 'People do comment. All the time. Do you know how hard it can be wearing a swimming costume when you're a size sixteen? I've heard all the whale jokes, and though *I* might know that whales are majestic ocean royalty, it still hurts.'

I'd had no idea. Kayla always acted so invulnerable, unafraid of anything except her dad accidentally drilling through a power cable when she was out.

Again. She was always the first person standing up for other people, so I never thought about there being no one to stand up for her. I never realized she might need someone to.

'Then why wear one?' I asked.

'Because the problem isn't with me; it's with them. Why should I have to hide who I am? I decided I couldn't just stop swimming just because some idiots got upset that I took up a little more space in the pool. All my life I've been telling myself to do the things I'm afraid of – telling myself to act like I don't care.'

She got up, sweeping a few of the glittery hearts that Jude hadn't taken for his craft project into the palm of her hand. 'But I do care. I just focused it all in on this one thing. In the end I stopped swimming because it was too hard to always keep my head above the water. I've just been hiding, Dylan, and . . .'

She paused, but I knew exactly what Imaginary Kayla would say. *'If you pretend to be someone you're not, you'll never know who would have liked you for who you are,'* I said.

'Exactly,' Kayla said, with a smile. 'Sometimes you're smarter than you look.' She looked down at me. I was in my oldest jeans and a Godzilla T-shirt that said 'Big in Japan'. 'Then again, that isn't hard.'

I threw her towel back at her. She dropped the hearts

as she reached to catch it, scattering them like an affectionate hailstorm.

'You do look good though,' I said. 'Not just less orange. More glowy.'

She pinched her lips around a smile. 'Thank you. And hey, it looks like that didn't get broken after all.'

She was pointing to my T-shirt. One spangly heart had stuck there, right over Godzilla's muzzle. It looked more like he was having a glittery nosebleed than some sort of mystical sign that I might one day be able to love again, but that was all right. I wasn't ever planning to try.

'So you're never wearing make-up again?' I asked, following her to the caravan door.

'I'm not wearing make-up *all the time*,' she said. 'Just when I want to. I've decided to stop wanting to be normal, Dylan. I'm going to make normal want to be *me*.'

Then she was gone, off to do the lotus position with a load of strangers on the clifftops. What she'd said kept replaying in my mind. Maybe that was my problem too. Maybe I had to stop wanting to be like everyone else, and start wanting to be myself. Whoever that was.

Jaw set in determination, I even managed to close the caravan door without looking over to see if Jayden-Lee was home, waiting to catch me watching him. I'd be totally happy if I never had to see his face again.

Today was going to be a day off from the world: calm and quiet, just me and the four walls of our bronze-class caravan.

'DYLAN!' Jude cried out, just as the door clicked shut.

And I looked up to see him covered in red from head to foot.

THIRTY-ONE

Sparkly red poster paint, it turns out, is not very easy to wash off clothes. Or furniture coverings. Or the skin of small children.

After an hour of alternating between panicking and scrubbing, the inside of the caravan still looked like it had been the scene of a bloody battle between two vicious but glitter-loving warlike tribes. Jude's clothes were hidden as deep as I could get them in the laundry bag, and we'd been in the shower until the hot water ran out just trying to keep him from looking like a hospital warning poster about extreme sunburn.

He was still a little bit rosy-cheeked, but I couldn't tell whether that was from the paint or all the effort of rubbing it off.

The only thing that really came out undamaged was the card Jude had been making for Nibbles.

We were both shivering when we got out of the shower. As soon as I realized the stuff all over him wasn't blood but an experiment in performance art, I'd rushed him under the water, fully clothed. My T-shirt and jeans were clinging to me, soggy and freezing.

Even my trainers sloshed when I walked.

'Can I have some towels?' Jude asked.

I wrapped him up in three formerly white, fluffy towels, and settled him on the newly pink sofa.

'Can I have Twinkle?' he asked.

I turned on some cartoons.

'Can I have blackcurrant and apple juice?'

'No.' I shook my head. 'No. You can never have any form of coloured liquid ever, ever again. I'm not sure about you having liquid at all. You might have to be like a koala and rely on leaves for hydration. Maybe you could go and live in a tree, as well. No one's going to care if you dye a few branches fuchsia.'

And then Jude's bottom lip started to wobble in a precariously getting-ready-to-do-proper-goose-honk-sobbing sort of a way, so I got him the tin of Iced Gems, and some juice that was safely inside a carton with a straw.

Then I picked up the I LOVE YOU NIBBLES card that was behind the whole mess, and evacuated to the top of the ramp outside to let the paint on it dry, and to try to figure out how I was going to tell Mum and Dad that our mega-bargainous £9.50 holiday was probably going to cost a little bit more.

How much could redecorating a caravan cost, anyway? It wasn't like it had been anything special to look at even before the beef and the paint had spattered it in interesting new shades.

Maybe it would be cheaper to buy the whole thing. We could install it in the back garden, and I could move in there when my parents disowned me for not being able to watch my brother for five minutes without something getting messed up or cut off. At this point I was probably lucky that Jude still had all his limbs.

Margaret the manager was right – I was a total incident magnet. Locking myself in my room and refusing to come out was almost definitely my best hope of surviving the rest of the holiday intact. It was only one more day. I could live like a tinned sardine for that long.

First, though, I was going to sit and feel sadly, damply sorry for myself for just a while longer.

There was a Starcross staff golf buggy rattling along between the caravans, and I thought I'd better wait for it to go past, just to make sure they weren't paying one of those courtesy housekeeping calls, where they check that your curtains match and your heating works, and that no one's accidentally tie-dyed the living area while trying to declare their love for a giant rodent.

If they were, I'd be waiting to tell them that everything was *completely fine.*

The sun was glaring off the front of the buggy like a

searchlight, so I couldn't tell whether Margaret and her clipboard might be inside, ready to inform me again what a complete degenerate I was, just in case I hadn't been listening hard enough last night.

I studied Jude's card and pretended not to care if she was. The hamster he'd drawn inside the big red heart wasn't too bad, for four-year-old art. All right, it was sort of just an orange ball with a face, but it definitely couldn't be a cat ball or a dog ball. If you knew Nibbles, you'd recognize him.

I knew I'd never be able to forget his big, furry face.

Somehow the hamster was always at the scene of my biggest traumas. Except he got to be the hero, not whatever Margaret had called me: the *common denominator*. I almost wanted to ask him if he'd noticed my life falling apart while he was busy doing silly dances and somehow saving the day all at the same time.

He probably had. It would show how low I'd sunk if a giant hamster thought *I* was the ridiculous one.

It was just lucky he couldn't talk.

'Hey!' a voice called out of the golf buggy's sunshine-glow, and I looked up to see a figure jumping from one of the open sides. Just my luck: they were definitely doing housekeeping calls.

The sun in my eyes meant I couldn't see who it was

at first, but the voice was much too deep, and the silhouetted outline much too tall, to be Margaret.

The hair was different, too. Instead of neat, crispy curls I could just make out a thick mane of dreadlocks, which hung to about his shoulders.

His shoulders were too broad to be Margaret's.

When he got closer, I could see that his skin tone was too warm and too dark to be Margaret. His legs were too long, and he strode easily where Margaret clipped along on her pointy heels. He was carrying a giant rucksack, not a clipboard. And where Margaret wore a forced, tight little smile, he had a grin that curled wide enough to brighten his whole face. I could feel myself smiling back at him without even thinking about it, like it was contagious.

Though, at the same time, I sort of wanted to tuck my head down against my knees, roll backwards through the caravan door, and hide for about a million years.

I knew who this was.

I thought I did.

He swung his rucksack on to the ground and sat down beside me. 'I had to get them to drop me off when I saw you. It's kind of a novelty to be able to say hey directly to your face.'

I'd been hiding in a hedge, last time, with my shoulders wedged too tightly between the branches to turn around. And before that I'd had the bum of my jeans for a head. I couldn't actually understand why he'd want to say anything to me at all. But he ducked his head a bit as I blinked at him, and his smile only got warmer, and brighter. It was like sitting next to a little piece of the sun.

'So, hey, Dylan,' he said.

'Hey, Leo.'

He squinted at me, like he was noticing something for the first time, and glanced up at the clear blue sky. 'Has it been raining?'

THIRTY-TWO

I'd completely forgotten how cold and wet I was, though when Leo mentioned it I was suddenly aware of a steady, chilly dripping as shower water spiralled down the back of my neck and slid under the collar of my T-shirt. It just didn't feel that bad any more. I'd even stopped shivering.

They should send people like him out to do mountain rescue. He'd be a thousand times better than one of those dogs with little barrels of brandy on their collars. One smile could turn all the snow to slush.

I wasn't even too flustered about looking like I'd decided to wash my clothes while I was still wearing them. If he hadn't thought I was a total weirdo who should be kept at arm's length after seeing me with jeans on my head, it probably wasn't going to happen now.

Shaking my head, I laughed as he ducked the little flecks of water that sprayed off me. 'It hasn't been raining, exactly. But is it possible to have a personal raincloud that follows you round all the time? Because I think I might have one of those.'

Leo looked up again. The sky was still endlessly blue. 'I'd say no,' he started, slowly. 'But the soggy evidence is on your side. Looks like your raincloud's hiding right now though.'

'Gathering energy for the next storm.' I sighed. 'Every time it seems like it's giving me a break, it just comes back worse.'

'See, that's your mistake,' Leo said, rummaging through a pocket of his rucksack, his hair falling forward into a thick curtain to hide his face. It seemed unfair: I'd only just seen what he really looked like, and I already felt like I wanted to make up for lost time.

'What mistake?'

'If it's giving you a break,' he said, pulling a small cloth-covered parcel out and offering it across to me, 'you should be using the downtime to prepare.'

I put Jude's card down between us, and took the blue-and-white-striped bundle.

It was an umbrella.

'See. Now you'll be ready.'

Nobody had ever given me an umbrella before. Just holding it made the next storm feel a very long way away.

'Do you think it'll help?' he asked.

I nodded. A drop of water dislodged itself from my hairline and rolled slowly down over my nose. 'Next time that cloud comes for me, I'll be one step ahead. I haven't got anything to give you though.'

'I'm not being stalked by my own personal weather phenomenon.' Leo rocked back on his heels. 'And you don't have to—'

'How about a biscuit?' I broke in. 'Mum's got this thing about guests and biscuits, so we've always got some around. Although the only guest we usually have is my nana, so I think it's really just a cover for Mum's addiction to custard creams.'

My mouth was doing that thing where it was running on ahead of my brain again. I knew words were happening; I just had no control over them until they were out in the wild. Trying to sound normal was like trying to lasso a bolting horse.

I pushed myself to my feet before Leo could protest, like I'd suddenly been possessed by the ghost of a housewife from hell. I didn't care about biscuits; I just needed to take a second to blush in private. 'I'll get some – wait here.'

Dashing into the caravan, I took two very deep breaths, and borrowed Jude's tin of Iced Gems before he could make himself sick in various colours of frosted pastel.

A waft of music from the TV accompanied me as I stepped back outside, hoping against hope that the word-horse was back in the vocabulary stable and I might manage to sound normal from here on.

It wasn't exactly the theme tune I'd have chosen to emerge to, but Leo was making a face of pleased recognition. '*Twinkle*! My littlest sister's mad on that; she's a superfan.'

'She'll have to fight my brother for that title, and he's vicious in a thumb war.' I settled down again, putting the tin on my knee. 'Iced gem?'

Leo was holding something too. He held it up to show me. 'Is this what *you're* a superfan of?'

I LOVE NIBBLES blinked at me in glitzy, smudgy red, and I felt the blush in my cheeks returning. But then I thought about it for a minute. 'I used to want to call pest control out on him. But now I've met some other rats and –' I shrugged – 'he could be worse.'

I looked across at the Dramavan without thinking, reaching into the Iced Gem tin to distract myself from dwelling on Jayden-Lee.

Leo reached in at the same time, and when his fingers brushed mine, I felt something.

Electricity.

We both caught quick hissed breaths at the snap of static between us, and I turned my head to find that he was laughing.

'Sorry—'

'Sorry—'

Even our apologies met in the middle. We both paused, looking at each other. My stomach didn't lurch, though, the way it always had when Jayden-Lee's eyes met mine. It just tied itself into a knot, and pulled tight.

'Are you going to the fair later?' Leo asked. His hand was so warm that my cold one was like a negative image. 'I heard you can get hamster selfies.'

Then, before it got too weird to be almost holding hands in a biscuit tin, he picked a blue gem out and crunched it.

'It's not really a selfie, though, unless he's taking it?'

Leo shook his head. 'Paws are too big for the buttons.'

I grinned, picking my own gem and dropping it into my mouth. Then I shook my head. 'I'm barred. Jude's going, though.'

'You're what?' Both his eyebrows lifted into perfect curves.

'I'm . . .' I tried to remember exactly how Margaret had put it, imitating the squeak of her voice. '*Banned, barred and prohibited from all gatherings and events within the park.* Until the Park of the Year Award's given out, anyway. And we'll be gone by then.'

It was quite a good impression, I thought. Leo looked like he couldn't decide whether to be impressed or outraged.

'What's she got against you? It's not like *you* peed in the pool.'

He was *there* too? I had to force myself not to think too hard about what he might have heard.

'No, but she thinks it's my fault. Every disastrous thing that's happened since we got here's been my fault – and Jude's not allowed into the Stardance, either, because his chair's a fire hazard.'

Leo let a breath whistle between his teeth. 'That's all nonsense. She's just looking for someone to blame if she doesn't get that prize, that's all. It's always madness here.'

'Riots, pool evacuations and rivers of puke?' I asked doubtfully.

'That's on a good day. It's never dull, but I'm not going to be sorry to get out of here at the end of the season.'

'You're leaving?' I realized too late I sounded upset at the idea. Which was even more stupid when I remembered we were going back to Woking tomorrow afternoon. It just felt for one moment like there was a chance for something good to happen, and I could already sense it passing me by.

'It's only a summer job. I don't go to school round here, so Mum likes having me close to her in the holidays. Plus they had a spare uniform lying around that turned out to be a perfect fit.'

'You don't go to school in Cornwall?' I *had* to stop repeating everything he said.

'No, I go to a dance college near London,' he said. 'Listen, If you—'

'EILEEN SLATER, YOU GET OUT HERE!'

A loud screech drowned out whatever Leo had been trying to say. A woman in a blue velour tracksuit was marching towards the Dramavan. She was dragging a small, greenish-looking child, and clutching an ornamental flamingo in the same way an ancient Japanese warrior might brandish a samurai sword.

'Don't you worry, Alfie,' she muttered as she passed us. 'If that little brat won't say he's sorry this time, this is getting shoved somewhere the sun don't shine.'

She dragged open the Dramavan door and vanished inside. Leo was already on his feet.

'Duty calls.'

I hurriedly put the card and biscuit tin down on the ramp. 'Do you need any help?'

'Better not.' He unclipped a walkie-talkie from his belt. 'I don't want to get you in more trouble. I'll have backup here in a minute. Besides, I'd really like it if you could manage not to get thrown out of the park before I catch up with you again. OK?'

'I—'

There was a roar from the Dramavan like a lion tackling a gazelle.

I nodded hastily. 'OK.'

Leo grabbed his rucksack and started to run. I watched him go. Watched him yell into his walkie-talkie about a *code red*. I watched the open top pocket of his oversized bag flap open, and stared at the giant, orange hamster head grinning soullessly out.

Swallowing hard, I stared back down at Jude's card.

I LOVE YOU, NIBBLES.

As a string of shrieked swear words erupted from the caravan opposite, I bolted back inside my own.

THIRTY-THREE

'My only love sprung from my only hate!' I whispered dramatically, throwing myself back against the closed door and slowly sliding down it to the floor. That was a quote from the Shakespeare play we'd done in English last year. I felt quite connected with Shakespeare: for someone that old he was really good at being miserable and romantic.

Jude shuffled along the sofa edge to peer down at me. 'What?'

'We'd better get you dressed or you'll be late,' I corrected, sighing. 'You don't want to miss your big hamster date.'

Shakespeare did rhyming couplets too. Maybe I'd found my calling, and thwarted love would inspire me to greatness. I'd rather it didn't though. All things considered, I'd rather be ordinary and have a boyfriend at least once in my life. Being thwarted was definitely not all it was cracked up to be.

Not that boyfriends were any kind of prospect right now. I couldn't even leave the caravan. And Leo seemed . . . well, amazing, but Jude had more chance of ever seeing him again. While my little brother was off presenting one secretly handsome hamster with a hand-made gesture of his affection, I was banned, barred and prohibited from the whole fair.

It was better that I didn't go, anyway. I'd embarrassed myself over a pointless crush enough for one lifetime already, let alone one week. Leo couldn't like me that way. The electricity we'd felt was probably just a static shock from sitting on metal steps in wet jeans.

So it was totally, utterly, definitely for the best that I didn't go to the fair.

Leaning over, Jude tapped me on the shoulder with something small and solid, then dropped it on my head. 'Mummy says you have to take me.'

'Mummy says what?' I scrabbled to dig whatever it was out of the back of my collar. My phone – I'd left it on the table while trying to de-pink Jude in the shower. I'd missed a call, and there was a message on the screen.

> Dyl Darling. Back later than expected, golf emergency. Pls take Jude to see his furry friend. We'll meet you there. Xxx. Mummy.

What on earth was a golf emergency? They weren't even playing with full-sized clubs. I didn't know whether I should be worrying more about the possibility that Dad had sat on a miniature windmill and got one of the spokes wedged somewhere uncomfortable, or the near certainty that Margaret would catch me at the funfair and string me up from one of the carriages of the big wheel.

From outside the caravan, I could hear yelling and thudding. Security must have turned up to intervene in the Mum-off at the Dramavan. If I went back out now I might get to see Leo again and check that he was OK. But I couldn't move.

If Margaret had anything to do with it, next time Security showed up they'd be coming for me.

I tipped my head back to look up at Jude. 'Are you *sure* you want to go to the fair? It can be a bad idea to meet your heroes. Remember when Dad met the Woking FC goalie in Pasta Pronto, and got mistaken for a waiter?'

Dad had stood there with his football scarf trailing in one hand, while having an order yelled at him: *I'll have el spag bol with un bottle of Chateau Magnifico por favore, garçon.*

'What if he's not the hamster you think he is, Jude? I just don't want you getting your heart broken over this. We could stay in and watch *Twinkle's Time to Shine,* instead. It would be safer.'

And it might distract me from thinking too hard

about whether my heart was capable of breaking again too.

Above me, Jude had wriggled across the sofa until he was lying flat on his stomach. He pulled himself forward like a swimmer crossing a channel of scratchy pinkish wool, and tipped himself over the side until his face was upside down in front of mine.

'I,' he said.

'*Want*,' he added.

'NIBBLES. I WANT NIBBLES! I WANT NIBBLES. I. WANT. NIBBLES!' he foghorned directly into my face.

It looked like I was going to the fair.

'OK, OK,' I muttered, getting to my feet and hauling Jude up into my arms. 'I've got the message. I've also got two burst eardrums, so thanks for that, but I've got it. You want to see Nibbles again.'

Then, while his cheering mostly drowned me out, I added quietly to myself, 'Me too.'

While I got Jude changed into his fanciest date-wear (and talked him out of the panda onesie that was his first choice), I sent a quick message to Kayla. If she checked it as soon as she'd finished yoga, she might be able to intercept me and take Jude before I was caught by Margaret and publically pilloried at the coconut shy.

I risked a glance out of the window when we were ready. The Dramavan looked as serene as anywhere guarded by a porcelain frog in a tutu and a dozen grinning garden gnomes could. There was no security hanging about. No Leo.

The coast was clear, so I checked Jude had his autograph book and Valentine's card, and opened the door.

'Why *has* your caravan got a slide, anyway?' Jayden-Lee asked, from where he was sitting in the grass.

THIRTY-FOUR

It was *our* grass that he was sitting on. Our ornament-free, slightly scruffy excuse for a lawn. He had his back against the side of the caravan. *Our* caravan. Pointing to *our* front door.

It was like he was waiting for me. Just sitting there with his knees drawn up and his football making a dent in the greenery. For the first time ever, looking at him made my skin prickle with irritation instead of adoration.

'It's for my *brother*,' I told him, standing at the top of the ramp. We had an accessible caravan, with extra-wide doors and a seat in the shower, and a ramp so people could get in and out without having to climb stairs.

I didn't ask Jayden-Lee what he wanted. If he'd decided that today was a good day to pay me back for being made to suffer a hygienic hose down at the Swim Centre, then he'd picked a seriously bad time. I had enough to worry about. He'd dropped right down my list.

But it didn't seem like he was out to pick a fight. He

didn't even get up. 'Oh, right. Yeah, I guess it might be fun for people like him.'

Now, I'm not an especially angry person. I don't pick fights with match officials, like my dad, and I don't smilingly tear people apart the way Mum sometimes does. I'm definitely not capable of destroying someone with a few carefully chosen words, the way Kayla can. But, sometimes, enough is just enough.

'It's not a *slide*; it's a *ramp*. It's something people use to get downstairs when walking isn't an option.'

Jayden-Lee just shrugged, but I was already pounding down the echoey ramp and heading towards him. I wanted to say this while Jude was still inside.

Stamping across the grass, I kept my voice low. 'His name is Jude, and from now on that's the *only* name you get to call him. And yeah, he has a disability. But he's not "people like him" – he's just a person. More than that, he's my little brother, and no one gets to make him feel bad while I'm around. So I'm going to take him to the fair, and you're going to keep your mouth shut, all right?'

I folded my arms over my chest just in case the nervous rumba my heart seemed to be dancing was visible from the outside. Jayden-Lee dropped a hand into the grass at his side and pushed himself up on to it. He drew one foot underneath him, then he stood up.

He was quite a bit taller than me, this close. For a second I caught myself thinking about the scar on his lip again, only this time I was wondering if he'd got it in a fight. It crinkled up and almost disappeared as he twisted his mouth into a scowl.

'Whatever. All I'm saying is, if it *was* a slide, it would be a crap one.'

I stared at him, wondering how he'd somehow missed my point as it whooshed right over his head. I'd tried everything but brute force. Maybe if just I left what I'd said hanging in the air it might seep into him slowly through his skin somehow, the way sunshine gets into plants.

'Fine.' I kept my eyes on him and dipped my chin in a sketch of a nod. 'If you've really got to insult something, it may as well be the ramp. Now I've got to go.'

'Wait.'

Turning, I found my shoulder grasped tight. He pulled me back round to face him, and he was looking at me with this weirdly intense expression – nervous, but intent. If this had happened yesterday afternoon I'd have been having an internal panic attack that he was going to go in for a Hollywood Kiss.

Now I felt . . . nothing. Except confusion, and a bit of worry that Jude might miss his selfie slot.

Jayden-Lee dropped his hand back down by his crotch and had a thoughtful scratch, then ran his fingers back through his still-perfect-but-maybe-a-bit-less-appealing hair. He cleared his throat. 'Is your mate around? I wanted to see her. You know, say something about last night. Sorry, or whatever.'

'Kayla?' I asked slowly. 'You want to say sorry to Kayla for what happened last night?'

'Is that her name?' He smiled, like I'd told him a secret. 'Yeah.'

'Last night, when you yelled about me being a gayboy to a hundred strangers in rubber rings and novelty hula skirts? You want to say sorry to Kayla for that?'

'Right.' He nodded readily. 'But more for just after that, when I said that thing about her face. It looks fine, really. I didn't know it was permanent.'

'*All those people didn't know I was gay.*' It wasn't that Kayla didn't deserve an apology too. I just couldn't believe Jayden-Lee was totally ignoring the gay elephant he'd let loose. It was as if all those years I'd spent trying to make it a completely invisible part of me had finally worked at the weirdest possible time. I flung my arms out to the side, practically doing jazz-hands of incredulity. '*Until you decided to tell them.*'

'Yeah, but they're not going to care, are they. It's not like you fancy them.'

He might as well have said *'What's the big deal?'* and without finding out one of his biggest secrets and arranging for it to be displayed in neon lights on the Starcross gates, I couldn't figure out how to explain.

Maybe it shouldn't have been a big deal. Nobody cares about people knowing they're straight. Nobody has to tell their parents about their straightness, or worries that their friends might think it's weird.

Straight people probably never look up the word 'straight' in the dictionary and wonder how something with such a totally different meaning could also define who they love.

So maybe it really shouldn't have been a big deal at all for a load of people who didn't even know me to find out that my dictionary definition wasn't: *adj. without a bend, angle or curve* but *adj. joyful or happy.*

But it *was* a big deal. To me.

I backed up a few steps, shaking my head. 'You know what – I can't do this right now. I've got a hamster to meet. Yeah, you do owe Kayla an apology, so come back some other time if you're actually sorry. But if you're just going to upset her again, then don't bother.'

Turning to head back inside and get Jude, I added, softly, 'And for the record, I don't fancy you any more. So you can stop caring about that too.'

He didn't say anything, just let me go. When Jude

and I came out he was still standing there. He watched as I locked the caravan door, then wandered back across to start kicking his football against the side of his caravan. We headed past him, towards the fair.

I looked back, once. I wasn't sure if what I'd said had been completely true. I couldn't just turn off all the things that had made me fancy him; he still had gorgeous eyes and nearly perfect hair, and a jawline that Greek sculptors could break a chisel on. I just knew that all those individual parts weren't enough any more. Once I'd put them all together into a whole person, it was like the same sum adding up to a different answer.

I'd never really understood maths, anyway.

THIRTY-FIVE

Twinkling fairground music broke into my attempts to figure out a precise calculation for true love. Where there had been nothing but a few fractured metal skeletons of tents and half-constructed attractions when Kayla and I had sat on the clifftops before, there was now a whole carnival.

Alongside the big wheel, a collection of stalls and clattering vintage rides were scattered through the meadow just below our bench, with its seagulls and signs to stay away from the crumbling edges. There was a carousel and a ghost train, a van selling ice cream, and another serving up burgers to massive queues.

It was all part of the big end-of-season celebration, and it was packed. Given the size of the crowd, it should have been easy to go unnoticed. That was, if I wasn't walking alongside a wheelchair containing a four-year-old in a hamster hat, clutching a card shaped into a huge, glittery loveheart.

Next time Mum took us anywhere, I was going to bring a range of wigs and false moustaches, just in case.

'Now, if you were a hamster, where would you

be holding your photo shoot?'

I hunched down over the back of Jude's chair as we looked around. Somewhere on the opposite side of the field, between the win-a-goldfish hoopla game and the ghost train, I could see a tent with a group of people gathered round it who were mostly too small to be allowed on the rides. Jude spotted it at the same time as me.

'There! In the hungry tent!'

On closer inspection, the tent flaps had been cut to resemble two big white buckteeth.

'That's definitely the one,' I agreed. Now I just had to get us in, get the picture, and get back out without being busted.

We were hiding in the shadow of a tall red-and-yellow signpost that read: *DON'T CLOWN AROUND – HAVE FUN RESPONSIBLY.* The words were painted on to a gigantic dangling clown's head, which was terrifying both in general and because, the way it was swinging, it looked like it could slice down and brain someone at any moment.

Just across the walkway, fair workers were trying to help two elderly Elvises who'd got stuck near the hook-a-duck pool. The ground around it was a waterlogged mud bath, and it had sucked in their blue suede shoes.

This was going to be fine. If there were any security

staff, they'd be looking out for things like that: *actual* problems. As long as Jude and I avoided making any trouble, who was going to come after two kids enjoying a funfair? All we had to do was act casual and style it out. I tapped on the back of Jude's chair and we started to head across the fairground like we owned it.

Until a hand clasped my collar and yanked me back. '*Got* you.'

Dragging myself free, I whipped round and narrowly avoided getting a face full of Mr Whippy. Kayla had ordered the planet's biggest ice cream, with raspberry sauce and sprinkles.

'Kayla! Where have you *been*?'

She took a lick of vanilla before replying. 'Um, yoga, obviously? I could have sworn that was you I was talking to about it this morning. Your evil twin hasn't got out of his cage again, has he?'

'No, but I might need that excuse in a minute. I sent you an emergency text!'

'Ice creaaaam,' Jude interrupted, reaching out with the hand not clutching his card.

Kayla bent down to allow him a few messy licks. 'Phone's dead, I forgot to charge it last night. What's the emergency? I thought you weren't even supposed to be here.' She snapped part of her flake off and Jude crammed it gratefully into his mouth.

'That *was* the emergency. One of the emergencies. I think I've managed to fit more emergencies into one morning than Mum and Dad do working on the ambulances.'

Straightening up, Kayla carefully kept her ice cream away from my anxious over-gesturing. 'Well, nothing seems to have flooded or caught fire, and I'm assuming neither of you have been arrested yet. You being here doesn't look like it's brought about the end of the world, so why don't you start with the biggest crisis and we'll work backwards from there.'

I thought about Jayden-Lee turning up out of the blue, and the fact that, once what I'd said had caught up with him, he might decide to object to being spoken to like that. I thought about Mum and Dad's mysterious crazy-golf crisis, and the pink couch, and about how I might be called in as a witness if Alfie's mum had actually rammed her flamingo where she'd said she would. And I said:

'I don't hate the hamster any more.'

Because I was going to have to see him again, any minute, and somehow that seemed like the biggest emergency of all.

Kayla pursed her lips. She handed Jude her whole ice cream, then took my hands from where I was anxiously

234

flapping them, and tucked them into my pockets.

'OK. Tell me all about it.'

So I did. I told her about meeting Leo in the loos, and in the hedge. About him giving me his umbrella, and me forcing biscuits on him, and about how warm his back was, and his smile. I told her about his eyebrow bar, and how I'd always wondered what I'd look like with one of those, but I got an infection in my ear back when I had the cartilage pierced and I now I was concerned about ending up with a Vesuvius of pus right in the middle of my face.

And she told me I was getting off the point, so I told her that when I touched his hand there was a real, actual spark between us. And I didn't even mean the static electricity – just a small, sweet shock.

I might have mentioned the way my stomach had gotten tied up in knots when Leo smiled at me, and how it hadn't undone itself yet.

Finally, when I'd got through all the important things, I remembered to tell her that I'd had a change of heart when it came to fancying part-time hamsters, too.

Kayla listened, and made approving noises in most of the right places, except for the snort of laughter at finding out Nibbles was Leo all along. Then, when I'd run out of things to say, she put her hands on her hips, businesslike. 'Right. Well, you'd better tell him you're into him, then.'

'You're so right.' I sighed, already mentally prepared for the takedown she was going to give me over my second crush in a week. 'I should just forget all about it and . . . wait. What?'

'Tell him you like him. Bite the bullet, take the plunge, go for broke, use any cliché you like but, as the Goddess Nike says, just do it.'

'Did you see what happened the last time I tried that?' This couldn't actually be the advice she meant to give me. She was supposed to be the practical one. All my impracticality depended on that balance between us. If Kayla started being reckless and impulsive, I was going to have to buy some cardigans and start going to bed before nine.

But she was smiling at me like there was nothing wrong at all. 'This time will be different.'

'You don't know that.' I should have factored in her obvious hamster bias. 'You're just letting yourself be fooled by his cute, fluffy exterior. When I thought I was madly in love with Jayden-Lee, you kept telling me I didn't even know him.'

'And you didn't, as I think experience proved. But you know this hamster.'

'I spent all week *hating* this hamster!'

Kayla clicked her tongue. 'And you've spent all week talking to Leo. Actual conversations, not just him grunting out a few words while you daydream about how swoony his eyes are. You don't hate the hamster now you know it's him, do you?'

I shook my head.

(Leo's eyes were pretty swoony, though. I just hadn't known before today.)

'Do you think you're falling for Leo?' Kayla asked.

I had to consider that one. I could easily remember the way I'd felt about Jayden-Lee. Which was sort of sick, and terrified, and excited all at once.

I didn't feel the same about Leo. Thinking about him didn't make me rush through the same weird combination of awful and amazing.

It was just really nice.

I shook my head. 'I don't know. I think I could like him, a lot. Like, really a lot. But I'd need to spend more time with him to find out for sure.'

'Perfect.' Kayla reached up to pat my head as if I was a puppy mastering a new trick. 'That's how sane people start relationships. Tell him.'

'But . . .'

'*Tell* him. If you'd like me to prepare a written statement clarifying the nature of your intentions, then I'm happy to go back and type one up. But I think it might be quicker if you just went to say hi.'

She nodded across to the Selfie Tent. The crowd of children was temporarily dispersing as Stacie hung up a sign outside reading *20 MINUTE BREAK*. 'There. Looks like the perfect time.'

THIRTY-SIX

The timing really did seem to be right. Twenty minutes would give Jude a chance to recover from the inevitable brain freeze that had followed eating an ice cream as big as his head, and it gave me some time to psych myself up outside the Selfie Tent.

The only thing it didn't give me was any idea about how to get in there alone.

Sitting at the ticket desk, Stacie looked up from behind a stacked pile of squeezable Squeaky Nibbles souvenirs. She'd had her face painted, and I couldn't figure out if the blotchy mix of black and white meant she was a cat or a cow.

'No admittance at the *moo*-ment,' she said, giving me a clue. 'Nibbles is having his hamster ham sandwiches.'

'I just want to swap this for a ticket – do hamsters even eat ham?' I asked, handing over the free voucher Kayla had demanded back at the children's party. 'I thought they were vegetarian.'

Stacie gave me a flat look. 'Can you think of a vegetable that sounds like hamster?'

I tried, for a minute. 'Not really.'

'Well then.' She stamped my voucher as if this closed the matter, and handed over Jude's golden ticket. I looked over my shoulder to see that Kayla had managed to wet-wipe most of the raspberry sauce off his face. She'd stopped to talk to a blonde girl I didn't recognize, but when she saw me watching they waved goodbye and she and Jude headed over.

Jude's focus was locked on to all the Nibbles merchandise like a hamster-seeking missile. I just hoped he wouldn't explode with happiness on impact.

I handed my wallet to Kayla while he dug into the toy pile, setting off a million squeaks. 'He can have one of them – just don't get blackmailed into coming away with a Nibbles army.'

Kayla gave me a funny look, jerking her head and shoulder to the side.

'And I give up. I'm not going to get into the tent while it's got a guard cow on the door.' It had always been an impossible dream. 'I'll just leave now, while the coast's clear.'

Kayla jerked her head again, and again, until it looked like it might actually roll off her shoulders.

'Are you all right? I'm not sure if you're doing some new yoga move or having a fit.'

As I tried to hold on to her shoulders just in case, she

growled at me, '*Look behind you and to the left, you utter, utter pillock.*'

'Oh, was that supposed to be pointing?' I asked. 'Kayla, you don't have to point at things with your face; that's why we have hands.'

The noise she made in response sounded like she was ready to bite my hands off, so I did what she said. And behind me, to my left, a sliver of orange fur was poking out through a flap in the back of the tent. It was a way in.

I turned back to Kayla, wide-eyed, and whispered, 'What do I do now?'

'Just go!' she hissed back. It sounded like we were having a conversation in fluent snake. 'Quick!'

Before I could protest, she lurched towards the ticket desk.

A shower of Squeaky Nibbles went flying in all directions as Kayla stumbled, then more while she tried to regain her balance. Jude squealed and tried to catch one as it rocketed past.

Kayla stood up with an armful of the things, her eyes wide and doll-like in a way I didn't know she could pull off. She even *giggled*. 'Oh my god, I slipped! They're just *so* adorable, I can't help wanting to hug every one!'

As children started to be drawn in by the squeaky bounty, Stacie pulled a megaphone from under the desk and put it to her mouth. '*NOBODY MOO-VE. THE TENT WILL NOT REOPEN UNTIL EVERY HAMSTER IS ACCOUNTED FOR!*'

I ran.

Bolting round to the back of the tent, I ducked in through the opening in the canvas and found myself squished up against a massive orange backside. I tried to wriggle past, but Nibbles moved with me, pinning me between his bum and the side of the tent.

So this was how I was going to die. Squished by the bottom of the hamster I fancied. It was definitely a tragedy worthy of Shakespeare.

I couldn't help picturing the funeral. Leo in a tailored black suit, flanked by police officers who'd be investigating him as a potential murderer, but who'd eventually release him after he confessed his feelings. '*I loved him,*' he'd tell them. '*From the heart of my bottom.*'

I was starting to run out of air. But I could hear something on the other side of the hamster.

The clicking of heels.

'He's been seen at this location,' Margaret the manager said. 'Attempting to accompany the boy in the chair. If he tries to sneak in at any point, it will be considered a sackable offence not to sound the alarm, alert the authorities and *release the hounds*. Do I make myself clear?'

Nibbles' bottom quivered a little bit and he tipped forward in the hamster equivalent of a nod. I gasped for air as quickly and quietly as I could.

'He must *not* be allowed to bring chaos to proceedings today. Understood?'

Another nod.

'Splendid.' The heels clicked briskly away.

Just as I was beginning to feel dizzy, Nibbles stepped forward. Without his ample backside to prop me up, I crumpled slowly to my knees, gasping for air. It wasn't exactly how I'd intended to say hello, but at least I was alive. And I understood now – he'd been protecting me.

Crouching at my side, Nibbles offered a paw to help me up. I took it gratefully.

'So, I know it's you in there,' I said, swallowing hard and trying not to avoid meeting his big, googly eyes. 'I should have figured it out as soon as you said you were a dancer. I saw you, you know, the other day in the showhall. You were brilliant. But I didn't quite get it, then. I haven't quite been getting it all along, have I? I could never figure out how you were always there, but I never saw you. At the party, the karaoke . . . the pool.'

I still didn't know how much he'd overheard at that last one. Wearing a giant costume head must have had *some* kind of muffling effect.

Nibbles splayed out his pink paws. Looking into his

wide, black, bucktoothed mouth, my stomach started doing gentle loop-the-loops.

'And I think I might need you to take that head off now, because it's really hard to talk seriously to someone with little sticky-up felt ears.'

The hamster costume shook in a way that I guessed meant the person inside must be laughing. Nibbles bowed down in front of me, bending his head so I could see the Velcro strap that held his head to his body. I slid a finger between the two sticky strips, and tugged.

When the hamster stood up again, Leo was peering over its shoulders. 'Sorry,' he said. 'I kind of get into character when I've been in there for a while.'

I looked down at the empty head in my hands. A few days ago I'd been daydreaming about decapitating him. Now it felt a bit traumatic. The strangest thing was seeing Leo and Nibbles in the same place at once.

'It's OK.' I carefully put the head down on the table and turned it so it couldn't watch us. 'Don't you get sort of cramped inside there, though?'

Leo looked shifty for a second, glancing round just to check no one else was there, before sighing and stretching both arms out through the hand holes. Nibbles' paws were fluffy pink gloves. The rest of his arms were covered by that skintight black outfit I'd seen him dancing in. He grabbed a bottle of water from the table and took a long swallow, then groaned in relief. 'Hot, sweaty, and *seriously* cramped.'

From outside the tent, I could hear Stacie on her megaphone again: *'TEN MINUTES UNTIL PHOTOS RESTART. CREATE MOO-MENTS TO TREASURE FOREVER!'*

I was running out of time. Leo must have noticed my nerves. Setting his water bottle down again, he turned back to me.

'So what was it you couldn't say to my ears?' he asked.

'I just . . . wanted you to know that . . .' I cut myself off. This was it, the point of no return. This was where I risked him freaking out and never talking to me again, or worse, reacting like Jayden-Lee.

Or this was where I could walk away silently and be *sure* I'd never talk to him again.

There was only one choice, really. So I made it.

'Just that I think I might like you, that's all.'

I took a deep breath, and waited for the world to fall apart, again.

THIRTY-SEVEN

'*FIVE MINUTES! JUST FIVE MINUTES TO BOOK YOUR MAGIC MOO-MENTS! SQUEAKY NIBBLES ALSO AVAILABLE FOR SALE – SLIGHTLY SOILED.*'

Stacie's voice crackling through her megaphone was the only way I knew time was still passing. Inside the tent it felt like it had stopped the instant I'd said *I like you*. Or, I *might* like you. After what had happened with Jayden-Lee, I was careful to pad out saying important things with words that made it sound like I didn't really care as much as I did.

Just in case.

Since time was standing still, it was impossible to tell exactly how long Leo spent looking back at me before he glanced away and smiled. 'Well. That's lucky, because I'm pretty sure I like you too.'

My shoulders had slumped the moment he looked away, and I got ready to say I was kidding, and pretend to laugh as I backed awkwardly out of the tent. I was planning to tread carefully to make sure I wouldn't trip over the slushy remains of my ripped-out heart. But that hadn't happened.

I didn't have a plan for what to do if it *wasn't* a disaster.

Slowly, my shoulders pulled upwards again, my head lifting like a puppet's when someone tugs on the strings.

'I mean, I *like* like you.' I needed to make it absolutely clear. I didn't think I could bear it if him liking me back was going to be followed up with *but not in a gay way*.

He laughed, carding his fingers back through his mussed-up dreads. 'Good, because if you'd just meant you wanted to be pen pals, that could have been embarrassing. I *like* like you, too. I thought it was obvious, but then –' he tapped a finger to the arch of a cheekbone – 'I guess I don't get too flushed.'

'You're blushing?' His skin was dark enough that it didn't turn his face into a neon announcement of the fact, unlike mine. The realization made me want to touch his cheek too.

'I'm just stealthy about it.'

The tips of my ears were starting to radiate an equal heat.

'But, every time you've seen me, I've been doing something weird.' My treacherous mouth was running ahead of anything my brain told it to do, and now it was busily trying to talk him out of what he'd said. Maybe him liking me back was just so unexpected that I needed to test it was for real. 'The first time you met me I was talking to you through my crotch.'

While I silently cursed my runaway mouth for managing to use the word *crotch* in the middle of a Very Important Conversation, Leo was shaking his head.

'The first time I met you, you were making sure your brother didn't get left out at the party. Do you know how many people our age I've seen let themselves get dragged into the kiddie dances like that?'

I bit my lip.

He held a single finger in the air. 'About the same number who'd hold a conversation while trapped inside their jeans like it was no big thing. And your name wasn't even on the list at the karaoke, was it?' he asked.

'It really, really wasn't.' I let out the breath I'd been holding while he spoke.

'So you still got up and sang, even though it terrified you. You're here now, even though my boss is out there organizing a manhunt. It doesn't matter what gets thrown at you, you keep going. I like that. I like you. Besides, if you can handle how I'm dressed right now, I can deal with a little weird on your end.'

My face was so hot I was worried about all that nylon fur catching fire if I got too close.

'The hamster suit's growing on me.' I swallowed

hard and smiled. 'I think you can carry it off.'

I couldn't believe I was still managing to form words. Usually around someone I liked my throat would have sealed shut by now, and I'd be left to communicate via frantic panic spasms. Maybe that summed up what was different this time. 'I like that you're so easy to talk to. It seems like nothing really fazes you, and that calms me down somehow. Because I might keep going, but I'm freaking out a lot of the time too.'

'Most people are,' Leo laughed. 'That's the big secret. You just need to realize that most of the people who look cool to you are flipping out on the inside too. Then you don't need to worry about yourself. That's what keeps me calm. Might even help with your anger-management problem.'

Oh, right, that. I scrubbed a hand across the back of my neck, feeling sheepish. 'Um, I don't actually have—'

'I know.' He grinned. 'I guessed it might be more of a freak-out problem when I found you hiding in that hedge. I wasn't going to push it. You don't know how long I spent hoping you'd finally turn round and look at me, though.'

My hands were pushed deep enough into my pockets to start worrying holes in the lining as I asked, 'Why?'

He stepped forward. Just one step. And he lifted a hand until it was almost brushing my cheek. I found myself tilting my head into the touch.

'Because you've got a nice face,' he said. 'And because I wanted to do this . . .'

Then he was leaning in, and I was leaning in, and there was a moment where we realized that if we both leaned the same way it was going to mean a painful bump of noses. So he tipped his head just slightly to the other side, and he kissed me.

I kissed him.

We kissed.

It wasn't how I'd imagined it.

Usually when I'd pictured my first kiss, it had looked like something from a film, or at least a soap opera: it was well lit and perfectly angled, and everyone had really great hair. I'd never thought about my first kiss happening in the dim light of a tent, with me having to make room for someone's snugly padded stomach. And Leo's hair was a little tangled when I caught my fingers in it, and mine was kind of flat.

It wasn't how I'd imagined. But I'd never really known what perfect looked like before. I don't think any amount of soft-focus lighting and violin music in the background could have made it feel better than it did.

He pulled back, a little, and I opened my eyes and smiled at him, and then kissed him again. Now that I'd started, I found I didn't really want to stop kissing him, ever.

Until I heard the swish of canvas tent flaps being pulled apart. And then my mother's voice saying, 'Jude, darling, that is *not* the way in. You'll just have to wait your turn with everyone else.'

I reeled back, grabbing Nibbles' head from the table and throwing it at Leo, who wrenched it on as I turned around. And there, framed in a triangle of light at the side of the tent, were Jude, Mum and Dad.

THIRTY-EIGHT

'Nibbles?' Jude asked. '. . . Dylan?'

He squeezed the squeaky toy in his hand, and for a second I had to check that the pitiful wail it made wasn't coming from me. Searching my parents' expressions, I said about twenty prayers begging that they hadn't seen.

I'd devote my life to charitable service, I decided. I'd move somewhere hot and earthquakey and spend the rest of my days building houses, or feeding orphans, or just swatting flies for people too weak to do it themselves. I'd muck out pigs at the city farm. I'd wipe the bottoms of the elderly. I'd clean my room and wash my own pants, and do all the dishes every single day. I'd do all of it, if only Mum and Dad hadn't seen.

'Well,' Mum said, putting her hands on Jude's shoulders. 'Just because your brother's decided to set a terrible example and jump the queue, it doesn't mean you can too. Come on now, you can meet Nibbles properly in a minute.'

My heart felt like it was rattling my ribcage with how hard it was beating. I didn't know what to do. I didn't know what had just happened, except that it was something important. Something I'd spent years waiting to pick the right time for, and now it had taken me by surprise and I didn't know what to *do*.

If Mum hadn't said anything about it, maybe it meant she hadn't seen . . .

'That's *not* Nibbles,' Jude said, putting his hand over the control panel for his chair so Mum couldn't steer him away.

'It *is* Nibbles,' I tried to argue, my voice sounding like it was somewhere distant from my body. 'How many giant hamsters do you think this park has?'

'It's not!' Jude said, stubbornly. 'It's not a real hamster *at all*.'

The rattling against my ribs started to feel more and more like someone going at them with a pneumatic drill. Any moment I was going to split open and spill my insides everywhere, in a way that I didn't think even my parents' medical training would be able to fix.

'It is *Nibbles*,' I said, through gritted teeth.

'Come on, darling,' Mum tried again, but Jude was set on it now.

'No! Nibbles is a *real* hamster. That one's got a boy inside him playing dress-up! I know – I saw! And *Dylan* was *kissing* him! With his *mouth*!'

I threw up my hands, turning violently away to pace

towards the back of the tent. That was it, then. The worry I'd had that the world might end when I told Leo I liked him must have been a premonition. It was just a shame that I was too blindly furious to think about my amazing new psychic powers.

Dad stepped forward. 'Come on, mate. I'm sure they were just having a chat.'

'They were *kissing*,' I heard Jude protest. He hated when people acted like he was stupid, so Dad doing it must have been a total betrayal. 'Kissing just like you and Mummy when Woking win in the football.'

'Jude.' Mum's tone ticked into something stern.

I turned around to look at her.

'No, don't. Don't tell him he's wrong when he's not.' Knotting my fingers together at the back of my neck, I stupidly wished Leo hadn't put the hamster head back on. Maybe he'd have been able to keep me calm.

'He's not wrong.' I couldn't understand why I felt so angry. I was boiling with it. 'There is a boy in that costume and I was kissing him. And I was going to tell you, when it was the right time. Probably. If Jude hadn't opened his big mouth, I might have had a chance to choose when that was.'

Jude let out a hurt yelp, but I couldn't look at him. I couldn't look at anyone. I'd just wanted one thing to be my choice. One thing to not get messed up somehow. I could just picture Mum telling her friends that she'd always been suspicious of children's entertainers. Dad's mates laughing about it in the pub.

I couldn't just stand there waiting for whatever came next. I had to get away, as fast as I could. Breaking into a run, I pushed my way through a curtain into the main part of the tent, and hurtled past the trail of children leading back outside. Shoving past the ticket table, I ignored Stacie yelling at me to come back and pay for all the squeaky toys I'd just knocked into the dirt, again.

I pounded across the fair, skidding past people and barely looking where I was going until I found myself in the dark alleyway between two tents, and stopped to catch my breath. Hiding again. I wasn't anything like as brave as Leo thought. It took high canvas walls surrounding me before I started to feel even a little bit less exposed.

I might have stayed there until the fair closed, if two people hadn't stumbled into my hiding place fifteen minutes later, laughing and shh-ing each other between kisses. I recognized the red-haired girl and the boyfriend she'd nearly broken up with at the karaoke, though that fight was obviously ancient history now. They didn't even notice me, they were so wrapped up in each other, but I couldn't stay there any longer. Just watching them made my chest hurt.

I bolted out of the other end of the alley, and crashed into someone full on.

'Oi!' Jayden-Lee brought a hand up against my chest and pushed me back in one very solid shove. 'Don't have to go throwing yourself at me, now.'

My luck was just amazing. If, right after my parents walked in on me kissing a giant hamster, someone had stopped to ask me exactly what might have made the moment any worse, even I would have struggled to come up with this one.

It was like I was being haunted by the ghost of stupid crushes past.

'Just leave me alone.' I tried to push past him and go.

He stuck out a hand and grabbed a handful of my shirt, the way you might pick up a kitten by its scruff. 'No can do. I want a word with you.'

I was too angry to feel scared. 'What? What can you possibly have left to say to me?'

He let go, and dusted my shirt down carefully. Confused, I watched him swallow down a lump in his throat. 'Have you seen her yet?'

If I didn't know better, I could have sworn that his ears were turning pink.

'Who . . . Kayla?' I couldn't focus on this. 'Yes, no . . . look, I'll tell her you're sorry, all right? I will. Now let me *go*.'

When I tried to move past him again, he sidestepped to put himself back in my way. He still had that football tucked under one arm, and with how quickly he was intercepting my movements I had to think he'd make a better goalie than a striker.

'Only I've got these, you know. Feelings. For her,' he said. 'Proper ones.'

I stopped trying to dodge him just to process that. Not that it helped much. My brain just kept throwing up error messages: failure to compute. 'Proper feelings? Are you trying to tell me you fancy my best friend?'

Jayden-Lee broke into the biggest smile I'd ever seen. He didn't look mean like that, just big and dumb and hopeful. I must have been smiling at him that way all week.

'She's gorgeous,' he said. 'And hard as nails. I like that.'

I raised my eyebrows.

'She could eat you for breakfast, with room for a round of toast after. But you're going to have to talk to her yourself. I don't have any good words to put in for you. *And* you'll have to find her on your own.'

'*Dylan!*'

Or, she could find us.

I looked round when I heard Kayla call out, but I didn't want to speak to her. She'd just try to turn the whole situation into a positive, and I wanted to wallow in my own misery for a while. She was running straight for us though. Jayden-Lee pushed in front of me, and for a moment it looked like she was going to leap into his arms.

I decided to make a quick exit before I was sick.

But she didn't run into Jayden-Lee's embrace. She totally ignored him, skidding across the grass in front of me. '*Dylan*, where's Jude?'

I sighed. 'Mum and Dad turned up; they've got him. He saw—'

'No, they haven't,' she interrupted. 'They were talking, and Leo had to go back to the photoshoot, and I got side-tracked picking up Nibbles toys. We thought he must have followed you.'

She made a grab for my arm. 'He's missing, Dylan. Jude's gone.'

THIRTY-NINE

'How can he be gone?' I asked between quick breaths as we pelted around the edges of the fairground, trying to spot Jude somewhere in the crowd. 'He's got a maximum speed of four miles per hour. He can't just *vanish.*'

Kayla was keeping up, her hand caught in mine. 'I don't *know*. Everyone thought someone else was watching him.'

Any other time, someone else would have been. Any other day, it would have been me. I pulled us up short, my attention caught by a gleam of sunshine on metal, but it was just light reflecting off the wing mirror of the ice-cream van. Jude's chair should have been easy to pick out, but the fair was getting busier as the afternoon went on, and all I could see were the tops of people's heads towering over anywhere he might be.

Kayla squeezed my fingers tight. 'We'll find him.'

'I know.' I said it automatically. We would find him. We *had* to. Because I didn't know what I'd do if we didn't.

He arrived when I was ten years old. I remember

resenting him a bit, at first. Mum had him sooner than she was supposed to, and Dad, Nana and everyone had gone around pretending not to be scared about it. Everybody was snappy with each other, and with me. I'd been promised a baby brother I could play video games with; I never signed up for those few weeks of quiet fear.

So when Mum and Jude came home, it was this big celebration. Jude was the miracle baby who'd survived against the odds, and I felt like my own superpowers were being unfairly slow to develop, considering he'd had his from birth.

But then time went on, and people started comparing him against me. He didn't sit upright, like I'd been able to. He was kind of floppy where I hadn't been, like a doll in your arms.

That was when he got his diagnosis. I still remember one of the nurses on the paediatric ward sitting me down to say what a challenge it would be, having a brother with a disability. And yeah, Jude's *definitely* challenging. Like, he went through this phase of chewing the corners off my magazines when his teeth were coming in. And he yells when we don't have the same number of fish fingers, even though I'm obviously twice his size. And he's always, *always* touching my stuff.

Having a brother is pretty challenging. But not for any of the reasons I was told.

So I'm kind of protective of him now. Not because he can't do things for himself, but because he's stubborn enough to insist on doing them. And I want to protect that, because I know how hard it can be to feel different. I've felt it approximately all my life.

Leo said he liked me because I just kept going, no matter what. I think I learned that from Jude, and hearing that he was missing made every part of me want to stop still – including my heart.

'Over there!' Jayden-Lee had inexplicably followed us, and just then I was grateful for his few extra inches in height. I followed where he was pointing, and there it was: the unmistakable mix of silver and black that was the back of Jude's chair, swerving wildly through the crowd.

'That's him!' Kayla dragged on my hand. I was still trying to put my finger on what was wrong.

'Jude's a better driver than that. He must be upset.' He'd been on two powerchair training days, and he could wheelchair slalom like a pro, but he didn't usually swing around like that.

Guilt spiked me in the chest. I must have upset him by getting so mad. I'd make it up to him, though, just as soon as we caught him. And we were almost there.

Until someone with crispy blonde hair and a shiny blue skirt suit clicked her way out from in front of the hook-a-duck pool. Margaret held her arms out wide on either side, one hand clutching a patent-leather handbag that she looked ready to do some serious damage with.

'Mr Kershaw,' she was saying. 'What a dubious pleasure it is to see you here today . . .'

I didn't have time to listen. I just kept running, glancing over at Jayden-Lee as I did.

'You take left,' he said.

I nodded.

He ran smack into Margaret's outstretched right arm, spinning her round in the slick mud that surrounded the pool. Two seconds later, I ran into her left arm and spun her back the other way.

Kayla ducked under both helicoptering arms and ran with us, leaving Margaret reeling like a revolving door.

None of us slowed down for a second, not even when we heard her dizzily tripping straight into the pool. There were splashes behind us, and a screech of outrage before she started yelling, 'After him! An incentive, reward and bonus to anyone who can apprehend that boy!'

One of the cooks from the burger stand climbed over his counter. Someone abandoned the coconut shy. The ice-cream van backfired and started playing a demonic version of 'Greensleeves' backwards through its speakers as it began reversing right into Jude's path.

'He doesn't know there's someone behind him!' I yelled, waving my arms to try and attract the attention of the van driver. He must have thought he was being mocked, because it only made him rev his engine louder. Jude was a few feet away from a collision, and he wasn't even trying to get out of the way. It was like he'd totally forgotten how to use his chair.

'The sign!' Kayla shouted. 'Dylan, the sign!'

She shoved something towards me, and I looked down to see that it was Jayden-Lee's football.

The sign. The huge *DON'T CLOWN AROUND* clown's head that was still creaking as it swung from its post. It was the only thing between Jude and the van.

I dropped the ball at my feet and ran backwards to give myself some momentum.

Then I kicked like I was in the Cup Final.

The ball bounced off the back of the ice-cream van and scythed upward, slamming into the clown's face and slapping it off the hooks that it swung from.

It dropped like the blade of a guillotine.

Either everything was happening impossibly slowly, or so fast that my mind couldn't cope with watching it in real time, but it seemed to take forever before the sign stopped twanging and shivering, wedged firmly into the mud.

The ice-cream van backed into this new obstacle with a sickening crunch, and as the driver realized he'd hit something, he finally, reluctantly, came to a halt.

Jayden-Lee reached Jude's chair first. He put a hand on the headrest, then growled, 'You little ...' and tipped the whole thing over on to its side.

Tumbling Troy out of the seat.

FORTY

'IT WAS MY TURN!' Troy roared, as Jayden-Lee dived to pin him down. 'HE'S HAD IT ALL WEEK.'

'People don't take *turns* in wheelchairs,' Kayla snapped, kneeling to one side of him. I caught up and dropped to the ground on the other. 'God forbid you ever meet someone who uses a pacemaker.'

'Where is he?' I demanded, breathless.

Chaos was erupting around me: a crowd had gathered to watch the ice-cream van attempt to detach its back wheels from the crumpled sign, while various fair workers were struggling to pick an equally crumpled Margaret out of the mud around the duck pool.

I was barely aware of it. There was only one thing I cared about. 'What did you do with Jude?'

Troy set his jaw tight, until Jayden-Lee leaned in so close that they were almost nose to nose. 'Either you tell him, or I pick you up by the ankles and shake it out of you.'

He said it surprisingly calmly, as though casually threatening children was a daily event.

'Like last time,' he added.

Screwing his face up like he'd just taken a bite of toilet-freshener flavoured candy floss, Troy spat out, 'On the bench! He's on the bench, and I'm telling Mum!'

'The bench?' I asked. The bench that looked like it was carved out of a fallen tree? The one where Kayla and I had decided to make friends again? 'The one on the cliffs? *You ditched my brother on the edge of the cliffs?*'

I was already racing to get to my feet. My blood ran slow and icy in my veins, and it felt like the tick of every second was lasting a lifetime. I knew Jude was smart; he wouldn't have gone too close to the rocky edge. But there was a persistent little voice in my ears whispering *what if?*

Behind me, I could hear Jayden-Lee let out a harsh breath as he swung Troy up into his arms like a small, aggressive sack of potatoes. 'You're coming too. And if you're lying—'

His voice was cut off.

In slow motion, something that looked like a mud monster from the Black Lagoon lurched towards me, letting out a monstrous wail of, '*Apprehend hiiiim.*'

I left her behind. I left behind the squelching and the string of swearwords as she smacked into Jayden-Lee. I left the jingling tune that started up as the ice-cream van revved its engine again, and the sickening crunch and squeal of grinding metal that followed.

I was barrelling towards the cliff, and the bench, and the edge.

The cliff, which I reached in record time, with people stumbling to get out of my way as I ran.

And the bench, which looked emptier the closer I got.

And the edge.

I had to do it. Even if Troy had been lying to freak me out. Even if this was just his idea of revenge. Even then. I had to go to the cliff edge. I had to look over.

I had to make sure.

Feeling sick with the thought, I jogged onward, trying not to focus on anything but the pounding of my own feet. It was easy enough to do, given that my eyes were stinging, my vision blurring into a wet, water-colour haze of green and blue, brown and orange.

And orange?

I blinked what I would definitely deny later was any kind of liquid out of my eyes and refocused, looking across the clifftop a little way along from the bench.

Sitting in the long grass was an overgrown orange hamster. And in his lap he had my little brother. They were feeding the seagulls.

'Dylan, look!' Jude called to me as I ran over. 'I found the *real* Nibbles!'

As relief washed all the panic I'd felt back out of my body, the excess adrenaline that had driven me so far turned into total, full-body exhaustion. For the second time in about ten minutes, I dropped to my knees.

Reaching out for one of Jude's hands, I squeezed it tight, making sure he felt as real as he looked. 'You're right. The other one was just a decoy lookalike. All the really famous hamsters have those.'

Jude smiled, but I couldn't, quite. 'I'm sorry I got mad at you in the tent. I'm glad you found Nibbles anyway.'

'The *real* Nibbles,' Jude reminded me. 'Who doesn't like *kisses* at all. But look!' His free hand swung high in the air, clutching a scrap of bread that must have been liberated from the remains of somebody's picnic. He pitched it over the side of the cliff, and within seconds a clever white bird swooped in and caught it. Jude squealed in delight. 'He showed me the seagulls won't eat me if they're already full.'

'He really is the hero this caravan park deserves,' Kayla called, arriving to join us on the grass.

It turned out that Jude actually had allowed Troy a turn in his chair, though I didn't feel very guilty for not having believed it. Nibbles found him waiting alone on the bench and had broken the first rule of being an animal mascot – never speak while in costume – to send someone to get my mum and dad.

They showed up not long after I did, carrying the twisted wreckage of his wheelchair.

'What *happened*?' I asked Kayla, while we watched Jude receive a series of smothering hugs, interspersed with lectures on when it's appropriate to share. Mum was hugging Nibbles too, squeezing tight enough to flatten his fur.

'Margaret's to blame for the chair.' Kayla crossed her legs like she was settling in for story time. 'She mud-wrestled Jayden-Lee straight into the path of the ice-cream van, so the driver panicked and backed up right over it. If you ask me, you've got an easy claim for the cost of a new one.' She considered for a moment. 'And maybe for some free raspberry-ripple ice cream.'

'She's going to try and blame me,' I said. 'I can see her version now: *heroic hamster rescues child after own brother tries to fling him off a cliff.* She'll say I was doing it just to spoil her celebrations.'

I kicked at a clump of grass, still sort of feeling like this was all my fault too.

'Well, it *would* have put a slight dampener on them if you had.' Kayla just smirked when I glared at her. 'Anyway, that sounds nothing like Margaret. You didn't rephrase all the important bits three times. Also, furthermore, and in addendum, I have a feeling the heroic hamster might not go along with that story.'

'He might.' I couldn't keep from smiling over at Leo. He still hadn't escaped from Mum's grateful suffocation attempts. 'The fame could go to his big, padded head. This time next year he'll be demanding they set up a big wheel just for him to run in circles on.'

'Why not.' Kayla laughed. 'He deserves it. I did tell you he was my hero.'

I couldn't believe how much things had changed. Two days ago the same words had made me storm off to sulk about rodent-based favouritism. Now I finally understood.

'Yeah,' I said, getting up to go and join in with the hamster hugs. 'Mine, too.'

FORTY-ONE

Jude got his hamster photo eventually. I was in it too, holding him up while he and Nibbles waved, and Kayla snapped us on her phone against the best backdrop ever. The whole clifftop scene, with the blue of the ocean and sky meeting behind us, made it look like one of the posters you see in travel agents' windows, advertising proper holidays to places outside of England where the sun shines more than once a month.

For Jude's photo, at least, Starcross Sands really looked like a dream holiday destination.

Kayla took one of just me and Nibbles together too, which made me blush so much I looked sunburned. I almost thought about using that as an excuse for why I was so flushed, except I didn't want Leo to think it might be painful if he wanted to kiss me again.

Because I really, really hoped that he would want to kiss me again.

Once he'd had a chance to take the hamster head off, obviously. I liked Nibbles a lot more now, but I definitely only fancied the boy inside.

He wasn't going to be free of the costume for a while

though. I didn't even get the chance to talk to him – as soon as we'd taken the pictures, he had to run back to finish his photo session. I hoped he'd get there before the children started rioting. A lot of them were in nappies, so it could have been a really dirty protest.

After Leo had gone, I tried to blend back into the crowds at the fair for a while. Mum, Dad and Kayla were getting involved in sorting out a temporary wheelchair for Jude, and I still felt like I needed some space to take a breath. The relief I'd felt over Jude being OK was starting to melt back into a strange, unsettled feeling in my stomach as I thought about all the things that weren't.

Things weren't exactly back to normal. I didn't know if they ever would be. Mum and Dad had seen me kissing Leo, and life as I knew it felt about as mangled as Jude's chair.

Carefully edging around the spot where I'd left Margaret the manager stuck in the mud, I headed for the rickety-looking ghost-train ride that stood next to Nibbles' tent, and bought enough tokens for a dozen rides. It was full of plastic skeletons and mannequins dressed in white sheets, and the screams of the other passengers meant I couldn't hear myself think for a while. It was perfect.

Then, after my sixth go round, someone opened the

carriage door beside me and asked, 'Is this seat taken?'

I sort of knew my parents would track me down eventually, but I'd expected the one doing the talking to be Mum. At home she was usually in charge of *feelings* conversations, while Dad was the go-to for terrible jokes and official backup that chicken in a bucket for dinner counted as part of a balanced diet.

It wasn't that Dad didn't do feelings. It was just that his emotional range usually swung from cheering and singing to sobbing and swearing, and both ends of the scale usually had something to do with sport. He once got them mixed up and cried while telling me how proud he was when one of my goals won us the Surrey Schools Cup.

'Oi,' he said, giving my shoulder a tap. 'I said, is anyone sitting here?'

As I shook my head, and he wedged himself in next to me, I realized just how much I didn't want him to ever tell me he was disappointed. The train took off through a curtain of witchy rags for the seventh time since I'd got on it, and as we shot into the dark I finally felt scared.

'*YOU'LL NEVER GET OUT!*' a voice screeched in my ear, before a ghost dressed in a powdered wig and light-up trainers ran off though a cobweb-covered door.

'That must be true,' Dad mused, leaning in to be heard

over the looping soundtrack of 'The Monster Mash'. 'You've been round on this thing five times already.'

'Six,' I admitted, staring ahead to where a collection of ghouls were resetting the bloodied blade that was going to almost fall on us a bit further on.

Dad gave a low whistle. 'Keep coming back for the Hollywood special effects?'

'I just needed some space, that's all.' The plastic guillotine swung into action, slicing downwards to dangle half a foot above our heads, before being hoisted back up by another ghost-worker. The torch he was holding under his white sheet accidentally illuminated the logo on his hoody. 'Before everyone started . . . you know.'

Dad gave me a deliberately blank look, eyebrows raised.

I sighed, pushing my hands over my face before I ended up glaring so hard at the Egyptian mummy creeping up alongside the train that he started to unravel.

'I'm gay,' I said, finally. 'Aren't you supposed to ask me questions, or something?'

'Like what?' Dad asked.

'Like . . . I don't know.' I *did* know. It was a list I'd run through a thousand times in the part of my mind I tried not to listen to. 'Like, *How long have you known?*

Like, *Are you SURE?* And, *Why?* And, *Do you know there are no gay players in the Premier League?'*

Dad was frowning by the time I'd finished. A vampire bat wafted right past his face and he didn't even blink. 'I don't know there *aren't* any gay players in the Premier League.'

That might have been true, but it wasn't the point. Dad held up a hand to stop me before I could say so.

'And it's nobody's business if there are, Dylan. Not if they don't want to talk about it. But you and your brother? You *are* my business. Now, aren't you supposed to ask *me* questions?'

I frowned, shaking my head slowly. 'I don't think so. Like what?'

'Like, how long have I known?'

I stared at him.

'Or you can ask how long I've loved you. It's a bit longer than the first answer, but it hasn't changed because of it.'

I didn't know how I was supposed to reply. I didn't know how I *felt*. Sort of like I'd been hugged and punched at the same time.

'You really knew?'

'It was more of a feeling.'

'Was it . . . really obvious?' Maybe I'd been setting off gaydars left and right. Maybe instead of me not telling the world, it had been the world not telling me that it already knew. That wasn't a good feeling at all. But Dad shook his head.

'No, but you're my son.' He paused, then added, 'And when that boy next door sent you a postcard from Berlin, you wrote *ich liebe dich* all over the back.'

I groaned louder than the mummy still shuffling alongside the train, and buried my head in my hands. 'You *found* that?'

Dad squeezed my shoulder. 'Maybe you should tidy your own room.'

The train creaked slowly back into the sunlight, and I got shakily to my feet. There didn't seem to be any point in using up my last few rides, now everything was out in the open.

'You're really OK with it?' I checked, as Dad joined me in evacuating the train.

'Since before you decided to learn German,' he said.

I still felt like I needed some time to myself, just to try and process everything. And I wanted to try and catch Leo again before the fair closed, if I could. I glanced over to the photo tent, but Dad was still talking.

'They have parades for this, don't they?' He rubbed his chin thoughtfully. 'Pride parades. Flags on buses, chanting, bit like the victory parade when someone wins the Cup.'

'Oh my *God*, Dad, I'm not a sport!' I could see it now: him decked out in rainbows like it was the Gay team kit.

'Just picture it.' He waved a hand in front of him the way a painter sweeps a brush across his canvas. 'Cheering crowds. You and me on top of a bus, waving a banner that says *I LOVE MY GAY SON . . .*'

Dad wasn't freaked out that I was gay. Not even a little bit. He was supporting me.

Exactly the same way he supported Woking FC.

My life was *still* totally over.

FORTY-TWO

Dad's phone rang just in time to save me from hearing the 'supportive' chant he was working on. It started out with *TWO-FOUR-SIX-HEY!* So I was really fine with not knowing where the rhyme scheme would take it.

While he stepped away, cupping the phone to his ear, I looked over to where a line of hyperactive toddlers was still snaking out of the photo tent – then smiled as I caught myself hoping for a glimpse of orange fur.

I could *never* tell Kayla exactly how gooey I was starting to feel about something that probably had 'Caution: highly flammable' sewn into its tail.

Dad tapped me on the shoulder and I looked round guiltily, hoping he couldn't tell from my face that I was having fancy-dress-related romantic thoughts. He didn't need to know *everything* about me.

'Mum,' he mouthed, gesturing to the phone. 'Got to go.'

From the face he was making, I couldn't tell whether he meant it was Mum on the phone, or someone else calling him about her. Like the time he'd had to collect her from the security office at the Tower of London after she'd kicked off about the lack of accessibility ramps and made one of the Beefeaters cry.

But it wasn't just Dad's face that got my attention. It was the arm he was waving about too.

'Right. I'll head back to the caravan in a minute too. Um, Dad . . .' I raised my eyebrows. 'What's that?'

Because I'd just noticed that he seemed to have picked up a new fashion accessory. There was something big and red hanging off his wrist where his watch should have been. Something big and red and varnished, which curved out at the sides into a splintered wooden smile.

Dad quickly hid that arm behind his back.

'Oh, that? Nothing. New toy for Jude.' He held the phone away from his ear, and I could just hear Mum's voice raised in the background.

'All right . . .' I watched him start to relax, then freeze up again as I went on. 'Just one thing though, Dad. You know that *golf emergency* that meant you couldn't take Jude to the fair? What happened, exactly?'

Dad forced his frozen face to crack into a grin. A lot like the grin he then accidentally smacked himself in the forehead with as he went to run a hand back through his hair. There was *definitely* a creepy clown smile stuck round his wrist.

'Now, before you say anything . . .' Dad started.

'Did it have something to do with one of the holes?' I asked.

'*Before* you say anything—'

'Because they have holes shaped like clowns at crazy golf, don't they?'

'*Dylan.*'

'Did you get your hand stuck in a clown, Dad?' I asked him, folding my arms sternly and trying to clamp down on the urge to grin. 'You were cheating, weren't you?'

'Blooming course is *fixed*,' Dad exploded, finally, waving his arm so that the mouth jangled round on his wrist. It looked like his own hand was laughing at him. 'All those castles and windmills ruining the game! How do you judge a shot that's got to make it through something's face before it gets to the hole, eh? This idiot clown was turning the ball in circles till I sorted him out.'

He shook his own fist, as though the clown could still hear him.

'You were cheating.' I tutted. 'Dad, you literally tried to take the crazy out of crazy golf. That's the definition of missing the point.'

'Improved the game, if you ask me.' Dad gestured to the mouth. 'And no one's asking him any more.'

I couldn't believe he'd punched a wooden clown.

Maybe Margaret had been right about me. I was starting to think a habit of getting involved in 'incidents' ran in the family.

'*NIBBLES IS TAKING A FUZZY FIVE, FOLKS!*'

I almost leaped into Dad's arms when Stacie's voice burst through the speaker behind me. '*BACK IN JUST FIVE MINUTES, EVERYONE. NOBODY MOO-VE!*'

I shot Dad a slightly desperate look. There was just five minutes for me to catch Leo before he got stuck pulling poses with playschool kids for another two hours.

'Well –' Dad tapped the phone, giving me a wise wink and wincing at the volume level Mum's voice had reached when he lifted it to his ear again – 'better not keep her waiting.'

I made a dash towards Nibbles' tent the second Dad turned to head out of the fair.

Reaching the backstage entrance to the tent with seconds to spare, I pulled the canvas to one side and stuck my head in to see Nibbles hurriedly velcroing his own back into place.

'*Leo,*' I hissed, stepping through before I could be spotted. The hamster jumped, turning in a clumsy circle to face me.

I knew I was grinning like an idiot. It hadn't been much more than an hour since we'd been getting pictures together on the cliffs, but I was so pleased to see him again.

'Can you take the head off?' I kept my voice low, too aware of the chattering of excited kids waiting in the other part of the tent.

Nibbles gestured in that direction, and shook his chubby cheeks. He didn't have time. If only I hadn't been waylaid by Dad's clown-assault story.

'It's OK,' I said, rushing my words together in an attempt to get them all out in time. 'It's just, tomorrow's our last day in the park. We're leaving right after the parade and I haven't even had a chance to get your number. Can you meet me?'

'*Here he comes, boys and girls. Get your selfie smiles ready – the one, the only . . .*'

'I'll be outside the showhall at three tomorrow afternoon!'

'*Nibbles!*'

I was left watching the hamster's familiar orange backside vanish through the curtain before Stacie could pull it aside. Behind it, what sounded like a hundred children screamed in delight to see him so close.

I knew exactly how they felt.

FORTY-THREE

The next morning I woke up not knowing if I wanted the day to go fast or slow. Three o'clock, the *stupid* time I'd decided to tell Leo I'd meet him, felt like it was an eternity away.

And four o'clock, the time when me, Mum, Dad, Jude and Kayla would get in the car and leave 131 Alpine Views forever, felt like it was crashing towards me at breakneck speed.

It was our last day at the Starcross Sands. Suddenly everything looked as friendly and welcoming as the brochure had promised. Even Mrs Slater's gnomes took on a rose-coloured tint when seen through my eyes: their tiny, wizened faces seemed to be wishing me well. I didn't want to say goodbye to Starcross Sands, not when I'd finally come to appreciate its 'stunning views', 'unique community' and 'dedication to your dreams'.

Most of all didn't want to say goodbye to Leo.

I'd even gone out looking for him, not wanting to stand around feeling sick while Mum packed up all our things ready for the car. She'd performed some Mum-wizardry and turned our sofa from pink back to beige and was on a whirlwind tidying blitz, throwing things into suitcases where they landed perfectly folded.

I'd ducked out of the path of the storm and gone down to the Pie-O-Ria to see if Leo was hanging out there, but strangely the whole place was closed all day. There was nothing to see but some rolled-down shutters and a scattering of Chicken and Sweetcorn Fiesta on the ground outside.

Kayla came to find me right when I was considering writing DYLAN ♥ LEO on the shutters in a smear of leftover tomato sauce. She tapped me on the shoulder. 'Ready?'

I checked my watch. The time I never wanted to come was finally almost here.

A few minutes later, we were heading towards the showhall, with Kayla dragging her feet as she tailed me down the path.

'Are you *sure* you want me to be there when Leo arrives?' she asked. 'You definitely want me to be the P in your PDA?'

The way she was pulling on my hand was slowing us both down, but I didn't mind. It didn't really feel like my feet were touching the floor at all, so having her as an anchor might have been the only thing keeping me from floating away.

'*Obviously* I want you to be there,' I repeated for the

thousandth time that afternoon. 'Why wouldn't I want the chance to introduce him properly to my best friend in the entire world? You've never met him when he's been able to speak.'

'I just think you might be overcompensating for ignoring me when you were all about Jayden-Lee.' She met the warning glare I flashed at her with a bland look. 'I know, I know, those are the dark days and we don't talk about them any more. But you know what they say about "two's company".'

Kayla's brain was made up of forty-five per cent legal mumbo-jumbo she'd cribbed from TV shows, five per cent Deathsplash lyrics, and at least fifty per cent weird old sayings no one uses any more. I thought I knew this one though. 'Three's a crowd?'

'No, three's company plus one person trying not to throw up in their mouth while they're stuck listening to the other two making gross kissing noises.'

'Who says we're going to kiss?'

I kept my focus on the path, but I could feel the look she was giving me. 'Oh, it's just a little hunch based on you talking about how amazing kissing him was for at least a thousand hours last night.'

Which was clearly nonsense. Nights don't even last a thousand hours, unless they're nights in one of the horror games I suck at, and then it takes me at least that just to get past the screamer zombies in the basement.

I didn't call Kayla out on it, though, mostly because she was right: I *was* trying to make up for what happened with Jayden-Lee. If Leo and me were going to become a thing, Kayla was going to be involved every step of the way.

Well, *nearly* every step.

She was right that I had told her a bit about what kissing Leo had been like too.

And when I say a bit, I mean a lot.

Like really quite a lot.

Like it had probably been my main topic of conversation since it happened, except for when Mum and Dad had brought Jude back in a rented chair (courtesy of the Starcross management) with two arms full of fish and chips. Last night's dinner had been an agonizing hour of trying to talk about anything *except* kissing.

Mum had silently popped her head around the door of my room afterwards, right when I was telling Kayla how kissing the right person felt like putting your fingers in an electric socket of love.

'Your lips, surely? Or was he kissing your hand?' Mum had asked, startling me so much that I'd fallen off the bed, then considered physically curling up and dying right where I'd landed. 'That's awfully romantic.'

She seriously had to not stealth into my private conversations, like some kind of grossly invasive superspy on the weirdest government mission ever.

Coming over, she held out both hands to help me off the floor. 'Your father told me we were supposed to have a list of questions prepared for this occasion. Were you expecting some kind of test?'

Shrugging awkwardly, I'd climbed back on to the bed and tried to half bury myself under the covers.

'Darling.' She pressed a chips-and-vinegar scented kiss to my forehead. 'There's no such thing as a right time – there's only when you're ready. I *am* sorry that you weren't able to choose. But I'm not going to test you. Nobody asks boys who like girls if *they're* sure.'

Which was sort of nice, even if I was starting to feel like I might have been ready for a while, and just hadn't known. Like I'd been wasting time instead.

It might almost have been worth the embarrassment of her having seen me kiss someone, until she turned on the way out and added, 'Now, if I thought it was *hamsters* you wanted to date, I might have a few questions.'

She and Kayla had giggled evilly for at least ten minutes after that. I'd just lain back on my bed and wondered why I hadn't arranged to meet Leo sooner, so I could stop talking about kissing him and maybe try actually doing it again.

If he still wanted to, that was.

It had been almost twenty-four hours since he said he *like*-liked me. That was plenty of time for him to have changed his mind.

It was enough time for him to have gone off me entirely.

In fact, it was probably long enough for him to have had a religious revelation and gone off *kissing* entirely. He might have hung up his hamster head by now and left the park to become a silent, kissless monk. Literally anything could happen in a day. For instance, yesterday already felt like it had changed my life.

I pulled up short just at the bottom of the slope that lead to the showhall doors. 'But what if—'

'No,' Kayla said.

'But—'

'Dylan, you've been through a *million* of these scenarios.'

I had. But it was no good – I had to go through another one or I was going to explode. 'But what if he *doesn't come*?'

Kayla groaned in frustration, catching me up and making a grab for my hand. She squeezed it, tight. 'Of *course* he'll come. You haven't been able to go for five minutes without running into him this entire holiday.

Do you really think he'd start avoiding you *now*?'

'But what if . . .'

What if he'd been lost in romantic daydreams about me on the cliff edge yesterday evening, and had fallen into the ocean?

What if one of the children in the photo tent had coughed on him and given him a terrible disease?

What if . . .

. . .

I'd run out of what ifs. Usually Kayla would have interrupted my thoughts by now, but she was strangely quiet. When I looked across at her she was staring, shocked, at something on her phone. My heart twanged anxiously.

'It's not your dad, is it?'

It would be the worst thing to have got through to the last day with no disasters, only to have knocked over the final hurdle.

Kayla gave a small nod, and passed her phone across.

The screen displayed a photo of her living room. There was a thumb hanging half over the camera, but beyond what it blotted out everything looked . . . completely normal. All four walls were still the right way up, and the roof hadn't fallen through. There were no scorch marks on the carpet; no noticeable holes or dubious stains. Even her two cats, Sid and Nancy, were present and accounted for, curled up on the sofa. I'd never seen her house look so un-chaotic.

When I looked up, Kayla was smiling.

'Maybe it *is* safe to leave him for the occasional afternoon without anything burning down, exploding or disintegrating,' she said. She looked different, all of a sudden, and it wasn't down to any change in her make-up routine. I think it was the first time I'd ever seen her really relax.

Then I checked her phone again, and panicked. 'Oh my god, fifteen minutes? Kayla, we can't be here fifteen minutes early. I'll look totally eager.'

'You *are* totally eager.' She artfully caught her phone as I flipped it into the air, mid-flail.

'I don't want to *look* it though. Maybe we could walk some circuits around the hall.'

'Dylan.'

'Or we could go and hide in the trees by the playground and come back in twenty minutes. Is five minutes late enough to look keen but not I've-been-waiting-here-all-day-actually keen?'

'Dylan, it's fine. I set the clocks on our phones backward last night so you wouldn't embarrass yourself. You're *already* five minutes late.'

My mouth dropped open. For someone who wanted

a job promoting justice, Kayla made a remarkably competent evil genius.

By the time I'd run, breathless, to the front of the showhall, I was nearly ten minutes late. *Ten minutes late* for the most important date of my life. And, as the horror of that slowly settled in, I realized that it meant something even worse.

Leo hadn't come.

FORTY-FOUR

He wasn't there. The doors were there, opaque in the sunlight. The yellow Stardance posters were there, brand-new ones that must have been pinned up in a hurry, with edges that curled and flapped in the wind. Twinkle the Talking Train was still there, motionless without Jude to fill her up with pound coins.

I was there.

But Leo wasn't.

It was just me. Standing in front of the showhall. Alone.

Or almost alone. Kayla wasn't far behind me. She sped up a bit once it was clear she wouldn't be interrupting a passionate reunion anytime soon.

'He's only ten minutes late,' I croaked as she joined me. I stared back up the slope the way she'd come, waiting for a head of dark hair to come into view, blotting out the sun and somehow brighter than it at the same time.

'Ten minutes is nothing,' Kayla said, putting on her perkiest voice. 'You were ten minutes late, and you've been waiting for this all day.'

'Exactly. I can't expect him to be on time when I . . .' I stopped, a shock of panic rushing through me. 'I was ten minutes late. Kayla. What if I missed him? He must have been here and assumed I wasn't interested!'

'In ten minutes? I think he'd have a bit more patience than that.'

'But you don't *know*. You reset my phone and I was late, and now I've missed him.'

Kayla had grabbed for my wildly gesturing hands as I spoke and was holding them steady, clasped between her palms. 'Or maybe *he's* late and you're having a heart attack for no reason. I'm sure he would have waited otherwise. Not everyone assumes the other person's been kidnapped by aliens or run away to become a monk if they don't turn up exactly when they're meant to.'

'How did you know about the monks?'

She raised an eyebrow.

I suppose I might have mentioned my monk fear once or twice last night. I shoved my hands into my pockets and stared at the ground.

'Maybe you're right. There isn't time for him to be running that late though. The parade starts in half an hour.'

Gradually, all my visions of my first encounter with Leo without a stuffed hamster stomach coming between

293

us were starting to crumble. Seeing him for just a few minutes would be better than nothing though. This was my last day – my last chance. I couldn't leave the park without getting his number.

'He'll come,' Kayla said decisively, climbing up on to Twinkle to swing her legs off the side of a carriage. 'I saw the way that hamster looked at you. Any minute now.'

I looked back up the pathway just as a shadow fell across the sun.

'Either of you seen that thieving little brat?'

Jayden-Lee jogged down the path towards us, out of breath and flushed in a way that, two days ago, I'd have found irresistible.

'I take it you mean your brother?' Kayla asked, leaning round Twinkle's engine.

Jayden-Lee nodded. 'He's taken Mum's reading glasses again. She's doing her nut.'

Kayla shot me a glance. 'What does he want those for? Illicitly reading small-print classics?'

'Ants.' Jayden-Lee sighed.

'Ants?' I tried, seeing if the word made any more sense as an answer the second time around.

Jayden-Lee looked at me like I'd asked him if the world was flat. 'If you get the sun at the right angle through a lens, you can set fire to ants with it. It's science.'

'It's animal cruelty!' Kayla exclaimed. 'Not a child's game! Where do you get his toys from? Murdercare? The Early Murdering Centre?'

Jayden-Lee shrugged. 'It's his hobby. But Mum needs them back for bingo. So he hasn't come past?'

'Believe me, you'd know if we'd seen him,' Kayla said, a low threat in her voice that suggested Troy would definitely know about it the next time he ran into her, too.

I gave up on paying attention to them, looking at my phone and then back at the empty space where Leo wasn't. He was fifteen minutes late, now. I wondered if there were any monasteries in Starcross. Maybe we could call in at one on the drive home, just to check.

Kayla's feet slapping the ground as she jumped off the Twinkle ride brought my focus back to the present.

'So, I was wondering if you felt like going,' Jayden-Lee was saying.

'With you?' Kayla checked.

'To the dance.' He gestured at one of the flapping posters, then pushed his hands into his pockets awkwardly.

'Oh my *God*,' I mouthed over his shoulder, as Kayla glared at me from the narrowed corners of her eyes. He was asking her out. The boy of my dreams-slash-nightmares was really, properly, asking my best friend out.

I checked myself for any slight twinge of jealousy, but I couldn't feel anything but the sudden, bubbling sensation that I was about to laugh. Choking it down, I stared wide-eyed at Kayla as I – and Jayden-Lee – waited for her response.

'Dylan's parents are leaving before the dance, actually. We're not going,' she said, briskly. I think I deflated as much as Jayden-Lee at the reminder of how little time we had left.

'But,' Kayla added, as Jayden-Lee's slumped shoulders straightened out again, 'even if we were, I don't think I'd feel like going with you. I don't think I'd feel like going *anywhere* with you, *ever*, not even if we were both at the bottom of a pit and you had the only stepladder out. Not if I was starving and you had the world's largest Cornish pasty. Not even if you had tickets to the Deathsplash Nightmares' next big show, *and* backstage passes, *and* Rick Deathsplash had personally promised to kiss every fan there.'

From Kayla, that was probably the biggest *no* you could get. She carried on:

'You see, unlike you and your little brother, I don't think it's very nice to torment things for fun.'

She folded her arms and tipped her chin in the air. She was more than a foot shorter than Jayden-Lee but still somehow made it seem like she was looking down on him. Mind you, the way he'd shrivelled up as she spoke did make that easier.

I almost felt sorry for him. Until he spat out a wodge of gum between his feet and snorted, 'Yeah, well, like I care. You two can stay here and hang out with that dancing freak.'

He stomped off around the back of the showhall before I could work out if his ears were turning red with anger or something else.

'Harsh,' I murmured, watching him vanish from view.

'It's no worse than anything he said to you. As *if* I'd want to dance with him after that. And what did he mean, "dancing freak"?'

'Oh, last time he was here we were watching Nibbles – Leo – practising his ballet moves. We could see him through the . . .'

The showhall doors. The way the sun was positioned meant it was impossible to see through them unless you pressed your face to the baking-hot glass.

Seconds later I was risking burning all the skin off my nose.

'He's there. Kayla, he's *here*. I can see him at the back of the lobby.'

The hall was crowded with performers getting ready to join the parade. Leo was in full hamster costume already, standing off to one side with a couple of people in security uniforms.

He must have been waiting for me the whole time. Dizzy with relief, I pushed the door open.

'Leo! I was in totally the wrong place!' I smiled, even though the security guards were looking at me like I'd just climbed the gates of Buckingham Palace dressed as Spiderman. 'I can't believe I nearly missed you!'

One of the guards stepped forward and grabbed my arm as I got close, issuing me a gruff command. 'No touching the talent.'

I frowned. 'It's OK, we had a . . .' I couldn't say *date* in front of everyone. 'We had plans. Didn't we, Leo?'

Nibbles looked back at me with cold, blank eyes.

'Leo?'

'The hamster must always be addressed in character,' the other security guard said, grabbing my arm before both of them started to march me back to the exit.

Leo didn't say anything. He didn't try to stop them at all.

Even Twinkle seemed to look embarrassed for me as they threw me out of the doors.

Kayla was still out there, and she must have seen what happened, because she looked as horrified as I felt.

Then she opened her mouth and screamed, 'FIRE!'

FORTY-FIVE

It was impossible to say where the fire had started, but it caught quick, tearing up the sparkly curtains. The hall evacuated in a glitzy stampede, pushing me and Kayla away from the doors. Most of the parade performers were still half-dressed, clutching props or hair curlers and trailing pom-poms. Some of the Elvises, who had been meant to be having a sing-off on one of the floats, were trying to stamp out the flames from their flares.

Nibbles rushed out with his security escort and was bundled into one of the golf buggies. He was probably the most flammable thing there, so it was good to know he was safe, even if he didn't look at me once as they drove him away.

Kayla pulled me away too. I walked back to the caravan feeling strangely singed.

Mum and Dad had rushed down to help at the showhall, but there weren't any casualties except the building itself. Dad said there was no known treatment for a blackened glitterball, so they'd come back to finish packing the car. Me and Kayla were doing our part by standing at the window of 131 Alpine Views and eating our way through everything in the fridge that wouldn't survive the long drive home.

'I can't believe Leo acted like that,' Kayla muttered through a mouthful of crisps. 'Do you want me to sue him for you?'

We were watching the latest screaming match to break out in the Dramavan. It had been going on for half an hour, at least, ever since a fireman had shown up at the door holding a pair of reading glasses.

'Because I could,' Kayla said. She'd been blazing hotter than the showhall ever since Nibbles blanked me. 'I could sue him for everything he's got.'

'Leo's fifteen,' I reminded her, scraping the remains out of a family-sized pot of yogurt and gesturing with the spoon. 'I don't think he has any valuable assets, except some nice trainers and enough orange fur to carpet a seventies disco. Besides, don't you need a real reason to sue someone?'

'I have plenty of real reasons,' Kayla snapped. 'Gross negligence. Dereliction of Dylan duties. Being an unfathomably massive jerk.'

She dug her hand down to the bottom of a jumbo bag of nachos and shoved the last few crumbs angrily into her mouth.

'All right, it was a jerky move to just blank me like that. And I'm not sure what dereliction means. But it's not like he was my boyfriend or anything. He didn't have a duty to kiss me.'

I was feeling surprisingly OK with it. Or, not *OK* exactly, but not like I was going to crawl sobbing into the showhall and beg to just be allowed to burn. Maybe I was getting used to rejection. Maybe I'd secretly known that Leo turning out to be my dream boyfriend would have been too perfect to be real.

Or maybe I was just feeling anchored by the solidly massed weight of cheese sandwiches and choc ices I'd been cramming into my stomach. I'd filled up the space where my heart used to be with stale Iced Gems, and now I was too full to mourn.

'I just thought he had *potential*, Dylan.' Kayla folded her arms and leaned against the window ledge. 'He was supposed to be the plot twist at the end of this story.'

'The beast turning into a prince.' I smiled.

'*Literally.*'

Opposite us, the Dramavan door flew open. Troy tumbled out, escaping just far enough to kick the head off a flamingo before his mum emerged like a Viking queen in her nylon nightie and dragged him back inside by his ear. Through the glass we could hear her screaming, 'AM I FINISHED? YOU'LL HAVE SIX KIDS AND A PENSION BY THE TIME I'M FINISHED WITH YOU, TROILUS-CLAY.'

'Troilus-Clay,' I repeated, slowly, once everything had gone quiet.

Kayla shook her head. 'You might be unlucky in love, but at least you weren't named by Mrs Slater.'

I nudged the side of her foot with mine. 'I'm not unlucky.'

I had her. I had parents who hadn't blinked twice over catching me kissing a hamster, and I had a little brother who didn't have a side career as an arsonist. On the whole, I was definitely luckier than most.

Kayla grinned, gathering up our empty snack packets and crunching them down into the bin. 'If we both end up single, I suppose we can just raise these food babies together.'

I groaned, rubbing a hand over my swollen stomach. 'What are you going to name yours? I was thinking Nacho-Melba sounded nice.'

'Still can't believe you dipped your crisps into that yogurt.'

I was about to defend my food choices when Mum swept in. 'Right then, we're in the car. Your dear brother insists he doesn't need the toilet. Have you remembered to pack your waterproofs?'

We'd been on enough family holidays for me to know those two thoughts weren't disconnected. I winced. 'I've got them in my backpack.'

Within easy reach for emergency shielding purposes. I really hoped Dad had remembered to program the satnav to detour past every Welcome Break on the way home.

Kayla grabbed the last of her things and we headed out to the car, where Jude was sitting with his arms folded and a Squeaky Nibbles toy tucked into the crook of one elbow. The unexpected reminder of yesterday at the fair knocked my zen-like, accepting attitude a little bit.

Kayla put a hand on my shoulder, but I shrugged her off. 'It's all right. At least one of us gets to have him.'

I took her bag and opened up the boot to toss it in, just as Jude called out, 'We have to stay for the parade!'

'The parade's been cancelled,' Kayla explained, not for the first time. The parade *had* been cancelled, and so had the Stardance, so at least we weren't missing anything. 'The costumes were all in the showhall.'

'The parade!' Jude insisted. 'The parade! The parade!'

I swung the boot closed to see Mum and Dad looking at each other. Jude had been promised a parade all week. He was really looking forward to it.

I leaned down to peer into the back seat. 'We'll have a parade when we get home, OK? I'll make costumes for me and Kayla, and you can pick the music.'

'We can have it at my house,' Kayla offered. 'And dress up the cats.'

Jude drew his lower lip between his teeth and chewed as he considered this. 'OK,' he agreed, finally. 'But is *he* coming?'

He pointed out in front of the car where, standing in the back of a golf buggy that was slowly steering towards us, was Nibbles.

I grabbed Kayla and we both stared, open-mouthed.

'I *told you* there was a parade!' Jude squealed, scrambling to lean out of the car window for a better view.

Parade might have been a slight exaggeration. There were no other floats, or characters. It was just Nibbles, dancing to the 'Happy Hamster' theme tune as the buggy crawled slowly along. Stacie walked behind, clutching her megaphone. As she got closer, the tinny sound it made transformed into words.

'*DUE TO UNFORSEEN CIRCUMSTANCES, TONIGHT'S STARDANCE HAS BEEN MOVED TO THE FAIRGROUND FIELD. I REPEAT: THE STARDANCE IS STILL SPARKLING. JOIN US FOR A DISCO INFERNO!*'

'Might be the wrong choice of words,' Kayla observed.

'*PLUS THE ANNOUNCEMENT OF THE PARK OF THE YEAR AWARDS! COME ONE, COME ALL TO OUR SPECTACULAR STARDANCE. ONLY TICKET-*

HOLDERS WILL BE ADMITTED.'

I couldn't help feeling like that last part was directed at us. Mum and Dad were standing in front of our car, watching the one-hamster parade pass by.

'Do they really still think they can win that award?' Kayla hissed in my ear.

'Maybe they're hoping for the sympathy vote,' I murmured, only half listening. I couldn't look away from the parade's solitary star: the giant hamster who was cheering and waving to rows of blank caravan windows as if they were all populated by adoring fans.

I didn't know if I really counted as a Nibbles fan any more, but as the golf buggy reached us, I lifted my hand to wave back.

Nibbles turned his back on me. While he sailed past, dancing and waving in the direction of the Dramavan, all I had was a prime view of his wiggling backside.

I felt a bit sick.

None of the food I'd eaten to try and squash my feelings had been enough to cushion my heart from breaking.

The buggy rolled on, Stacie's voice slowly falling silent. I could feel everyone watching me. Mum, Dad, Kayla, even Jude. It's weird how feelings can sometimes seem like a physical force. Like sadness. Like pity.

I slid into the back seat beside Jude. I'd had more

than enough of both those feelings for one holiday.

Silently, everyone else did the same. Only the satnav spoke, confirming that we could leave the park by driving in the opposite direction to Nibbles and his entourage. Good. I never wanted to see that buck-toothed face again. I never wanted to see the showhall again, or the Swim Centre, or the neon-lit gates telling me to LET THE DREAM BEGIN.

But we had to drive through the gates one last time to leave the park. And there, standing under them, with his hair swept up into a wild ponytail, wearing jeans and a white shirt and giving no signal that he might have made a quick change into them within the last five minutes . . .

Was Leo.

FORTY-SIX

Dad wordlessly swerved the car over to the pavement just before I threw myself out of it. Leo must have started running at about the same time, because we met somewhere in the middle, each of us skidding to a stop inches away from crashing into each other.

I really wanted to crash just a little further, but first I seriously needed to know what was going on.

'I thought I'd missed you,' Leo said, trying to catch his breath.

'I thought you'd just waved your bum in my face.'

That needed some explaining, so I told Leo how I'd just seen him – hamster him – totally diss me. He shook his head, biting down one corner of his lip in a way that I thought might mean he was trying not to laugh.

'I'm not Nibbles any more. I got fired yesterday, right in the middle of the photo session.'

I gaped. 'Why?'

And who had I been daydreaming about sweeping off their little pink hamster feet?

'Dereliction of duty,' Leo said, sounding less than impressed and nowhere near sorry.

I thought about the reasons Kayla suggested she sue him. He couldn't *actually* have been sacked for standing me up, could he?

'According to the new rules, my priority should have been the kids who wanted overpriced photos, not the one who might have gone over a cliff. Margaret stripped me of my buck teeth on the spot. *She's* in the costume now.'

Full-body-shuddering at the thought of the moony eyes I'd been making at Margaret the manager, I spared a glance back to where Kayla and my family were sitting with the car doors wide open, not even trying to be subtle about listening in.

'No wonder she blanked me. When you didn't come to meet me at the showhall I thought—'

'Meet you?' Leo looked confused. 'I've been avoiding the park so I didn't run into her. Mum even shut the Pie-O-Ria in protest. We heard about the fire, though, and I had to check you weren't caught up in it. This was the only place I could think of to wait – I knew you'd have to come through these gates eventually.'

I couldn't believe it. He must have been fired before I even caught up to him in the tent yesterday. I groaned painfully.

'What's wrong?' Leo asked.

'Oh, nothing. I just might have also asked Margaret on a date.'

Leo tipped his head back and laughed properly, then, and I couldn't help staring at the long arch of his throat and how quick his pulse was beating, there. Like he was nervous too. He never seemed to let anything but calm show on his face, but gradually I was learning his other tells.

When I looked up, he was grinning at me again. 'Tell her I'll fight her for you.'

I exhaled a laugh of my own into the frustrating half-inch of space between us. The tiny distance that was keeping me from knowing how warm his skin was, or exactly what he smelt like up close. The distance between a conversation and a kiss.

It was a painful amount of space, but I was still wishing I could stay in it forever when Mum yelled from the car, 'Dylan – Dylan, darling!'

Her voice pulled me back to earth and the harsh reality that I was about to be dragged away too early, *again*. Ready to die of frustration, I sighed miserably. 'We're leaving.'

'We're going back to the caravan!' Mum called at the same time. I whirled round to stare at her.

'What?'

'Jude needs the bathroom!'

'And I forgot my straighteners,' Kayla called over, before tipping the most obvious wink ever in my direction.

They were being *so* embarrassing. But I was so lucky they were my embarrassments. After Mum checked whether I wanted to walk back to the caravan with Leo or get in the car next to a little brother on the verge of turning into a human sprinkler system, they headed back into the park without me. Dad tooted the horn as a cheery goodbye.

The half-inch distance suddenly seemed even more difficult to cross with no one watching. Staring down at my feet, I could see just how close Leo was standing to me.

Carefully, he bumped my trainer with his toe.

'So if you're *sure* you don't want to reschedule your hot date with Margaret . . . How about going to the Stardance with me?'

I snapped my head up so quickly that I almost smacked my forehead into his nose. Which would have been brilliant of me, obviously. It's probably just some kind of careless oversight that none of the famous Hollywood kisses feature an unstoppable nosebleed.

But, as quickly as I felt my hopes soar, they came crashing back down to shatter at my feet. The Stardance had been off-limits ever since the corned beef casseroletastrophe.

'We're still banned. Jude's a fire hazard, remember?' I thought I could feel my heart physically wrench over having to say no.

'That was when it was going to be held in the showhall, right? I think the damage there's already been done.' Leo grinned. 'They can't accuse Jude of blocking any exits in a field. And I might have been sacked, but I've still got my ticket, and a plus-one.'

My mind raced back to Mum's stand-off with Margaret, trying to remember if she actually threw the tickets back at her. I didn't think she had. So, if Leo had one extra . . . that would mean we'd have enough for everyone. Mum might actually agree to go.

Margaret *definitely* wouldn't want us there: as far as she was concerned I was still barred from everything until after the Park of the Year announcement. But that was going to be at the dance itself. She'd never notice a few of the names from the top of her blacklist creeping into the party under cover of night.

Besides, we could be subtle.

Or, we might manage not to get anyone run over or sprayed with meat this time, anyway. And I really wanted to see Leo dance again, the way I'd glimpsed before – all flawless lines and more grace than any normal human should be capable of. Most of all, though, I really wanted him to dance with *me*.

'Dylan?' The soft way Leo said my name was coupled with his hand wrapping gently round my wrist. His fingers tucked just under my sleeve and set off a billion tiny electric shocks all across my nerve endings. I caught a quick, involuntary breath.

'Yeah?'

'That was kind of a question. And you still haven't said yes or no.'

I really had to stop spending so much time visualizing the way situations might go in my head, and forgetting to actually live them. Leo was right there, the gap between us neatly bridged by the reach of his arm. I slid my hand slowly upwards until I could press my fingers between his and let them curl tight.

Leaning down until his lips were so close to my ear that I could feel his breath against my skin, he asked again. 'Will you come to the dance with me?'

'Yeah.' I smiled. 'Of course.'

FORTY-SEVEN

Mum and Dad didn't take much persuading to postpone leaving for a few hours. Even if part of it was only to spite Margaret, once Leo told them about his extra golden ticket they were delighted to have an excuse to shake the mothballs off their cringiest outfits and get down to the fairground field. They vanished as soon as we got there, getting lost among the gang of dancing Elvises who were trying to bully the DJ into playing songs from before the dawn of time.

One of them had lent Jude a big plastic quiff to cover up his bubblegum buzzcut, and was teaching him how to hand jive with the rest.

I walked through the crowds hand in hand with Kayla. In a field lit with fairy lights and the blinking lamps of the fairground rides, she was the sparkliest thing there. She had glitter eyeshadow to match her sequin dress, and her pink curls were braided and pinned into a crown around her head.

'It's not too fairytale princess?' she asked, catching sight of her reflection in the polished surface of a bumper car.

I shook my head instantly. 'No. More like the world's best fairy godmother.'

Both of us were trying to spot Leo. He'd had to go to hand in his staff uniform – the one he wore when he wasn't dressed as a hamster – but he'd promised to meet us, and this time I wasn't busily running through all the reasons he might not show up. That had already happened once. I knew I'd survive.

And I knew for sure I'd have someone to dance with. I'd already promised Kayla. Nothing was going to spoil how beautiful this night was.

'There's your boyfriend.'

A voice I half recognized cut in through the music, and both Kayla and I froze. For some reason I found myself turning round half expecting to see Leo waiting there.

It was Jayden-Lee. He was standing with Kev and Leroy and Dean, and he didn't look like he was having fun. They'd formed a sort of semicircle, with him on the outside.

'Couldn't even get a kiss from *him*,' Dean said, leering my way.

'Have you *ever* actually got off with anyone, Jay?'

'He so hasn't. It's all talk.'

I made a move towards them, wanting to weigh in on the boyfriend comments at least, but Kayla's grip on my hand tightened and held me back.

'You've not seen me at home,' Jayden-Lee was saying. 'It's different. They're lining up.'

He sounded younger somehow, like a kid making up lies in the playground. It wasn't working, either.

'Yeah, lining up at the exit. Like when you cleared the pool,' Kev jeered. The others laughed. The huddle around Jayden-Lee closed tighter as we watched.

Kayla pushed herself on to tiptoe and whispered in my ear, 'Back in a sec.'

Then she stalked across and tapped Jayden-Lee on the shoulder. As he turned around I prepared myself for one of her lectures, but it never happened.

Not unless she was lecturing directly into his mouth.

For one brief moment they were pressed together: her glowing like starlight and him leaning down to meet her, golden and just as beautiful. He was gasping for breath when she pulled back from the kiss, smiled, and walked away – to a chorus of woops and whistles behind her.

'You're going to have to become a lawyer for the defence, not the prosecution,' I whispered as she joined me. 'You're *way* too good at saving people.'

'My defence skills only go so far,' she said. 'If he thinks he's going to kiss me again, he'll have to present a very strong case for it. And spend at least two years

315

doing some serious growing up.'

'Well, I still think you're a miracle worker.'

Not far away, Jayden-Lee's friends were clapping him on the back. The way he was smiling, it looked like she'd made his whole year.

But Kayla was pulling away from me again.

'Hey,' I said. 'Where are you going now?'

'Oh, I thought I might see if I can find someone to kiss that I actually fancy.' She smirked at me. 'Maybe the blonde over there's more my type.'

I looked over to where she was gesturing, trying to keep it discreet. 'The only guys over there are about ninety, Kayla.'

A small smile caught at her lips. 'Who says I meant a guy?'

I looked again. There was the blonde girl I'd seen Kayla with at the fair. She was about our age, and dancing with her eyes closed, like she could live inside the music that way. When the song changed she looked across, and waved shyly at Kayla.

'We made friends at yoga,' Kayla said. 'Her name's Summer. She's nice.'

She watched the realization slowly dawn on my face.

'You never said.'

'You never asked. And I've never really worried about it, much.'

Patting me on the shoulder, she smiled and started to walk away.

'So you're just leaving me on my own?' I called, grinning too much to look like I really minded.

Kayla turned back for a second and pointed. 'You're not.'

'Dylan?'

I pivoted slowly on my heels in the direction of the voice. Low and soft, it was one I'd come to recognize.

Like he always seemed to, Leo had found me.

The fairground lights caught on his cheekbones and lit his eyes in shifting colours, the same way they were probably lighting my skin. He'd thrown on a leather jacket over the shirt he'd been wearing before. I wanted to twist my hands into it and pull him in.

So I did.

He stepped forward easily, smiling, but now I'd learned how to check for nerves. With the backs of my hands brushing his chest, I could feel his pulse race in competition with mine.

'What is it?' he asked, tilting his head to assess the way I was looking at him.

'Oh, nothing. Life is just *so* much better when I can see your face.'

His hand smoothed up my arm, fingers curling over my shoulder as he asked, 'So it's goodbye to the hamster?'

'Good *riddance.*' Nibbles really had been my arch-nemesis all along, keeping Leo hidden. Although he'd sort of brought us together, too, just in a slow, backwards kind of way. I didn't know if I'd ever have gotten to know Leo if I'd had to do it face on, but now that I had, I couldn't care less if I never saw his fuzzier alter-ego again.

On the hastily erected stage, a loudspeaker crackled to life, pumping out the 'Happy Hamster' song as Stacie's voice announced that the Park of the Year prize was about to be awarded. '*SO PLEASE WELCOME TO THE STAGE OUR MYSTERY JUDGES, ALONG WITH THE FURRY FACE OF STARCROSS SANDS: NIBBLES!*'

The giant hamster bounced his way on to the platform as everyone under four foot began to scream. A group of adoring toddlers mobbed the front of the stage, arms in the air. Nibbles wobbled precariously close, looking like he might roll off the edge and steamroller them any minute. It was only now that I could appreciate just how coordinated Leo had managed to be inside that costume.

'Do you think it's still Margaret in there?' I yelled into Leo's ear, over the noisy delight of a hundred high-pitched playschoolers.

Leo nodded. 'I don't know how she's doing it. It gets so hot.'

Nibbles was trailed on to the stage by the three undercover judges, who turned out to be the bald Elvis who'd given Jude his quiff, a hen-fairy still wearing her 'bride to be' sash, and a woman dangling a little girl from either arm. Minnie and Winnie's mum.

It was the twins' mum who stepped forward to the microphone, while a man with a camera dived down in front of her, presumably broadcasting the award results to other dances at other caravan parks across the UK.

Nibbles quickly retreated to dance at the back of the stage.

I thought I got it, now. I leaned over to tell Leo. 'She's wearing the costume because she doesn't want anyone seeing her face when she loses.'

'The Park of the Year Award rewards destinations with the ability to make holiday makers' dreams come true,' the twins' mum was saying. 'This year's winner has faced challenges, and overcome them. It's shown that, even in the face of adversity, it can still bring people together. So – with a special runners-up mention to Joyful Valley, which is recovering well after being quarantined for a vomiting virus – I'm delighted to announce that the award goes to . . .'

She left a dramatic, game-show pause, which was completely ruined by the twins standing on tiptoes to yell into the microphone: 'STARCROSS SANDS!'

A huge cheer went up. It was the kind of moment you'd expect to be accompanied by explosions and a boy-band power ballad, except that the fireworks had all gone off when the showhall caught fire, and the DJ had been bribed by the Elvises to play something called 'Heartbreak Hotel'.

Instead, Starcross Sands' victory celebration saw Stacie running on to the stage to pull the string on a party popper while, from behind everyone, a gigantic hamster stumbled dizzily forward.

'It's mine.' A black slit had opened up along Nibble's neck, and he pulled upwards on his cheeks, trying to rip his own head off. The toddler's screams were starting to change in tone from joy to fear.

From deep inside the costume, a woman's voice could just be heard. 'I've done it. I've *done it*. It's *mine*.'

Nibbles swayed dangerously while, trapped inside the costume, Margaret held her hamster arms out to receive the award.

And tumbled over backwards, in a dead faint.

FORTY-EIGHT

In the moments that followed, I saw my parents storm the stage yelling that they were medics, helping Stacie to carry Nibbles off so they could treat him without causing further trauma to all the children in the crowd.

I saw Kayla, catching my eye as she stood smiling beside Summer, their arms linked.

I saw Jude, who already knew the *real* Nibbles wasn't the one with a fake head. The twins dashed down from the stage to join him playing Ring a Ring o' Roses with the Elvises.

Not far behind them Troy was looking sullenly on, his hand kept in a vice-like grip by Mrs Slater, who seemed to be wearing the frilly nylon nightie she kept aside for special occasions. While I was watching, Jayden-Lee came up and hooked his elbow through his mum's other arm, looking hazy and happy, as though his whole life had turned around in one night.

But, wherever I looked, my attention kept circling right back to Leo, a steady anchor point amid the lights and noise. Though even he was a bit dazed. 'I can't believe she actually won it. *We* won it.'

Starcross Sands must have still felt a little bit his, even though he was leaving it behind, and by September he'd be back at his dancing school miles and miles away from here. A dancing school, coincidentally, a little bit nearer to me.

'For overcoming adversity and bringing people together,' I said. My hands were still caught in Leo's jacket. 'Can't argue with that.'

It was strange because, even though I'd stayed for less than a week, Starcross Sands felt a little bit mine now, too. At least, this moment did. This moment was going to be mine forever.

Leo, tilting his head just a little to the side, leaning in towards me.

'No, I can't argue with that.'

Me, leaning my head just a little the other way, tilting closer too.

This moment that was top-of-a-rollercoaster terrifying and brilliant all at once.

This kiss.

This time at Starcross Sands. I was keeping it forever.

Dream boy. Dream holiday. Dreams coming true.

THE END

ABOUT THE AUTHOR

Before writing her first novel, Birdie dabbled in the theatre, sold books at Waterstones, ran drama classes for children, and dispensed romantic advice to internet daters. She studied at two universities cunningly disguised as stately homes, taking a BA in Creative and Professional Writing at St Mary's, Twickenham, and an MA in Writing for Young People at Bath Spa, where she gained first-class degrees in-between looking for secret passageways and dodging peacocks.

Birdie is pro-body positivity and anti-bullying, and believes in kindness above all things. She lives in Surrey, where she writes despite the best interruptive efforts of her pets, Ziggy Starcat and Moppet the Wonder Dog.

ACKNOWLEDGEMENTS

This book is for my beautiful mum, who brought me up with books and showed me worlds beyond the wardrobe, and for my brilliant dad, who made toothbrushes and bath towels talk, and in whose voice I can still hear the most infuriating line from the end of my favourite pony comics: 'But that was another story'.

I always wanted to know what those untold stories would be.

Because of both of you, I'm getting to tell my own.

This book was sometimes tough to write, because it's not easy to write warm, funny things when the world around you isn't feeling very warm or funny. So this is for the people I lost along the way: for my Nana, who thought I shone no matter how dark I felt, and for my Grandma and Granddad, who were every childhood holiday I ever took, and who were – all three – the personifications of warmth, humour, love and acceptance.

It is also for my punk rock kitties Sid and Nancy, who were with me for fifteen years, and purred through most of the writing of this book. And it's for the newer additions to the family: Moppet the Wonder Dog and Ziggy Starcat. It's for my crowd of aunts, uncles and cousins, who are too many to name, but each of whom hold a shard of my heart.

This book wouldn't be here without a village comprised of mentors, guides and co-explorers. I'd like to thank my BA Creative Writing lecturers, Russell Schechter and David Savill, who believed in me long before I believed in me – you changed my life.

Thanks to CJ Skuse, who fought for this book against the siren song of my other works-in-progress, and is a wonderful mentor. And to my writing partners, readers and friends: Ruth Griffiths, Cordelia Lamble, Roz Stimpson, Kathryn Clarke, Sarah House, and Julie Pike. You are all marvels.

Plus the friends who put up with my occasionally angsting my way through writing funny: Camila Tessler, Ruxi Iordache, Gee Mumford, Maria Pluzhnikov, Rebecca Hart, Lindsey Cohick, Ashley Parsons-Trew. I love you so and I really hope I've spelled all your surnames right.

Thanks to Steph Carfrae for all your positivity and powerchair tips, and to Ellie Bailey for your enthusiasm and kindness. This book is for Aurora Bailey, too. Thanks to Erica, Joff, Sam, Jackie, Micky, Nat, George and everyone at the best day job a writer could ask for.

To my wonder of an agent, Molly Ker Hawn, who I'm pretty sure destiny brought me around to, full circle: thank you for every second of your support. Thank you to Gemma Cooper for all your help and good advice. Thanks to Linzie Hunter for the gorgeous cover art, and thanks to Venetia Gosling, George Lester, Kat McKenna, Bea Cross and the crack team at Macmillan for your wisdom and for whipping my words into shape.

But back to my mum for a moment. I had these acknowledgements all nicely written out before I realised you were going to die on me, Mum, and now I can't change them too much or I'd write the whole thing about you. My smart, funny mother who knew the answers to every quiz show question on the radio before the contestants did, and got me into 'retro' music (thank you forever for Joan Baez and Leonard Cohen), who knew how to be terrifying with a smile, and who loved me fiercely no matter what.

When I first started to let people read this book, the piece of feedback I heard most often was 'I really loved the character of the mother'. Well, so do I. You're in every word I've ever written, Mum. You'll be in every word I ever write.

An un-book-related thank you to Mr Jay Chatterjee and Mr Andrea Scala, the kindest surgeons I've ever met, and to all the doctors and nurses whose care for Mum was incredible and who helped more than they can know during the hardest time of my life.

This book is for anyone who has ever felt different. Which I'm almost sure is everyone. Thank you for reading.